A Venture into Murder

Also by Henry Kisor

Other Steve Martinez Mysteries

Season's Revenge, 2003

Cache of Corpses, 2007

Hang Fire, 2013

Tracking the Beast, 2016

The Riddle of Billy Gibbs, 2017

Nonfiction

What's That Pig Outdoors: A Memoir of Deafness, 1990

Zephyr: Tracking a Dream Across America, 1994

Flight of the Gin Fizz: Midlife at 4,500 Feet, 1997

A Venture into Murder

First published in hardcover by Forge Books, 2005
First published in Great Britain by Robert Hale Ltd., 2006
First published as an e-book, 2011
First published as a CreateSpace paperback, 2016

A VENTURE INTO MURDER

A Venture into Murder

For Will

ONE

"Start at the beginning," I said, stepping gingerly away from the corpse in the sand. It had a hole in its chest. But Elmer Knapp had none, and he proceeded at full throttle and with a bottomless fuel tank. Mr. Knapp had found the body.

"Me and the wife are from Bloomville, Wisconsin," the octogenarian said, sweeping off his threadbare fisherman's porkpie and mopping his head, its bald white pate divided neatly from his stubbly cheeks by a deep farmer's tan. Like many vacationing heartland country dwellers of his generation, he dressed not in the Lands' End shirts and stonewashed jeans of midwestern Baby Boomers but in faded military khakis and a flap-pocketed blue chambray work shirt buttoned all the way up, collar gaping around his tanned turkey neck. From his frayed pants cuffs jutted stained, scuffed work boots with lug soles. Dead center on his rawhide string tie lay a bright Navajo turquoise clasp, no doubt a souvenir from a vacation in the Southwest. He looked utterly authentic, and for the most part sounded the same way.

"That's down near Antigo in Langlade County, you know. Last Saturday, that's two days ago, we were going to go to Bayfield—that's out by the Apostle Islands, you know—because Aunt Pearl has been poorly with the arthur-itis, and the wife wanted to get something pretty to cheer her up. But I can't stand that gift-shop junk—you know, Bayfield is becoming touristier and touristier with every passing year, and all it's doing is attracting the wrong kind of people from all over, you know, the ones who throw McDonald's trash all over the highway, and . . ."

By this point most other police officers would have

rolled their eyes and said in so many words, "Yes, yes, can we get to the point?" But I believe in letting witnesses rattle on, even elderly ones no longer inclined or even able to distinguish relevant from irrelevant. You never know what might spill out when a witness charges along under a head of steam.

"And?" I said in an encouraging tone.

"And I managed to persuade Elfrieda, that's the wife, that her Aunt Pearl, who loves pretty stones, might like an agate or two from the shore of Lake Superior. So we decided to drive to Porcupine City and rent a cabin for a few days, as we've done a week or so every other year since 1957 or thereabouts, and hunt up some stones on the beach. That was last Friday. No, I said it was Saturday, didn't I? What day is today?"

"Monday," I said.

"Yes, that's right, we have eggs Monday mornings," Mr. Knapp said firmly. "It's definitely Monday. Sunny side up."

"Then what happened?" I said.

"After breakfast we started walking west down on the beach looking for agates. In the morning when the sun is low it's best to keep it at your back so you can see the pretty rocks sparkling ahead of you, you know. It was kind of foggy, though."

I nodded and jotted a word in my notebook. Foggy.

"After about an hour we heard a sport fisherman raise its anchor and start its engines maybe half a mile off the beach. That was probably the *Mary-El*. You know, that's a party boat, takes people fishing."

"Yup." Another jot. *Mary-El*. A thirty-six-footer out of Silverton, just about the only sizable commercial sport fishing vessel along the 150-odd miles of nearly deserted Lake Superior shoreline between Ashland, Wisconsin, and Houghton, Michigan. I'd been aboard her myself a couple of times, on forays for lake trout. "See her?"

"Just barely," Mr. Knapp said.

" 'Bout what time was that?"

"Eight-fourteen. I just happened to check my watch. It's a Timex, you know, the best twenty-dollar watch in the world, never stops running. I got her at a garage sale. You know what I paid?"

He leaned toward me conspiratorially. *"Two bucks."*

"Wow," I said. "That's a buy."

"Damn right," he said. Another thrifty child of the Depression, the kind who hunts for mail-order and garage-sale bargains, clips coupons, never pays retail, and always buys a used car. I admire those who are careful with their money because they have to be, as I suspected Mr. Knapp was, and pity the tightwads who don't need to scrimp but still boast about their steals at Costco and Sam's Club. The rich man who walks a mile to save a penny is a sad human being indeed.

"Was that Central time or Eastern time?"

"Central. I don't change my watch up here. Makes me late to supper."

Though it lies seventy-two miles farther west than Chicago, Porcupine City, seat of Porcupine County, runs on Eastern time, like the rest of Michigan except the four counties along the Wisconsin state line. Michiganders who live next to Wisconsin just find it easier to live by Central time. In Porcupine County, however, being on Eastern time means late dawns and late sunsets during the summer. Often last light doesn't fade until ten-thirty.

"What happened next?"

"By and by, maybe ten minutes later," he said, "Elfrieda tapped me on the shoulder and said, 'Elmer, that's odd.' I looked up and saw a bunch of crows, half a dozen or so, way up the beach pecking at a log half in and half out of the water. Now crows don't usually do that. They're not shore birds, you know. I said to Elfrieda, I did, 'You're right, that's odd. Let's go have us a look.' "

—

Elmer sighed. "When we got there, Elfrieda said, 'Elmer, logs don't have arms nor legs.' And I said, 'This one don't have eyes neither.' The crows had been at it a while."

He shuddered and looked back on the beach, where other Porcupine County sheriff's deputies stood over the body, trying not to gag as the sun rose higher in the June sky and accelerated the processes of putrefaction. To my eye the half-naked corpse, a large and burly male lying faceup and clad only in jeans and a single sneaker, had not been in the water long, judging from the bluish skin and lack of bloat. The chill of Lake Superior most likely had slowed decomposition.

"And that's when we went to that cabin over there and, you know, asked them to call the arthur-ities."

For a moment I thought Mr. Knapp had said "arthritis." I took a deep breath. One more "you know" and I'd go nuts. Young people have corrupted the everyday language of many of their elders with that useless locution, and "like" isn't far behind it. I was sorry. If it had not been for that I would have been persuaded that Elmer Knapp was an utterly pure and unspoiled old-timer from the midwestern countryside. They're hard to find nowadays, what with television and the Internet turning the speech of too many people between the Hudson River and the Sacramento Valley into that of cookie-cutter Middle Americans of the youthful persuasion.

"Thank you, Mr. Knapp," I said. "You've been very helpful. Now I don't think we'll be needing you any more today. Could you give me your address and telephone number in Bloomville, just in case?" He did so, and I shook his hand gravely. "Maybe you'd better look to Mrs. Knapp. She seems unwell."

Mrs. Knapp sat disconsolately on a log nearby, as if she had suddenly been told that her salmon-colored double-knit pantsuit, set off by a bright yellow chiffon scarf, had been out of fashion for thirty years. It looked almost new, as if she wore it only on special occasions, like vacation days. Probably it was another product of the pinched thriftiness of the lower

10

middle class. But I suspected that what really ailed her was the unexpected sight of an eyeless corpse.

"Who is it, do you think?" Mr. Knapp said. "What happened to him?"

"I don't know," I said. "Maybe a fisherman who fell out of his boat a few days ago."

I didn't tell Mr. Knapp about the dimpled perforation directly under the stiff's left nipple. I'd spotted it when I arrived on the scene an hour earlier. I would have bet good money the hole had been made by a bullet, although it was possible the corpse had been punctured postmortem by a snag as it rolled in the shallows. I'd told the two deputies who followed me on the scene to let the body lie as it was, then called my immediate boss, Gil O'Brien, Porcupine County's undersheriff, and told him the facts. Right away Gil phoned the state police post at Wakefield, a little more than fifty miles southwest of the sheriff's department in Porcupine City. Rural sheriffs rarely have the means or manpower to investigate suspicious human deaths in these semi-wilderness parts and generally let the better-equipped troopers do the job.

I looked out on the beach. Here, not quite halfway along the fifteen miles between Porcupine City and the vast Wolverine Mountains Wilderness State Park in western Upper Michigan, some fifty feet of sand spanned the distance between tree line and water's edge—a fairly wide beach for this stretch. The lake was still this morning, the gentle lap-lap of the waves barely audible in the soft breeze. Heaps of skeletal white driftwood thrown up by spring storms spotted the beach like a bleached wooden boneyard, an ossuary of dead pine and cedar—except along the three hundred or so feet that belonged to the owner of the cabin Mr. Knapp had hailed. Evidently the owner was an anal-retentive sort. Unlike most lake shore property holders, who tended to prefer nature's helter-skelter design and let their beachfronts alone, he had raked the sand clean so that it shone spotlessly white, like Waikiki Beach on Sunday morning. But there was no fringe of stately palms, only a thick line of birch and aspen broken by a few towering white pines left over from the logging days of a century ago.

Through the trees I saw oncoming flashing red, blue and white lights, and checked my watch. It wasn't even an hour since I'd called Gil. The state cops must have covered the fifty miles from Wakefield at ninety miles an hour, even though there was no life to save, only a corpse to investigate. The big Ford cruiser fishtailed to a stop on the access road in a cloud of sand and gravel. Smokeys like to make dramatic entrances, as if to emphasize their exalted status on the law-enforcement food chain, several links higher than their not-too-bright country cousins in the sheriff's department.

"Okay, girls," said a gruff voice as a beanpole in blue blazer and khaki slacks emerged from the passenger side of the cruiser. "It's ours now. Skedaddle."

I laughed. Sergeant Alex Kolehmainen, the smartest state police detective and evidence technician in all of Upper Michigan, loved to play the stage bully with sheriff's deputies. At first he spooked rookies. At a skinny six feet six he was all elbows and knees and Adam's apple, like Tony Perkins in "Psycho." His mock bombast, coupled to fast-growing gray stubble on his cadaverous cheeks, made him look like the Grim Reaper in a coat and tie. Sooner or later, Alex's hamminess tipped off even the greenest probationary deputy that his fierce manner was all a put-on.

Alex, who had grown up in northern Wisconsin and served in the Army after college, like me, had started his law enforcement career as a lowly sheriff's deputy himself, and he showed great respect for the kind of work we did. "You couldn't ever get me to handle a domestic dispute again," he often said of a common task country deputies hated. It's a frustrating scenario: The abusee calls the cops. The cops arrive and attempt to restrain the abuser. The abusee suddenly feels loyal to the abuser, and the cops end up getting hammered by both sides. Occasionally the abusers—and even their mates—

are armed as well as drunk or drugged. "That's worse than wrestling a crocodile," Alex says.

And like me, he had not yet married. Women quickly see past his lanky homeliness and set their sights on him, but Alex is a choosy sort. He likes women but loves the bachelor life more. Women invite him to dinner and sometimes he spends the night, but he's always gone after breakfast. Still his paramours forgive him, for he is dashing and generous and dumps his ladies so gently and magnanimously that they are barely aware of the end of the relationship. I doubt that Alex has ever been dumped himself. At least that's how it seems. Though he and I are good friends, he has never talked about the women he has known. He likes and respects the ladies too much to tell tales out of the bedroom.

Alex stepped over to the body. "What have we here?" he said, broadly including me and my brother deputies in the pronoun. Not "What do we got?", the hackneyed query of the movie cop. Alex is as careful with his grammar as he is with his tools. "Fill me in."

As the responding officer I did. Alex nodded as I finished my much-edited tale of the Knapps' discovery of the body, then went to work, photographing the corpse from several angles with an Olympus digital camera for quick results and a Nikon thirty-five-millimeter film camera for legal backup. He also gathered samples of sand and measured the water's temperature, leaving no pebble unturned.

"Anything else turn up on the beach?" he asked after an hour of meticulous labor.

"Nothing we could see. We searched it for half a mile in both directions."

"Okay, shall we bag him and drag him?" The Porcupine County Hospital ambulance waited behind the cruiser to transport the body to Houghton forty-eight miles east, where the medical examiner would perform the postmortem. Porcupine County has a coroner, but he's an internist, and all questionable cases needing a pathologist go to Houghton. Suspicious ones often end up at the state police forensics lab in Marquette, the only one in the Upper Peninsula.

Alex stood up. "Most likely a homicide," he said, officially voicing what we on the scene all thought of that hole in the man's chest. "The doc'll decide."

"How long ago, do you think?" I asked.

"Hard to say. Could have been just a few hours, but maybe a couple, three days. I'll have to get a range of water temperatures at this time of year."

From June to mid-September Lake Superior's inshore waters are often warm, sometimes topping seventy degrees Fahrenheit, but a sudden shift of wind can roil the lake, bringing up colder waters from the bottom and dropping the surface temperature into the low fifties in a couple of hours. It often takes hours of studying weather and temperature charts to arrive at just a rough time of death.

Alex stripped off his crime-scene gloves and tossed them into a hazmat container in the trunk of his cruiser. "I'll call you when we know anything," he said. "Probably be at least a couple of days, maybe a week."

I nodded and shook his proffered hand.

"Thanks for keeping a clean scene," Alex said as he shut the door of the cruiser. "That helps a lot. Honest Injun."

He winked at me.

I winced only a little.

TWO

That evening, in civilian attire, I dined alone on lake trout at George's Supper Club in Silverton, five miles west of my log cabin on the shore. George's, the dining room of the big inn that catered to hikers and skiers in the Wolverines state park on its doorstep, was the closest thing to a gourmet restaurant in Porcupine County, and that isn't saying much. Its menu was heavy on deep-fried everything, the favorite of north country natives, but at least the salad-bar veggies were fresh, and George's broiled lake trout was as good as anything I'd had in the seafood emporiums of Boston and Chicago.

That was because Rudy Makinen currently was in residence as executive chef, or whatever George's called its head cook. Though Rudy is not a graduate of the Culinary Institute of America, he had learned his trade in one of the toughest kitchens in the world: the galley of a nuclear submarine, where tight storage space means a simple menu of a few items prepared perfectly.

Every year or so Rudy has a fight with the manager of the inn, usually over accounts. He quits and hangs up his shingle, or skillet, or whatever it is chefs hang up, at O-Kun-de-Kun, the restaurant in the mall at Lone Pine, the old copper mining community six miles south. As soon as the local diners discover Rudy has dumped George's, they emigrate en masse to O-Kun-de-Kun, and George's is left with only the tourists. By and by Rudy has a fight with the owner of O-Kun-de-Kun, quits, and takes his skill back to George's, the local clientele again in tow.

One year Rudy decided to be his own boss and opened the Starlight Inn on the highway in the countryside seven miles east of Porcupine City. For two years his seafood restaurant was the brightest constellation in the Upper Peninsula's dining firmament, for Rudy ranged far and wide for the best and freshest salmon, trout and whitefish he could find. In the summer he'd catch lake trout on his day off Monday and serve it to a few lucky friends Tuesday, and his Friday night fish broils—even the shrimp were broiled, not battered and deep-fried—drew diners from all over the U.P. and northern Wisconsin. A meal at the Starlight was worth a two-hour drive.

But the economics of the restaurant business are always shaky, and they are shakiest of all in the hard-luck boondocks where the clientele is constantly shrinking. The bank foreclosed, and Rudy went back to his shuttling between O-Kun-de-Kun and George's.

And that was why, after a slab of broiled trout exceptional even for Rudy, I was feeling content with the world. Then, as I was just leaving the restaurant, a neighbor placed her hand on my arm.

For the last couple of years Mary Ellen Garrigan, a wealthy and fortyish divorcee who lived in Winnetka, Illinois, an upscale Chicago suburb, had been a summer resident at a huge, brand-new, and expensive six-bedroom beach home built for her by a Wisconsin contractor with imported labor, not Porcupine County carpenters, on the lake shore just half a mile east from my cabin. I had not yet encountered her, for she was not the kind who mixes with locals, who meet and greet each other daily at the town's modest supermarket. She didn't shop there but had gourmet foodstuffs delivered at great expense from chichi stores that served the resorts around Eagle River and Rhinelander two hours south in Wisconsin.

Her meager relations with Porcupine County residents bordered on the imperious. To them she was haughty, rude in the unconsciously and sometimes deliberately belittling manner the very rich often display to those lower on the economic and social ladder. Next to people like her on my scale of annoyance are the self-absorbed second-rate urban intellectuals whose snobbish disdain for rural Americans is born less from ignorance than desperate striving to be superior to somebody — anybody. I had known both kinds of twits in my youth and in college and despised them equally.

Mary Ellen Garrigan's social life at her lakeside mansion was unsurprising for her kind. It consisted of weekend house gatherings with others like her, often attended by much younger hunks in BMWs and Jaguars, college boys with too much money and too little supervision. They were noisy and wild occasions, and rumors of debauched parties were beginning to emerge.

All these things Joe Koski, the sheriff's department's chief dispatcher, one-man intelligence service, and unofficial town crier, had told me. Nothing escapes Joe. He can tell you — and will tell you whether or not you want to know — who's been occupying a bed they shouldn't have, who's visiting their relations in New Mexico and whose dog has just had puppies that need a home. He's a terrible busybody. I wouldn't have been able to tolerate him if he hadn't been a nice guy, a poster child for Officer Friendly. He helps old ladies across the street, kisses children's boo-boos and lends broke deputies a tenner till payday. Everyone knows Joe. With their scanners, as common to a Porcupine County household as a color television, they listen to him all day on the police radio as he sends deputies to accident sites and takes their license and registration queries during traffic stops. The only person they listen to more than Joe is Annie Tollefsen, WPOR's motherly morning personality, who gets half her gossip from the dispatcher anyway.

I didn't need Joe to tell me that Mary Ellen Garrigan stood out wherever she went. She was still a knockout. Her boy-short bottled blonde hair set off a deep tan. Her ears, wrists and neck dripped with diamonds and gold, a rare sight in a place where an embroidered sweatshirt is considered dressing up and jewelry is left mostly to the pierced generation. The few times she appeared in public places like George's, she wore skimpy spaghetti-strap outfits designed to show her lack of tan lines as well as display a bust that just had to have been surgically augmented. For everyday wear she preferred snug slacks, high-cut shorts and jerseys not from the Wal-Mart at Houghton but from Bergdorf Goodman in New York and Marshall Field's in Chicago. One doesn't often see expensive clothing in Upper Michigan, except for the Timberland boots and top-of-the-line down parkas North Woodsers save up for because the warmest winter garments give them the best chances for survival in deep snow.

Mary Ellen often took the summer sun in the nude on the sand behind her house, barely concealed from the shoreline by a low dune. More than once that summer Sheila Carnahan, the hefty middle-aged widow who was my immediate neighbor to the east, had happened upon Mary Ellen either sunbathing or swimming on the not quite deserted beach in what Sheila delicately called "the altogether." Sheila, who often played hostess to two adolescent nephews from Arizona, had asked Mary Ellen not to go about without clothes when they were visiting, but the reply was succinct and rude.

Now, skinny-dipping is hardly a federal offense. I often indulge in it myself on warm summer days, when Sheila is out of sight in her house and nobody else seems to be on the beach. I suspect Sheila sneaks an occasional peek at me with the big Pentax binoculars she keeps on her kitchen counter for birdwatching. Anyway, she has never complained.

"That woman makes no effort to cover herself!" declared Sheila, who, like so many Upper Michigan women, is deeply modest. I had not felt the urge to investigate, having no law-enforcement reason to do so, but gently suggested to Sheila that she keep that information to herself.

"If it gets out that Mrs. Garrigan likes to go about outside without clothes," I had said, "every horny teenage boy

———

18

in the county, let alone your nephews, is going to be stomping around on the beach trying for a peek. Let's see if we can avoid that."

Sheila, who is as sensible as she is straitlaced, agreed. So far, so good. The beach remained largely deserted, except for the few residents and occasional out-of-town visitors who liked to hike for miles along it. Mary Ellen had not yet become a celebrated part of the scenery, let alone a familiar one. Sooner or later, however, that was going to happen.

All these things ran through my mind when Mary Ellen's brown and bejeweled hand suddenly grasped my arm in the parking lot just outside George's. No one else was about.

"Hello, Steve Martinez," Mary Ellen said, her eyes shining into mine as she leaned uncertainly toward me. They glittered from the pitcher of martinis she had downed with two other wealthy matrons at a table near mine. I could almost see olives instead of pupils in her eyes. Inside George's she had glanced my way several times, a few of them with bold interest. "You're the Indian deputy, aren't you?"

"Ah, yes, Mrs. Garrigan," I replied, trying to maintain a friendly tone although the unnecessary mention of my ethnicity irritated me. "We're neighbors on the beach. I've meant to introduce myself, but never got around to it."

"You live in that cute little shack to the west, don't you?"

"Shack" is hardly the word for my modest but well-constructed four-room cedar log cabin on the shore, but I let it go. People like Mary Ellen Garrigan just can't help patronizing their neighbors.

"Yes, that's the one."

She belched discreetly and giggled. "Sorry."

She was drunker than I had thought. I suddenly felt as if I had become the quarry of a woodland beast, and said hurriedly, "It's nice to meet you. I'll be seeing you around."

That was a dumb thing to say, considering what I'd

been told about her. It gave her the perfect opening.

She leaned even closer to me and whispered conspiratorially, "I don't pussyfoot around. Come on down to the house tonight. You'll see a lot of me."

She hiccuped. "You'll be my first Indian. "

I drew back, pretending I hadn't heard.

"I'm a *very* good lay," she insisted, pressing her considerable cleavage into my arm. "I'll bet you are, too."

For an instant she touched my male vanity, I have to admit, but I've never been interested in winding up as a one-night notch on a predatory female's bedpost—especially in these sparsely populated parts, where everybody's private business tends to get broadcast as soon as it is transacted. Besides, although she didn't know it and probably would never understand why, she had insulted me profoundly. I don't mind being hit on—I enjoy that as much as any other red-blooded American male does—but I just can't stand being thought of as a novelty lay, a piece of exotic meat. Suddenly the well-fed feeling I had carried out of the restaurant dissipated.

"Good night, Mrs. Garrigan," I said as severely as I could, turning on my heel. I did not look back as I walked out to the Explorer.

"Jerk!" she called after me, loud enough to be heard inside the restaurant. "You don't know what you're missing!"

THREE

My full and official title is Deputy Stephen Two Crow Martinez, Sheriff's Department, Porcupine County, Michigan. Genetically I am 100 percent Native American, born to the Lakota nation — one of the Teton Sioux tribes — but culturally and emotionally I am the white-picket-fence Eastern Methodist I used to be. I was adopted as an infant by well-meaning white missionaries from the poverty-stricken and dismal Oglala Lakota reservation at Pine Ridge, South Dakota, and was brought up as a seemingly well-tanned preacher's kid in middle-class Troy in upper New York State, listening to Mötley Crüe in my bedroom when I was not belting out "Battle Hymn of the Republic" in the choir of the church my father pastored. My middle name is the only remnant of Indian heritage my devout parents allowed and my last name is the echo of old Catalan settlers in Florida. Nobody in our family has spoken Spanish for generations. But my dark skin and Spanish name often make people think I'm a Latino.

Red on the outside, white on the inside — that's why I take offense when thoughtless and self-absorbed twits like Mary Ellen Garrigan think they know all about me just because I'm a ringer for the Indian on the buffalo head nickel. If I haven't made myself clear, I *hate* being pegged that way. Of course, decent folks do the same thing out of well-meaning ignorance, and if I want to have any friends I've got to cut them some slack. I spend a lot of time gritting my teeth. Here's what I'd tell them if they showed any interest in my history, and sometimes they do.

At eighteen I attended Cornell on an Army ROTC scholarship, then after graduation studied criminal justice at

City University of New York, picking up a good deal of street knowledge from the New York Police Department officers who moonlighted as instructors. After a year at CUNY I served three years as a lieutenant in the military police and herded Iraqi POWs into Saudi camps in the aftermath of Desert Storm. Afterward, on an impulse—and who wouldn't be impulsive after receiving a Dear John letter at the height of battle from a girlfriend who said she was pregnant?—I took the first police job that came my way. It was in the absolute basement of law enforcement—a low-paid rookie deputy in a backwoods sheriff's department, a position well beneath my education and capabilities, or so my horrified Army superiors said. In a short while, realizing that I'd simply engaged in a silly exercise of dramatic self-laceration, I'd expected to move on to a city job after a couple of years.

But this beautiful and isolated part of the country, and the people who live here and keep it that way, slowly wormed their way into my soul, and I am still here after almost a decade.

Part of the reason, I'll have to admit, is what I can describe only as a spiritual call to the blood. The Lakota and their kin, the Dakota and Nakota, lived in this place hundreds of years ago, before the more warlike Ojibwe crowding in from the East under European colonial pressure forced them out onto the Great Plains. In sentimental moments, when I'm feeling most Indian, I sometimes imagine that I've come home to my nation's ancestral hunting grounds. But that doesn't happen often.

Nor am I much of a hunter, unlike most Yoopers, as the people who live in the U.P. jocularly call themselves. I'm still just too much of an Eastern city boy to be attracted to deer or bear hunting, though both of those pastimes are ways of life, often necessities of survival, in the Upper Peninsula. Still, having inherited a heirloom shotgun—a beautifully engraved 12-gauge Browning over-and-under—from my father, who loved hunting upland birds with dogs, I do go after partridge and grouse when they're in season. Not that I've had much success — I'm just not that good a wing shot. But I cherish the eternal rhythm of the hunt, the careful preparations, the long walks in the fields and woods with dogs, the cool evenings before a roaring fire with a spot of brandy and a dollop of good fellowship. I often think my Lakota forebears felt the same way as they sat around their council fires celebrating after a long day of harvesting buffalo.

There are other attractions. Upper Michiganders, especially those who live in Porcupine County, tend to take care of each other in ways almost unheard of elsewhere. This is a land of high unemployment, the last copper mine having closed a decade ago and the last tall pines having been logged out almost a century before. Slowly younger people have moved elsewhere in search of jobs, leaving behind mostly the elderly and those who scratch livings in whatever way they can, like cutting second-growth pulpwood from the Ottawa National Forest for the paper mill. After its last count the Census Bureau declared Porcupine County a frontier county, meaning its population had fallen to fewer than seven people per square mile. McDonald's, Wal-Mart, and Starbucks have not seen fit to open stores in Porcupine County — that's how thin we're spread.

People up here may lose more and more of their neighbors every year, but that just seems to make them cherish the remaining ones as best they can. Old folks no longer able to get around easily often wake up to a bag of groceries on the doorstep or a fresh cord of split maple in the woodshed. Middle-aged matrons volunteer to watch their young neighbors' kids so Mom and Dad can spend a couple of days camping in the Wolverines, a cheap and popular date hereabouts.

Not that Porkies, as we call ourselves, are angels. We are no less prone to violence and depravity than those who live in the cities, but since there are so few of us, major felonies just don't happen often. Especially during the long and lonely winters, people do get drunk and take pokes at each other in the town bars. So do husbands and wives at home, and since every household in hunting country contains at least one rifle, one shotgun and lots of ammunition, enforcing the peace can get hairy. Fortunately battling couples are almost always too pie-eyed to hold a steady aim, though we cops of course can't count on that. Our motorists are just as aggressive or inattentive as those anywhere else, and they keep us busy writing tickets. Now and then a citizen gets desperate enough to grow marijuana or set up a cat lab to make methcathinone, or poor man's methamphetamine. Much as I despair over the nation's futile and self-lacerating war on drugs, the law's the law, and I'm paid to enforce it.

Porcupine County is nearly all white, descended mostly from the Irish, Cornish and Croatian miners who arrived in the 1840s and 1850s during the copper boom and from the Finnish woodsmen who came here between the 1870s and the early 1900s when the Upper Peninsula shipped millions of board feet of lumber south to rebuild Chicago after the Great Fire. There is a smattering of Jews and Latinos and, according to the last census, exactly three African Americans. So few blacks are seen in these parts at any time of year that Porkies automatically assume they're tourists from the cities. There also are quite a few Indians, mostly casino-rich Ojibwe who have spilled over into Porcupine County from the reservations at Baraga to the east and Lac Vieux Desert to the south.

At first most Porkies thought I was Mexican because of my name, but when they learned I was Lakota shrugged and figured me for just another odd bird who had washed up on the beach and stayed. They sometimes include me in their grousing about the casino Indians — "you all look alike, you know" — but the few instances of outright hostility I have experienced have come more from my job than my biological origins. People everywhere are just uncomfortable around cops. There's a little larceny in everyone, and they just don't

———

24

want to be reminded of that.

Slowly, however, over the better part of a decade I've come closer and closer to acceptance as a true Porky. And by none prettier than one Virginia Anttila Fitzgerald, the red-headed director and only paid employee of the Porcupine County Historical Society. Ginny is an extraordinarily wealthy woman, thanks to her late husband, an industrialist, but nobody in Porcupine County except me knows that.

We are naturally an item, and not merely a romantic one. Ginny is both lovely and loving, not to mention shapely, and the gravy is that she owns one of those encyclopedic memories that pops out in conversation like a drawer from a card catalog at the library, and it specializes in everything and everyone in Porcupine County. Ginny is blessed with the ability of almost total recall. Having read a document once, she can forever repeat its contents—a handy talent for a historian and a godsend for a boyfriend who is a low-ranking law enforcement officer needing to find out things about people in a hurry. With Ginny's knowledge and moral support, I have occasionally been able to solve the infrequent mystery that crops up in this cold and lonely land where felons are few and far between.

And that is why I found Mary Ellen Garrigan so easy to turn down. Why should I settle for stew on the road when there's sirloin at home?

That's everything about me worth knowing, and what isn't wouldn't fill a thimble.

FOUR

"I know something you don't," Alex chortled.

I heaved a mock sigh into the phone. "Why do you torment me so?"

"Because it's so *easy*."

His call had come while I was at my desk in the squad room of the sheriff's department gathering my monthly reports, seemingly ninety-nine per cent of which had to do with traffic stops, the usual country deputy's main task. Now, I liked my work, but sometimes its stultifying sameness got me to toying with Alex's idea that I should consider applying for a state trooper's job and moving up the ladder of law enforcement. But though I had the credentials, I hadn't the desire.

Alex chuckled. "That stiff on the beach last week? We've made him."

"Yeah?" I said.

"Just enough skin left on his fingertips for good prints. He is—was—a small-time mob muscle out of Chicago and Las Vegas named Danny Impellitteri. Long rap sheet for extortion and battery. One short stretch in Joliet for aggravated assault, but they never were able to get him on anything else. He was pretty slick. The DEA was looking at him as a drug courier but never made a connection. No relations, no family. The *capos* in Chicago and Vegas naturally say they never heard of him. Nobody to claim the body."

"Do tell." This was interesting. "Go on."

"That hole in his chest was made by a thirty-ought-six." A .30-'06 is a common rifle cartridge—just about everybody of hunting age in the Upper Peninsula owns a weapon chambered for that round. "There was no exit hole. That's rare for a powerful round like that, you know."

"Did the examiner find the bullet?"

"Yes." That meant the law very likely would be able to match the bullet to the rifle that fired it, if it ever could be found. But .30-'06s being as common in Upper Michigan as Frenchmen are in Paris, I doubted that anyone would search hard for the weapon.

"The entry hole was not round but oblong, slightly flattened," Alex continued. "Most of Impellitteri's ribs were shattered and one lung was cut up by the slug and contained blood. Both lungs were full of water. What does that tell you, Junior?"

"An oblong entry hole suggests that the bullet glanced off something, perhaps water, tumbled and lost some of its velocity before hitting the subject," I said in as professorial a tone as I could muster. "That and the broken ribs explain why there was no exit wound—the bullet bounced around in there. Water in the lungs means he lived for a while, then drowned. Considering his—ah—trade, first thing I'd think of is a mob hit. Maybe another hoodlum invited him fishing and carried out a contract."

"You know, Steve," Alex said, frank admiration in his voice, "you should have been a *real* policeman."

"Don't start," I said. "How long was Impellitteri in the water?"

"Coroner thinks from eight hours to three days, maybe a little more."

"Where'd he go into the water?"

"Hard to say. Could have been right off Porcupine City, could have been off the Apostles."

That island archipelago lay more than fifty miles west of the point where the body had washed up.

"But the Keweenaw is full of slow eddies, and he could've floated into one and spun around for a while."

The Keweenaw Current runs west to east from the westernmost tip of Lake Superior near Duluth in Minnesota

—

27

all the way to the tip of the Keweenaw Peninsula, the thumb that juts out into the lake some sixty miles northeast of Porcupine City. The current meanders along in most places at about five miles per hour, but at certain points offshore can reach eleven miles per hour, a pretty good clip.

"What makes it tougher to pinpoint the site, " Alex continued, "is that the fellow's chest and pants had postmortem abrasions and tears that makes the coroner think the body got caught on a snag in the shallows for a while somewhere before rolling back out into deeper water. Could've been anywhere."

The inshore waters of western Lake Superior are full of rocky shoals, toothy underwater escarpments linked to the copper-bearing ridges inland, as well as scores of old shipwrecks and vast sunken rafts of waterlogged hardwood and white pine lost in storms while being towed to the sawmills at Sault Sainte Marie a century ago.

"Anything else?"

A moment of silence at the other end, then a rustling of papers. "Yes. We found a bag of marijuana in his pants pocket. World-class stuff, too — absolutely loaded with delta-9-trans-tetrahydrocannabinol. About 15 per cent by dry weight, almost unheard of."

I whistled. "That's a lot of THC." Tetrahydrocannabinol is what gives pot its pop.

"Probably doesn't mean anything," Alex said, "except that Impellitteri could afford the best of everything."

"Or was peddling the best of everything."

"Yes. There was a fragment of peyote button in his pocket, too."

That was odd. The use of peyote, a mild psychoactive bud from a cactus, is mostly a Southwestern Indian religious custom followed by members of the Native American Church. Most Upper Michigan Ojibwe are either Catholic or follow the traditional Ojibwe religion. I doubted that there was much of a market for peyote in these parts.

"Maybe he'd been in New Mexico, traded a few ounces of pot for a button, wanted to see what it was like," I said.

"Whatever," Alex said. "There's still more."

"What?"

"*Banisteriopsis caapi.*"

I sighed. "You're going to lecture me, aren't you?"

"You need to complete your education, sonny."

"All right. Slide me down the banister-whatsis, willya?"

"Very well. It's a giant woody vine found in the Amazon rain forest. In Ecuador and Peru they call it the 'vine of the dead,' or in their word, *ayahuasca*. When its crushed leaves are combined with those from another plant, usually one called *chacruna*, or *Psychotria viridis*, the result is the brew also called *ayahuasca*. It's like LSD—it sends you to the moon. The natives of the Amazon valley have used it for millennia as a psychotropic drink for healing, divination and black magic. But it's almost unheard of in North America, except among scientists."

"You're reading from a book, aren't you?"

"How did you know?"

"Cop's intuition."

"Yes, well, bits of the vine of the dead were also caught inside the stiff's pocket seams with the pot and peyote."

"That's odd. Wouldn't they have been washed out when the body was rolled around by the waves?"

"Nope. The forensics guys found weeny grains of the stuff caught inside the stitches. These guys can find microscopic evidence in clothes even after several washings. Anyway, what does all this tell you?"

"Maybe this stiff was a well-traveled courier, a middleman who dealt in a whole drugstore of high-quality happy powder for upper-crust users. Maybe he got into a disagreement with a mob supplier over something, say, quality or price, made a threat he shouldn't have, and got wasted."

There was a brief silence, then Alex said, "Works for me, too."

"What are you going to do with the case?"

"Put it in the freezer," Alex said.

"What about the Feebs and the DEA?"

"They don't care." I knew that the FBI had enough on its hands hunting al Qaeda, and that the Drug Enforcement Administration had more to do than investigate another dead small-time Midwestern hood, even if he apparently had been in the drug business, unless the known facts promised to lead to big game.

"Let me know if anything turns up at your end, okay?" Alex added.

"Okay," I said. We both knew that the Porcupine County Sheriff's Department, let alone the Michigan state police, was not about to expend money and manpower on a homicide victim nobody cared about, especially a homicide victim on the wrong side of the law. Such legal triage was not justice, true, but it was common sense. We in law enforcement are stretched thin enough. And so Danny Impellitteri would go into the bulging cold case file, eventually to be forgotten.

Still, Alex was reminding me of something: Although the case was officially a state-police problem, and not a very urgent one at that, he was unofficially inviting me to stay involved as a brother officer if new facts came to light. After all, a corpse *had* washed up in my jurisdiction, and I had been the first to catch the case. Alex was quietly performing a professional courtesy, the unspoken kind that comes from mutual trust and respect.

"But," I said.

Alex's voice perked up. "But?"

"Assuming I'm right and this was a mob hit," I said, "what would a Chicago or Vegas hood be doing aboard a boat in Lake Superior? It's more than seven hundred miles from Chicago up Lake Michigan to the Soo and then out here."

"Flies don't grow on you," Alex said.

"You've checked already."

"The Chicago mob squad says only a couple of hoods own boats big enough to make the trip, and they haven't left harbor for weeks."

I sat silent for a while, contemplating.

"You still there?" Alex said.

"Yes."

"What's on your mind?"

"Doesn't seem that there would be a reason for mob activity way up here in the middle of nowhere," I said. "Nothing to extort. Nothing to steal. The only thing I can think of is it's drug related, especially with that stuff in the stiff's pocket, but that's so unlikely. Especially now."

Upper Michigan, with its long and sparsely inhabited Lake Superior shore, was a hotbed of smuggling during Prohibition, when Canadian rumrunners raced cases of gin and Scotch across the lake in powerful Chris-Crafts from Port Arthur and Fort William under cover of darkness. Lately there has been drug-running from the same places, but much less than a short time ago. Ever since the al Qaeda attacks in 2001, Air Force eyes-in-the-sky have constantly patrolled the Canadian border, watching for unauthorized flights from the north. No longer is Washington Island, just west of Isle Royale in the northern stretches of Lake Superior, a favorite drop zone for small planes carrying loads of marijuana and cocaine to be transferred to pleasure boats and carried to inlets on the U.S. side. Lately dope smugglers had been stowing their stuff in the noisome cargo of garbage trucks carrying Canadian waste over the border at Sault Sainte Marie to landfills in Upper Michigan. The hazmat scanners and drug-sniffing dogs at Customs can't detect such contraband amid the smelly garbage. Only poking about by hand worked, and the Customs people had to limit their searches to random checks. Lots of cocaine and other hard stuff got through that way, but the politicians south of the border were now demanding that the Canadian authorities check the loads themselves and guarantee their cleanliness.

"Yeah," Alex said. "No point in keeping this case active, is there?"

"Right. Now would you mind going away? I've got paperwork to do."

"Didn't know shitkicker deputies knew how to read and write."

"Screw you," I said, but I couldn't help laughing.

FIVE

That reminded me. I'd forgotten to drop by Silverton to check out the *Mary-El* and see if her skipper, Tom Whiteside, had seen anything while fishing on the morning the corpse of Dan Impellitteri had washed up on the beach. It wasn't important, just a loose end to nail down for the files, really a useless bit of work considering the item would likely be forgotten in the cold case drawer, but I was grateful for any excuse to leave my desk behind on a warm sunny day. Grabbing my garrison cap, I checked out on the board and headed in the department's Explorer thirteen miles west to the small settlement at Silverton.

Silverton is an old mining town named for an undiscovered lode of silver whose existence was suggested only by metal flakes that had drifted down the Iron River during the middle of the nineteenth century. The town consists mostly of a large chain motel with a restaurant— George's, of course—a general store with gas pumps, a bunch of tiny gift shops that cater mostly to summer campers and winter skiers and snowmobilers, and a warren of dented secondhand mobile homes intermixed with small, old miner's houses. Most everybody who lives there just scrapes by. Many of them are former miners at the old Lone Pine copper mine and smelter several miles south.

Tom berths the *Mary-El* at a dock at the mouth of the Iron River, one of the few waterways for hundreds of miles along the Lake Superior shore that doesn't turn into an impassable sandbar after the spring runoff. Even so, the mouth is so shallow that at times of lowest water the good people of Silverton often laid bets on whether the *Mary-El* would ground on the shifting sandbar going out or coming in, requiring Tom to winch her off with a stout steel cable fastened to an onshore oak.

The *Mary-El* was in, and as I strode down the rickety planks of Tom's dock I saw that her big diesel engine lay in pieces next to the boat, its crankcase split open to reveal the innards. Tom lay snoozing in a deck chair, soaking up the sun, but stirred as he heard my tread on the boards.

"Steve!" he called. "What can I do for you?"

"If you guarantee that I'll catch a thirty-pound coho today, I'll hire the *Mary-El*," I said. I'd had pretty good luck aboard her a couple of times in the past, going out for lake trout on county-sponsored outings in the days not so long ago when the county could afford such treats for its workers.

"Sit down, Steve," Tom said. pointing to a ragged deck chair across the dock from his. I sat.

"I can't guarantee you'll catch a thirty-gram minnow," Tom said, "not with that Cummins in the shape she's in." He pointed a wrench at the engine.

"What's wrong?"

"Cracked the crankshaft a couple of weeks ago," he said. "Do you have any idea how goddam long it takes to get a new one? And how much the bastards cost?" This, I knew, would make the difference between black ink and red on Tom's meager balance sheet for the year.

I sighed. "That's tough, Tom," I said. "And not much time, is there?" No matter if his boat returned to the lake by the following week, he couldn't make up the time he had lost. The Lake Superior sportfishing season is short. The tourists don't arrive until after Memorial Day and are mostly gone by Labor Day, except for folks who prefer the quiet silence of the cool early fall in these parts. By the end of October, the autumn storms would begin, locking the *Mary-El* in her berth for the winter.

"You said the engine broke down two weeks ago?"

"That's right."

That was a week before the hoodlum's corpse had washed ashore.

"You weren't out on the lake a week ago Saturday?"

"In what?"

"The guy who found that body on the beach last week said he'd seen the *Mary-El*, or maybe a boat that looked like her, just offshore the morning that body washed up on the beach. Thought you might've seen something." I didn't need to remind Tom about that day. Everyone in Porcupine City had heard about the corpse and the prevailing theory that it had been a mob hit.

"Sure wasn't the *Mary-El* out there," Tom said, reaching into a grimy file folder and pulling out a copy of a fax from a Milwaukee marine dealer acknowledging a similar communication from the Lumbermen's State Bank of Porcupine County, which kept a fax machine for its customers. The original fax was an order for a new crankshaft, and the reply was stamped with a date five days before the body had washed onshore.

"You're not a suspect in anything, Tom," I said, but I was glad for the proof anyway. Eliminated a possible lead.

"Might as well be one," he said wearily. "Don't have nothing else to do anyway."

"Okay, if we can't find a better perp, we'll let you know so you can apply for the job."

"I could use one," he said.

"Yeah." Off season, Tom kept himself housed, fed and clothed by repairing snowmobiles at the Polaris dealer in Porcupine City. But it would be another two months before enough snow had fallen for steady work there.

"You'll make out," I said. "You always do." I twirled my cap and rose to leave. "But what boat could that witness have seen that morning?"

"Don't know," Tom said, rubbing his stubble. "The *Mary-El*'s the biggest party boat in these parts. Maybe your witness saw another boat with the same shape." The *Mary-El*'s profile was distinctive, with a high flying bridge set closer to the stern than most, lake trout rods stuck vertically into holders at her fantail.

"What could that be?"

"The *Lucky Six* out of Porcupine City is one," he said. "But she's a private forty-footer that belongs to Morrie Weinstein and he says she's been in Lakes Huron and Michigan all summer on charter."

"Um." I knew Weinstein. He was a transplant like me, a wealthy entrepreneur from Chicago, scion of an old Upper Peninsula mining family, who in the last few years invested in all sorts of startup outfits in the area, the *Porcupine County Herald* front-paging every one of them. For a long time, as far as I knew, few if any of his efforts paid dividends, except for one. Three years ago he had opened up an old copper mine that had been in his mother's family for generations and turned it into an underground nursery, raising high-quality flowers and seedlings as well as experimental plants for the pharmaceutical industry. Slowly the enterprise had expanded, and now he employed thirty-odd Porkies and a dozen horticultural specialists from Chicago in two shifts. Everyone considered Weinstein a godsend to the county. Another year or two, and he would be its second biggest employer after the paper mill on the river across from Porcupine City.

I didn't know his motives, but it was not unheard of for independently wealthy people who had fallen in love with Porcupine County to invest in it and its people for reasons other than raw profit. I slept with one of them.

"Who knows?" Tom said. "That boat could have been from anywhere, come inshore that morning in hopes the trout were maybe running in the shallows."

"Could be," I said, "but it's probably not important."

Nevertheless, I jotted a few lines in my pocket notebook. You never can tell.

On my way back to the Explorer I spotted Olga Wennerstrom standing in the doorway of her single-wide across from Tom's dock. I hoped she hadn't seen me, but she had, and I quailed. Olga is an overimaginative old lady who, like so many aged and lonely folks, shows little self-restraint in her conversation and never misses a chance to express herself. To hear her talk, Silverton is a reeking Sodom of crime and sin, and it all washes up the Iron River from Lake Superior. I had no doubt that over the decades Silverton had seen its share of rumrunners and drug couriers from across the water, but today there were easier ways of making a nefarious living. There are a lot of Olgas in Porcupine County, and they are largely harmless, although Olga's habit of writing garrulous, mean-spirited and meandering letters to the editor of the Herald—letters that were printed verbatim, complete with unsubtle remarks about "the homosexuals" and "the colored"—caused me to avoid her when I could. Being a member of a minority group makes me sensitive about the slights others must suffer, and sometimes I can't watch my tongue. I often had to bite it, because in rural America the letters columns in country weeklies often are the only free outlet for citizens to sound off, other than on radio rant shows, where words disappear into the air as soon as they are uttered. Readers often turn to the letters columns as soon as their newspapers arrive in their mailboxes so they can find out who's pissed off this week, often by a letter or two in the previous week's edition. In the countryside the letters-to-the-editor page is the nearest thing people have to a legal dogfight, complete with blood and snarls. Letters columns sell newspapers, too. "They're better than Fox News," Alex once said, "for the crackpots." Alex is a liberal, a rarity among cops, city or country.

"Deputy!" she called. "Steve! Martinez!" I sighed, squared my shoulders, and strode to Olga's trailer.

"Yes'm?"

"You're too late!" she said, her voice ringing with accusation.

"Too late for what?"

"The white slavers!"

"The white slavers?" That was a new one.

"They landed last night, at that very dock there, and they brought in prostitutes, a lot of 'em," she sputtered.

"Who's they, ma'am?" I asked politely, turning to a fresh sheet in my notebook.

"You know, those people. The ones who come in every other day bringing all sorts of evil to good Christians."

"Right, those people," I said, jotting an imaginary note. "Where did they take the, uh, ladies of the night?"

She pointed across the road to Moriarty's, a tumbledown tavern whose closest brush with evil came with the penny-ante poker half a dozen wrinkled retirees played every afternoon. In the course of police work, aiming of course to dredge up possibly important information on slow crime days, I'd sat in on a couple of games—and hadn't arrested the players when they cleaned my pockets of loose change, chortling at having put one over on the law.

"I'll check 'em out," I said. "Thanks for the heads-up, Olga."

"Steve!" she called before I'd gone ten yards. "If there's a reward, I want it!"

"Sure thing, Olga."

Tom was standing by his pickup, the vehicle cheek by jowl with the Explorer. "Olga go on about hookers?" he said with a broad grin.

"Uh huh."

"Warm day yesterday, and there were tourists in bikini tops. Some of those tops weren't very big." He rolled his eyes in mock horror.

"Uh huh."

"Moriarty's could use some new scenery."

"I'll say."

SIX

The second corpse turned up in the middle of July, and this time it was not on the beach but deep in the second-growth forest in the southern reaches of Porcupine County. I was wrestling paperwork in the office when the radio call came in from Joe Koski.

"Chad just called," said Joe. Large, rawboned, good-looking, and amiable, young Chad Garrow was the deputy on shift in the southern and eastern half of the county. I liked him although I sometimes couldn't stand him. Chad is a clumsy sprawl of a lad, all knees and elbows, unkempt red hair and loose shirttails, the kind who unconsciously bulls into your personal space even if he may be standing six feet away. Women steer him away from antique chairs and gently take dishes out of his hands so he won't break them. Whenever we go out together in a sheriff's cruiser, Chad drives and I sit in the back seat — it's safer that way.

Chad is the newest hire in the department, and the nephew of Sheriff Eli Garrow. This wasn't quite a case of out-and-out nepotism, although it came close. Chad had been the only Porcupine County resident who applied for the deputy's job when it fell open the previous Christmas season, thanks to the arrest and conviction of its former occupant in a celebrated revenge killing. There had been smarter and more experienced applicants from outside, but Porcupine County prefers to hire its own when possible. Chad had just barely qualified in the other requirements, and as a green deputy he sometimes did not seem the sharpest axe in the woodshed.

We could have done worse. Chad, whose heart always occupied the right place even if his head didn't, tried hard to follow instructions. In his six months in the department, he had not embarrassed us. That gave Eli Garrow a lot of good-old-boy pride even though it caused the rest of us to shrug. When I was partnered with Chad on the same shift, as I was now, I tried, as we all did, to teach him the finer points of police work. The lad always put forth his best efforts, although there were times I wondered if he'd survive his year's probation.

"Body in the woods out back of Coppermass," Joe said. "Looks like it might be Saarinen."

"Out back of Coppermass" is a tangled wilderness where over the decades many people had disappeared without trace, so many that the locals called it "the Yooper Triangle." Frank Saarinen had gone deer hunting there one frigid weekend the previous November and never returned to his wife and four small children, who he had long supported, as so many Porkies did, by scratching out meager odd jobs. Saarinen was a familiar hard-luck case. He was a diligent worker skilled at many trades, but his drinking had cost him good jobs, one at the old Lone Pine Mine, the last Upper Peninsula copper mine to close, and another at the paper mill. Recently he had sobered up enough for Morris Weinstein to take a chance on him and put him to work at the nursery buried deep in the Venture Mine.

Saarinen's disappearance was not an uncommon occurrence in the northern wilderness. Hunters and hikers, even those native to the county, sometimes get lost, suffer heart attacks, and shoot themselves or each other by accident or by design, usually suicide. When bad things happen we find most of the bodies, but now and then one never turns up — or turns up only long afterward. The forest is large, deep, and thick. I had spent three days in the department's battered old Cessna four-seater, exercising the pilot's license I earned in the Army and hunting for Saarinen. I hoped he had found a clearing and possessed the mother-wit to build a smoky fire and wait for rescue. I didn't complain at the assignment.

Searching by air is infinitely more pleasant than pounding the ground through snow and bitter cold.

"Here's the Saarinen file, Steve," Joe said. He didn't have to tell me to get going—I was already on my way out the door to the Explorer. Among other things, the file would inform me what Saarinen's wife, Sally, had said he was wearing when he disappeared, helping in the identification of skeletal remains.

Forty minutes later I pulled up behind Chad's cruiser, an ordinary Ford sedan the local dealer had converted into a poor man's police car, on a gravel track four miles off State Highway M-26 and set off into the woods. Chad had called in the coordinates from his hand-held GPS, these days a standard item on a wilderness deputy's equipment belt, but it was easy enough to follow the old deer trail into the forest. I knew exactly where the scene was—on the edge of a cut-over meadow in old mining country, part of the Ottawa National Forest. In fifteen minutes I joined Chad and Tommy Goodkind, the veteran woodsman who had stumbled over the corpse while foraging for downed hickory to cut up for pulpwood to sell to the paper mill.

"No wonder we never found him last year," Chad said unnecessarily. The body lay nearly hidden by the boughs of a fat blue spruce Terry had brushed aside while shouldering his way through a thicket.

"I stopped when I heard the rattle of bones," Terry said, "and there he was."

I squatted and held aside a spruce branch. The body lay face down in matted leaves and spruce needles, almost completely skeletal. Even though the leaves concealed most of it, I could tell that the skull had been shattered. The stock of a rifle protruded from under the body.

"Stop fucking up my crime scene," a familiar voice cut in as a lanky shadow loomed in the sunlight on the spruce. I jumped slightly. For all his love of noisy arrivals, Alex Kolehmainen, a veteran woodsman, knows how to sneak soundlessly through the forest. He'd make a better woodland Indian than I would.

"Who says it's a crime scene?" I asked mildly as Alex took a pair of latex gloves from his kit bag. I fished a pair from my shirt pocket and handed an extra set to Chad, motioning to him to put them on. It was probably the first time he had ever needed them, and he had not thought to carry a pair with him. I sighed, but I also knew it wouldn't happen again. You had to show Chad only once—thank goodness for that.

"It's always a crime scene until I say it's not," Alex said. "Can't you get that through your thick heads?"

Chad and I grinned at each other.

"Up yours, Sergeant," Chad said affably. Even though he was still a rookie, he had already learned that Alex's fierceness was entirely theatrical.

"There'll be time for that later," said Alex just as amiably. "Let's get to work."

Enough remained of the clothing on the skeleton to match it with what Sally had said her husband was wearing the day he had disappeared. "Green canvas jacket," I said, riffling through the papers in the file. "Orange-and-black Pendleton wool shirt. Green cord trousers. The teeth ought to clinch it."

"Maybe not necessary," Alex said as he carefully fished a wallet from the wretched little pile of bones and rags with large tweezers. With latex-gloved hands he opened it. "Driver's license. Frank Saarinen, all right. Hunting license, too. The usual stuff, all in his name. Thirty bucks in tens. Here's a wooden cross, too."

The hand-carved hickory cross, inlaid with copper, matched the list in the folder.

Before touching anything else Alex photographed the scene from all angles with his digital camera, as always taking pains not to disturb the corpse. Macabre his task may have been, but I always admired the professionalism he brought to every case. Fifteen minutes later, satisfied with the prints, he squatted for a closer look. He brushed the leaves from the skull.

"See the hole?" he said, shining a penlight on a clean, slightly puckered indentation on the right temple. The left temple—indeed, most of the skull on that side—was missing, the edges of the bone rough and shattered. Alex reached for the camera.

"Bullet?" said Chad, grasping the obvious.

"Yup," said Alex, who did not suffer fools but showed patience with greenhorns. "Let's turn him over."

That was easier said than done. Bone by bone, sleeve by sleeve, Alex rearranged the skeleton on its back, constantly dictating what he saw into a small tape recorder in his pocket, microphone clipped to his collar.

"Right foot missing. Left ulna missing. Most of left arm gone."

Scavenging animals and birds had carried away parts of the corpse. Bodies discovered in forests are rarely ever complete.

"Where do you suppose the bullet went?" Chad asked.

"Probably hundreds of yards away," Alex said. "If this was a high-velocity deer round, as I suspect it was, it would just have kept going."

We contemplated the corpse for a while.

"One of three things happened here," Alex said presently. "An accident, suicide, or murder." His conclusion, painfully obvious to me, was meant for Chad, although addressed to us both. Consciously or unconsciously Alex was a born teacher, and all the cops and deputies who worked with him benefited from his subtle mentoring. "I don't think he shot himself accidentally."

"Why?" Chad said. He was paying attention.

"Look," said Alex, standing up.

Frank Saarinen—if the body indeed was his, and there was no reason to think it wasn't—had fallen over his rifle. That was clear from the original arrangement of the bones and scraps of clothing.

Alex picked up a stout branch four feet long and pointed it at his right temple, extending his right arm so that his finger rested on an imaginary trigger in the middle of the stick. "If you shot yourself this way," he said, "the recoil would catapult the rifle away from you and the impact of the bullet would drive you in the other direction."

Alex abruptly tossed the branch aside and lurched sidelong, well away from the spruce.

"See? It's unlikely that happened here. Besides, people who commit suicide with rifles almost always shoot themselves in the mouth, often with their toes on the trigger. That's easier than any other method. It shortens the distance between the head and the trigger."

I riffled through the file. "Nothing here that makes me think Frank was despondent," I said. "No obvious reason for suicide. Besides, he had a brand new deer license. You don't need one of those to kill yourself."

Alex nodded and looked at Chad, who was absorbing it all.

Alex picked up the rifle. A year's worth of rust had crept over the blued steel of the Remington .270 and its four-power scope. It had been an expensive rig, especially for a man like Frank, but like so many poor but proud Porkies he had spared no expense on the tools that kept his family alive. Frank, I felt sure, had fed his wife and children with lots of venison, both in season and out.

"This was a valuable rifle," said Alex. "If this had been a murder, the killer most likely would have taken it and Frank's wallet as well."

"Nothing in the file to suggest anybody had it in for Frank," I said. "No orange, either."

Frank had not worn a fluorescent orange vest or hat, as do most sensible, safety-minded hunters, to keep others from mistaking them for game. It's the law in Michigan. Deer are color blind, but some hunters won't take that for granted, and refuse to wear orange. Some don't want to be seen in the woods, perhaps because they're poaching, perhaps because they don't want other hunters to discover their favorite spots, and perhaps because they just don't want the government to tell them what to do. Porkies tend to be fiercely libertarian. They mistrust official bodies of all kinds, especially the Michigan Department of Natural Resources, whose statewide one-size-fits-all policies they consider unsuited to the special needs of dwellers in the remote wilderness, most especially Porcupine County. I was sympathetic. I knew how bureaucracies work, being a member of one myself.

"All right," Alex said. Holding the rifle in front of him, butt against his shoulder and muzzle pointed forward ahead, he took up position by the tree and peered ahead between boughs. "Frank is waiting at the ready for a deer to come by on the trail. Another hunter over here" — Alex pointed to the right across the clearing — "sees Frank's shape against the tree and thinks he's a deer. Bang! Frank's head explodes and he falls forward into the tree with his rifle in front of him.

"The other hunter sees his target fall, runs over, and discovers it isn't a deer. He panics and clears out as fast as he can. A lot of people would. Think about it. Thousands of hunters in Upper Michigan every November and we have no idea where most of them go. The bullet's away in the woods somewhere, and so are lots of other bullets hunters have fired over a hundred years. He didn't mean to kill Frank, but it'll be a terrible mess for him if he calls the cops. It's easier just to run away. 'Course, sooner or later it'll hit him that he killed a human being, maybe one with a wife and family, and he'll have to live with that the rest of his life.

"And it's entirely possible that didn't happen. Deer hunters don't aim for the head. That'd ruin the trophy. They aim for the heart. Maybe the shooter had no idea that he had hit anything and never came over to find out. And of course that bullet could have been just a stray. It happens."

There was nothing more to do except search the area

45

for a few yards around the tree. Chad turned up two large skull fragments, and Alex found a human finger bone an animal had carried away to gnaw upon. There was no point in hunting for more. We had enough for a burial, anyway.

"We're done here," Alex said after half an hour. "Let's bag the remains. Not enough left for the medical examiner to work on. I'll send them to forensics in Marquette for confirmation. For now it's a hunting accident."

Chad, Terry and I helped carry what remained of Frank Saarinen in a body bag to Alex's cruiser. The bag felt remarkably light.

"Be good, girls," Alex said as he drove away.

I raised Joe Koski on the radio. "It's who we thought, all right," I told him discreetly.

"Steve, stop by the next of kin," the undersheriff cut in. I hate that assignment. None of us like being the bearers of bad news. But it has to be done. I hurried so I could get there before Sally Saarinen heard it on the grapevine. No one should have to learn about the death of a loved one that way.

SEVEN

Sally Saarinen was just thirty-eight years old, but she looked fifty. Like so many single mothers who teeter on the edge of destitution in Upper Michigan, she had suffered from years of just getting by. She had once been an attractive woman, but now her puffy features — and those of her four children, ranging in age from six to fifteen — bespoke the usual fat-loaded, carb-heavy diet of rural food-stamp poverty, mostly day-old bread, a little hamburger and a lot of venison. Their clothes, faded and threadbare, came from the fifty-cent racks at St. Vincent De Paul's, the big charity store the Catholic church operated in downtown Porcupine City.

But the shirts and pants were clean and mended, the shoes freshly resoled. Sally, I knew, scraped up enough money each year to pay the minuscule property taxes on her battered single-wide mobile home and the half acre on which it sat at the edge of the woods on Quarterline Road, eight miles outside Porcupine City. The broad yard around the trailer was carefully swept, the grass trimmed right up to the concrete blocks bearing the junked '79 Ford pickup and '83 Chevy sedan in the back. Only two of the four cars Frank had been stripping for their parts to sell before his disappearance remained. Sally, who knew her way around vehicles — she had been a transcontinental eighteen-wheeler driver when she met Frank — had expertly completed the scavenging, and only the frame of the pickup and rusty shell of the sedan remained. She did what she could to survive. And she kept up appearances. That allowed her retain her pride. Often that was all some Porkies owned, but their neighbors respected them for it.

Sally was out hanging up the wash on a limp cotton

clothesline strung between the trailer and a stout oak branch a few yards away, and when I got out of the Explorer she calmly finished pegging a child's jersey to the line before she turned to me, her face set in resignation.

"It's Frank, isn't it?" she said.

"Yes. We found his body this morning in the woods south of Coppermass. Looks like a hunting accident."

She took a deep breath, but her careworn face remained carved in stone, the crow's feet around her eyes deepening but remaining dry. "You'd better come in," she said.

Two children, four and ten years old by the look of them, stood in the doorway. "Take Janie out back to the sandbox, won't you?" Sally said to the older one, and the two skipped down the steps and scooted gaily around the back of the trailer. I was glad they were too young to suspect the reason I had come to their home.

"Okay," said Sally as she sat on a lumpy couch in the tiny living space, I in an equally ratty overstuffed chair. "What did you find?"

I was honest but terse, editing out unnecessary details. "We can identify him by his teeth, of course," I said.

"He never went to a dentist in his life," Sally said. That was unsurprising. Poor rural people often never get physicals or dental care, unless they spend some time in the military or in jail.

"Then at some point we'll need you to come down to identify the clothes. There's a carved wooden cross, too."

She nodded.

"While we're pretty sure it was an accident," I added, "I still have to ask some routine questions. I can come back later if you'd rather."

"No. Let's get it done now."

Over the next twenty minutes I took Sally through the contents of the folder, step by step, reviewing what she had told us a year ago. Her answers remained the same. That impressed me. Memory being chancy at best and unreliable at worst, details change over time. A red sweater becomes a blue one. Brass belt buckles turn into steel. Loafers transmogrify into tennis shoes. Some cops, not understanding these common quirks of the mind, become suspicious that their interviewees are deliberately changing their original stories, and the interviewees wind up as suspects themselves. A lot of time gets wasted sorting out memories and facts. But Sally Saarinen changed nothing. Every detail remained the same.

"I'm sorry, but I've got to ask some personal questions," I said. I hated this part of the interview, especially with people like Sally. They have so little except their privacy. To take that away from them is to strip them of their final belongings. But there was no choice.

Sally shrugged. "Yes?"

"Was everything okay between you and Frank?"

"Yes. When he joined AA almost two years ago, we stopped fighting all the time. We got along pretty good. He was good to the kids. He had a steady paycheck. He came home every night instead of going out to a bar."

"Frank didn't seem depressed or unhappy, did he?"

"Nope. That man loved life. When he drank he often was down and when he sobered up he said he was no good. But he'd been sober for quite a while. He loved that job in the mine growing flowers and plants. He told me they were the first beautiful things ever to come from his hands."

"Then I guess there wasn't anything wrong at work?"

"No," she said, and after a beat, added, "Well . . ."

"Yes?"

"I didn't really think about it at the time. Frank was never one to bring worries home from work. But I think something was bothering him there."

"What could that have been?"

"I don't know. But a couple of weeks before he disappeared in the woods, he said he didn't want to go to the company picnic. I talked him into it, 'cause the kids don't get much chance to go out and have a good time—it's too expensive to go anywhere. We did go, but he didn't want to talk to anybody and played with the kids instead. When I asked afterward, he said nothing was wrong and to forget it."

I waited, but she had nothing to add.

"Probably doesn't mean anything," I said. I suspected it did, but I doubted that she knew why.

"Not anymore, anyway," she said.

I stood up. "Thank you, Mrs. Saarinen," I said. I knew her familiarly as "Sally" — I'm on first-name terms with most law-abiding people in the county — but this was a formal and sober occasion. Now I had to finish the formal and sober questions. "In a week or so we'll release Frank's remains. Do you have a preference for the funeral home?"

"I don't know," she said. "We can't afford one."

"I think something will be done about that." The Evangelical Lutheran church to which the Saarinens belonged most likely would come to the rescue. Devout churchgoers up here are loath to let their brethren depart this world in potter's fields. When accidents happened to the poor, religious charity took care of most of them. There was a lot of that in the Upper Peninsula, for the impulse to do God's work helped hold together the dwindling population.

"Yes. Thank you." Her expression remained calm.

I walked out to the Explorer.

"Deputy." She usually called me Steve.

"Yes?"

"There's one more thing I just remembered."

I waited.

"About a week before Frank disappeared, he held me close in bed and made me promise to take care of the children if anything happened to him."

I stared at her.

"I'm sorry, Deputy," she said. "I didn't think anything of it at the time. I thought he was just having a fight staying sober and had to unload his worries. But now . . ."

I examined her strained face carefully. She was not

dissembling. This was not a last-minute panic attack, a clumsy attempt to forestall accusations of concealing evidence. To her this was truly a revelation that had come only with the passage of time and the jogging of memory. Whether it was significant or not was anybody's guess. I made a guess, anyway.

"It's all right," I said. "Knowing that wouldn't have helped us find him, anyway."

"It was an accident, wasn't it?" she said, her cheeks beginning to tremble from the effort of keeping a brave face.

I nodded. "So far as we can tell, it was. Thank you, Mrs. Saarinen."

She closed her door.

Just as I started the Explorer, I heard sobs start up in the trailer. They were deep and ragged, the letting-go kind.

EIGHT

I was in bed with the brains of the outfit when I told her what I had been doing at work that day. For reasons I have never quite been able to divine, our skull sessions often take place after what she archly calls "physical therapy on the fitness bench," her term for happy activities under the coverlet of the oaken four-poster on the second floor of her roomy, exquisitely furnished log house on the shore a few miles east of my snug cabin. With my finger I traced an imaginary line through the perspiration covering the ample curves of Virginia Anttila Fitzgerald's person, fine and firm in its early forties. Still panting lightly, as I was, she let the finger advance on its objective for several inches before she giggled and slapped it.

"So what's the trouble?" she asked. "Sally Saarinen is made of hickory and steel, and if any poor single mother's going to manage to raise her children well, she's one of them. I'm sorry about Frank, I really am, and those children do need a father, but things could be a lot worse for them."

"Yeah. But it was what she said about Frank maybe having trouble at work that makes me wonder."

"What's that got to do with the accident? It's fairly obvious that's what it was. Besides, Steve, everybody has difficulties at work at one time or another. That doesn't necessarily lead to murder."

"Who mentioned murder?" I demanded.

She sighed. "I know how your mind works. You get a pebble in your shoe and it grates on your instep all day. Suddenly it becomes a boulder on your brain. One cross word from somebody's boss in the morning and by midafternoon it's a motive for homicide."

"But what about Frank asking Sally to promise to take care of the kids if anything happened to him?"

"You've never been a father, Steve," she said. "Every man, in the wee dark hours when scary molehills grow into terrifying mountains, worries about his family's future. Frank probably woke up from a bad dream and looked to Sally for comfort. You've done that more than once yourself."

"All right, all right, ma'am," I said. "You have me there." I began to retrace the alpine route my finger had traveled.

"That tickles. Stop it." She made no move to halt my progress. I stopped anyway.

"But I'm curious," I said.

"Don't stop," she said. "About what?"

"Frank's boss, Morrie Weinstein. Now that we mention it, I don't know anything about him, other than that he lived in Chicago, spent his summers here as a kid, came back a few years ago, tried his hand at a few things and finally opened up that nursery in the old Venture Mine. What do you know about it, Ginny?"

She lifted herself up onto one elbow and turned to me, the sheet dropping from her body. I closed my eyes, hoping to retain on their dark backdrop as long as possible the delicious image of her hip's graceful curve and the shadow beneath.

"Is that a rhetorical question or a serious one?" she asked.

"A serious one." Suddenly the languorous spell broke.

"All right." She sat up and hugged her knees. I could almost hear locks clicking open and drawers sliding out.

"Now then. Weinstein's mother, Edna, was the daughter of Gordon Holderman, the last magnate to operate the Venture Mine. Actually, 'magnate' is too splendid a word for Holderman. By the time he bought the mine from its owners in New York City sometime in the 1920s, it was moribund. Not even the demand for copper to make shells and rifle cartridges during the First World War could bring it back from the dead. There was still copper down there—there still is all over the Keweenaw Range—but it's just not economical to bring up, compared with the ore in those huge open-pit mines in the Southwest."

As Upper Michigan copper mines went, the Venture, founded in 1849 by a consortium of Manhattan investors, was a small one, but bigger than most mining enterprises, which tended to peter out when digging failed to uncover either rich seams of ore or mass copper, almost pure metal scattered in boulder-size chunks throughout the ridges of the Keweenaw.

"The Venture had a single vertical shaft about twelve hundred feet deep, with one skip that served seven drifts."

"Skips? Drifts?"

"A skip is the elevator car that's lifted up and down a mine shaft. A drift is a horizontal tunnel driven into the ore from the vertical shaft. Sometimes several drifts branched out from a single level. Sometimes a drift expanded from a low tunnel into a huge room. It all depended on what the miners found."

"Ah. Go on."

The old Venture owned a stamp mill for crushing ore hoisted up from the drifts where it was carved from the rock, often with the help of explosives, but it had no smelter. Once crushed, the ore was packed into barrels to be drawn by horses to the docks at Porcupine City for shipment by schooner to smelters in lower Michigan. Later in the century it was trundled to a horse-drawn tram line that served several mines along the Keweenaw Range and ended at the bigger and much richer Minesota Mine at Rockland, twelve miles east of the Venture. At the Minesota—that's one *n*, by the way—the ore was smelted and loaded into hopper cars to be hauled by locomotives to the harbor at Porcupine City for transshipment to the Soo and points east. Not Minnesota. Minesota. I wanted to know why there was only one *n*, but I wasn't about to deflect Ginny's head of steam.

"Profits at the Venture were always modest, even during the wartime booms of 1861 to 1865, 1898 and 1914 to 1918, when the demand for copper wire and shell casings was high, and to protect their investors during the lean decades the owners converted the property to a tribute mine. That means the miners were given no wages but themselves sold the ore they mined and paid the owners one-eighth of their proceeds in tribute. Nobody got rich, but everybody could keep their heads above water that way."

What's more, Ginny said, tribute mining wasn't terribly good for either the mines or the miners. The miners worked only the best rock, shoving the poorer ore aside under the ground—a practice the industry called "gophering" or "mine robbing." They also skipped a lot of safety measures, such as stout timbering of the drift ceilings, endangering themselves. Many tribute miners perished in cave-ins deep underground.

"By the stock market crash in 1929 the mine was all but played out. The owners had sold off the stamp mill machinery, and most of the other equipment—except the steam-driven shaft hoist—when Holderman bought the property for a song. He had been the manager since 1907, running two decades of tribute mining even after the scandalous deaths of several miners under his supervision. At first it seemed that he intended to expand the mine's operations—it was rumored briefly that a large mass of pure copper had been discovered deep at the end of the lowest drift—but he could not find investors. After the Second World War he turned the mine into an operating museum, taking skiploads of tourists down two or three levels. By 1955, however, the tourists had lost interest, so Holderman closed the museum and shuttered the mine. He died a year later at age ninety."

The mine stayed in the family, passing down to Edna Holderman, Gordon's only child. She had married a well-connected Chicago Cadillac dealer, and upon her death, her only son, Morris Weinstein, inherited the deserted property from his mother. Weinstein, who had also been handed down a pile from his father, had founded and sold a string of small businesses in Chicago, then invested the proceeds in a number of Internet start-ups. Presciently he had pOtherulled his considerable fortune out of the stock market just before the technological bubble burst.

"He seems to be the kind of man who in a small way can often spot a sure thing," Ginny said, "and capitalize on it, like Warren Buffett."

A Canadian mining company's promising experiment with growing pharmaceutical plants deep inside the Lone Pine Mine, just south of Silverton and fourteen miles west of the Venture, had piqued Weinstein's interest. Surely, he announced, he could use the Venture to produce high-quality seedlings and flowers for the suburban Chicago market as well as his own pharmaceutical plants for university experimenters, and by the turn of the twenty-first century the Venture Underground Agricultural Company had become a going concern. Every week, summer and winter, an eighteen-wheeler or two pulled out of the Venture property carrying sturdy young plants to the south.

"The mine now employs twenty full-time nursery workers and about the same number of part-timers," Ginny said. "Weinstein has been a lifesaver for Porcupine County."

"How did you know all that?" I said. I am still amazed by the things she comes up with. I sometimes think our relationship is like sharing a bed with a human database. At times that can be very helpful in my profession.

"It's my job, dummy."

I pinched her. She slapped my hand. But not hard.

"Did you know that I love you for your mind, not your body?"

"Do you expect me to believe that?"

"Not really."

"Then show me."

I did.

NINE

"We're ready to call the Saarinen case an accident," Alex said, sneezing into the phone and hurting my ear.

"God bless," I replied. "Yeah, but there's one more thing I have to do before we close it," I said. "I ought to go say hi to Morrie Weinstein and ask the routine questions about Saarinen's work record."

"You do that. It'll give you rare practice in good law-enforcement techniques."

"Screw you," I said, and put the phone down. I dialed headquarters and told Jerry Koski where I was going and why.

"Wrapping up the details," I said.

"Cool," Jerry said.

Gil did not bother to add the usual vexed grunt from his cubicle.

I drove out of town and then south on Norwich Road, a paved but potholed track that led twenty-four miles south to the hamlet of Matchwood. At the fifteenth mile it weaved through the steep forest-clad and copper-bearing escarpments, some of them almost a thousand feet high, that made up the western stretch of the historic Keweenaw Copper Range. The range, which bisects Porcupine County from east to west, runs more than a hundred miles from Fort Wilkins on the eastern end of the Keweenaw Peninsula, a thumb of land jutting out into Lake Superior, to the Wolverine Mountains fourteen miles west of Porcupine City.

After a twenty-minute drive I arrived at the Venture Mine, as everyone in the county still called the place deep in the thick woods. The mine nestled in a hollow hundreds of yards broad. One end of the hollow lay open, a two-lane gravel road running a mile east from the mine to Norwich Road. A rough Forest Service track climbed the far end of the hollow and headed west through the Ottawa National Forest.

An assortment of single-wide and double-wide mobile homes had replaced the tumbledown wooden structures that had housed miners and their equipment from the turn of the nineteenth century into the twentieth. Ancient stone and brick foundations still protruded, like loose teeth from a skeletal jaw, out of the scrubby brush and grass of the hollow.

Only the tall grey stone hoist house remained from the original mining settlement, and it had been tuck-pointed and refurbished, fallen stones carefully recemented into the walls, and its old steam engine replaced by a huge, modern electric motor. Its whine greeted me as I opened the Explorer's door outside Weinstein's office, occupying one end of a spartan double-wide on concrete blocks next to the hoist house. This was not a fatcat chief executive officer who liked to gild his nest with stockholders' money, although profits seemed to be flowing constantly out of the mine on skids, carried by forklifts from the hoist house to two waiting eighteen-wheelers. Today the skids bore hundreds of flats of low, gnarled plants. A score or more workers scurried busily before my eyes.

"Ginseng," Weinstein said from the door of the mobile home as he followed my eyes to the activity outside. "Bound for China. I think we'll do pretty well with it this year. What can I do for you, Deputy?"

"We've found Frank Saarinen's body," I said. "Tying up all the loose ends."

"I heard," Weinstein said with a sigh tinged by regret. News gets around fast on the north woods' jungle telegraph. Everyone has either a hand-held or table radio that continually scans radio channels, official and unofficial, all over the Upper Peninsula. We don't bother with standard police radio code because everybody knows it anyway.

Weinstein shook his head in mournful commiseration. A tall, burly, handsome man dressed in what Yoopers jocularly called "woods formal" — worn jeans and woolen shirt — he was relaxed, open-faced and friendly. With heavy features, olive skin and dark curly hair, he reminded me of a Mossad agent I had met in Tel Aviv on my way to Riyadh during my Army days. Like that fellow, Weinstein projected an air of amiable but alert watchfulness, as if welcoming you into his presence but remaining ready to act if you, God forbid, turned out to be an enemy. He was the kind of genial, outgoing person who was liked immediately, and I myself had taken a shine to him when we had met at a spaghetti dinner at the volunteer fire department two years before. We had exchanged commonplace pleasantries over a handshake, and I remembered his hearty, unpretentious grasp.

Today we sat in cracked old leather easy chairs in Weinstein's office.

"This is routine," I said, opening the Saarinen file. "Just a few questions, then we'll be able to close the case and send Frank on his way."

"Shoot," Weinstein said, chin in hand, elbow on armrest.

I led him through Saarinen's employment history according to the file, and like Sally Saarinen, Weinstein offered exactly the same answers he had given the deputy who had investigated her husband's disappearance the previous year. Nothing had changed. I was glad. That made things ever so much easier. I closed the file.

"So you'd say he was a good employee?"

"Absolutely," Weinstein said. "Knowledgeable, hard-working and extremely reliable, especially after . . . Deputy, it's no secret that Frank was in recovery. In the beginning of his employment, when he'd gone off on a toot he'd miss some work, but not since he joined AA. I was very sorry when he vanished. People like him are always difficult to replace."

I nodded. "Mr. Weinstein, Sally Saarinen told me that a

few days before Frank disappeared, he'd seemed upset about something at work. He wouldn't tell her what it was. Would you have any idea?"

Thoughtfully Weinstein leaned back in his chair and looked at me directly. "I don't really know," he said, "but from time to time Frank could get into it with his foreman, Roy Schweikert. Another good man lost."

My eyebrows rose. Schweikert, a veteran nurseryman Weinstein had brought up from Chicago shortly after he turned the mine into a hothouse, had drowned the previous winter in a freak accident in neighboring Gogebic County. Like so many who should have known better, he had gone drinking and snowmobiling one weekend. Out on a trail in the deep woods, he missed a curve at sixty miles an hour and plunged with his heavy and powerful machine through the thin ice of a frozen creek, so stupefied by alcohol that he drowned in less than four feet of water. Death by misadventure, the coroner ruled. Every winter in the Upper Peninsula a dozen snowmobilers bite the big one, usually against an unyielding tree but sometimes clotheslining themselves on barbed wire.

"I don't like to speak ill of the dead," Weinstein said. "But Roy and Frank didn't get along very well. They were temperamental opposites. Frank was a careful, meticulous worker, but Roy was a Type-A guy who always wanted folks to move faster. Basically they got along, but from time to time Roy would push Frank just a little too much, and you could almost hear them yelling all the way down in the seventh level of the mine."

"They ever get into fisticuffs? Threaten to knock each other off?"

"No, no, things never got that far. Just pissing matches, over almost as soon as they began. 'Course, things between them would be tense for a while, but sooner or later they simmered down. They were proud men, but they were grown men, too."

"Was there a dispute about the time Frank disappeared? That might explain why Sally thought he was upset."

"I don't know," Weinstein said. "Possibly. I don't remember, really. Those things come and go, you know — forgotten as soon as they're over. Wish I could help there."

I waited a moment, but he had nothing further to say.

"Okay, I guess that does it," I said, standing up to leave. "Thanks for your time, sir."

"Oh, don't be in such a rush," Weinstein said. "It's time for lunch. Have some with me. And don't call me sir. Call me Morrie."

I hesitated, as I always do at such an offer, suspecting the offerer's motives. Currying favor with the law? Patronizing an Indian? Or just being friendly?

Weinstein's smile was direct and guileless.

"Okay," I said. "And thanks. But please don't go to any trouble."

"Won't," Weinstein said. "We've got a little fridge and a kitchen here. Plenty of sandwich makings. What would you like?"

"A ham sandwich would do me," I said. Then I realized what I had said, and added, "I'm sorry. I don't know if you keep kosher."

Weinstein grinned widely, as if I'd walked right into a trap.

"Noooooo," he said slowly, "but there was once a time when I didn't eat meat on Fridays."

"You're not . . ." I said dumbly.

"Not since my paternal great-grandfather, also called Morris, was baptized by an insistent Jesuit sometime in the 1880s. He didn't change his name. He was proud of it. We've been Catholics ever since, although some of us of course are lapsed. Except for the genes I'm no more a Jew than you are a Sioux." He smiled at his ironic rhyme.

I sat down in mild embarrassment.

"You know about that?"

"It's hard not to," he said, "with your track record here."

Not to be immodest about it, but I've had a few successes as a police officer. Word gets around.

"Thanks," I said.

"So I know a little about what it feels like to be you," Morrie said.

It's rare anybody understands what it means to be one thing but look like another. Morrie did, and in my book that made him an all-right guy.

"*Ess, ess, mein kindt,*" he said, mimicking a Jewish mother, as he spread the sandwich makings, including a well-carved ham. "Eat, eat, my child."

"So you know a little Yiddish."

"Of course," he said. "Just like you know a little Lakota."

"*Hoka hey,*" I said, echoing Crazy Horse's call to battle: "It's a good day to die."

"It's a good day to *eat,*" said Morrie, who needed no translation. "We are who we are."

"No argument there," I said, tucking in. We ate almost silently, now and then pausing for a banality about the weather. Presently, after we had polished off the sandwiches, Morrie said, "Ever been down in the mine?"

"Not yet," I said. From time to time Morrie, proud of his enterprise, invited the public to an open house at the Venture, taking small parties on tours deep into the mine.

"Time to rectify that," he said.

"Why not?"

He led me to a large map, four feet high by seven feet wide, behind his desk. It was a chart, dated 1998, of the entire mine, showing the single vertical shaft and seven long drifts, the dimensions carefully called out in printed legends underneath. On it were stuck colored push pins, paper tags with handwritten names and dates tied to each pin. There were a lot of pins, so many that they almost obscured the outlines of the drifts.

"Each pin shows what we're growing down there, when it was planted and when it's being harvested," Morrie said. "Now let's go see."

TEN

At a low double-wide next to the hoist house Morrie led me into a locker room that could have served a high school football team. Instead of steel lockers for jerseys and pads, dozens of pristine white coveralls, emblazoned with the word VENTURE in bright red letters, hung from hooks lining one wall. A row of pegs on another wall carried yellow miner's helmets. Cardboard boxes of clear plastic booties stood on the floor. Three washing machines and three dryers, all of them running, lined a third wall. Two long changing benches bisected the room.

Morrie tossed me a pair of coveralls and a couple of booties.

"Suit up over your clothes," he said, "and put these booties on over your shoes."

"Okay. Why?"

"We don't want contamination to get into the mine or out of it. It's not absolutely biosecure, like a biological weapons lab, but we try to keep things as clean as we can. We ask our guys to shower before coming to work, and we ask them to leave their used coveralls here for washing."

I stepped into the voluminous coveralls and took a freshly scrubbed miner's helmet and a pair of dark-lensed goggles from Morrie's hands. He checked my equipage the way an astronaut examines another's, then we stepped out of the locker room into the hoist house proper. A few steps away lay the steel skip, twelve feet by twelve feet and protected on all sides by a twelve-foot-tall mesh cage. A perfect cube, I thought for no reason at all.

"The skip can hold fifteen men or nine four-by-four

skids of plants," Morrie said. "More if the plants are low and we can stack the skids on top of each other." He spoke with proprietary pride, as he did during our entire time underground.

With a screech of machinery and a whine of cables the skip descended slowly down the vertical shaft past a long ladder of bare lightbulbs, following a line of thick black electrical cables affixed to the roughly carved basalt walls every few feet. The lamps at the top of the skip illuminated frequent glitters of shiny quartz with greenish threading — veins of copper. It was the first time I had ever descended into the bowels of the earth, and the fascination of adventure enveloped me. I felt like a small boy being introduced to a natural wonder.

"How far down are we going?" I asked as we passed first one, then two drifts hacked out of the grey stone, workers inside waving to us as we dropped. A gentle breeze whooshed up the shaft.

"More than a thousand feet, all the way to the seventh level," Morrie said. "That wind you're feeling comes from a two-foot air shaft the original copper miners drilled down from the top of the hill. We've got fans and filters up there. Mine air tends to be full of carbon dioxide. We don't need that, though the plants love it. Photosynthesis, you know."

The air grew warmer as we descended, until about halfway down, when the temperature seemed to stabilize.

"Not going to get any hotter until we hit the molten center of Earth?" I asked.

"Nope. It's a constant seventy degrees throughout the mine," Morrie said. "The grow lights bring up the temperature. Perfect for growing most plants. No cold snaps, no heat waves, just a steady, boring, pleasant temperature. Plants love sameness, just like sheep."

With a small bump we reached the seventh and last level and Morrie swung out the skip's tall steel-mesh door. We stepped onto a pathway of wooden boards laid over the bumpy rock floor. The jagged ceiling of the drift loomed just a few inches above our heads.

"Mind your noggin," Morrie said. "Lots of big rocks jut from the overhead." Those safety helmets aren't for just in case something bad happens. As we walked along, the ceiling rapped my well-protected head despite my best efforts to stay clear of stony perils.

Twenty feet into the drift we fetched up against a heavy wooden door.

"Put on your goggles," Morrie said. "It's bright in there."

He swung open the door into a huge irregular chamber, its ceiling supported by dozens of rock pillars, the lumpy walls spray-painted a blinding white.

"Ninety feet wide by two hundred feet long," Morrie said. "This was the mine's richest seam of copper back in the nineteenth century."

Even with the heavy smoked goggles my eyes hurt. Rows and rows of fluorescent grow lights, hovering over rows and rows of seedlings in flats and tubs, made the place seem as if it nestled next door to the sun. A loud hum from the lights filled the room, several degrees warmer than the passage outside the door.

"Thousand-watters," Morrie said. "We keep the temperature steady with metered air from the shaft. These are mostly tropical plants, so they like a little extra warmth."

I am no gardener, but even with dark goggles I could tell that the seedlings stood a uniform height, about a foot, above their flats. Their thick stems, smooth broad leaves and deep color suggested vigorous health. I recognized hibiscus, roses, basil and other herbs, and a distinctive plant with huge leaves. It looked familiar, but I couldn't think of its name.

"What's this?" I said.

"Tobacco," Morrie replied.

My eyebrows rose.

"This isn't for Philip Morris," Morrie laughed. "They're

66

a special, genetically modified variety we're growing for a drug company that's experimenting with a protein extracted from them. It fights bone cancer. Over there we have some sweet wormwood, *Artemisia annua,* which produces a drug called artemisenin, used as an antidote for malaria. We're experimenting with new varieties of corn to make hepatitis vaccines, and with alfalfa against rabies.

"Just about all the plants in this room have been genetically modified. We call this the biosecure room. Actually, everywhere down here in the earth we're far away from insects and disease and wind and drought."

"Bioengineering protesters, too," I said. A lot of people hate the idea of genetic modification of living things — to some, that's playing God, and to others, it's risky to experiment with Mother Nature. As in every group of protesters, a few can get violent. Some ecoguerrillas have committed spectacular acts of sabotage, torching fields of designer corn and bombing agricultural laboratories.

Morrie nodded.

"True. But it works the other way, too. We don't sell living bioengineered plants. In fact, except for that tobacco — we carefully pack the harvested leaves in plastic for shipping — we don't let them out of here to get loose in the wild and contaminate ordinary plants. For the moment in this room we're just experimenting, seeing what we can do to improve certain species. There's nothing to trouble these babies — we don't even need to use pesticides — and they'll all grow up proud and strong. Because they're so healthy, every successive generation stands prouder and stronger. And they grow fast, because they're given a steady supply of nutrients and they stand under those grow lights eighteen hours a day. See those birches over there?"

Two dozen or so white birch saplings, six feet tall, stood in large plastic pots against the rock wall.

"Those are normal birches, not genetically modified. We started them from seed just one year ago. In the wild it'd take five or six years for them to reach that height."

"How come they grow so fast down here?"

"We don't know all the details yet. Some folks think electromagnetics have something to do with it. Those vary at different depths in the earth. There's still a lot of copper in the rock around us. Copper is known for its conductivity, and that could pump up the electromagnetic fields down here. Last week a biologist told me he thought the slight natural electrical current that copper carries discourages slugs from coming down here and eating the plants. Maybe the slight increase in air pressure from the fans helps increase the rate of photosynthesis. But personally I think the biggest thing is that the highly controlled environment just takes the stress out of growing. These are laid-back plants. They're fat and happy."

I'd not heard much about plant bioengineering. It's not the sort of thing one reads about in the daily papers.

"Why aren't the big drug companies interested in these plants?" I asked.

"Simple. It's hard to patent new drugs made from plants. That's why Abbott and Lilly and Pfizer generally stick to synthetic chemicals."

"Where does the research money come from?"

"Universities, mainly. They farm out their lab work to us, so to speak." He chuckled.

"You must use a lot of electricity," I said presently. "The lights, the hoist."

"The pumps, too," Morrie said. I could hear a low rumble from somewhere deep below. "We've got heavy-duty sump pumps keeping groundwater out of the mine."

"Doesn't all that cost?"

"Yes. It wouldn't be economical to grow ordinary seedlings and vegetables down here. But everything's absolutely top premium quality, and many people are willing to pay premium prices. We're now selling to upmarket greenhouses all over the United States and even foreign countries."

"Looks like a perfect place to grow very, very good pot," I said jokingly. A pioneering Canadian company raised medicinal marijuana, quite legal and government-controlled in that country, in an abandoned copper mine in Manitoba. The company had been in the news recently, for its first results were uneven, either too strong or two weak. The problem, the company said, was that it had to obtain confiscated marijuana seeds of unknown origin from the Royal Canadian Mounted Police. U.S. government sources owned pure strains of pot, but for political reasons — the hard-core drug warriors' influence reached everywhere — refused to share them with the Canadians. And the Canadians, forced by their own laws to obtain seeds only from licit sources, couldn't just buy good stuff from an illegal grower in, say, northern California.

Morrie laughed. "I hear that all the time. Everybody who comes down here looks around for weed. But you won't find it. We're inspected all the time, even by the DEA. Those guys like to look for trouble where there isn't any."

"Amen," I said. I'd been on plenty of useless forays with the feds into the countryside for small-potatoes pot growers and do-it-yourself meth labs. We expend a lot of money and manpower that way. One reason it's hard to alter the scattershot aims of the so-called war on drugs is that the law-enforcement bureaucracy that has grown up around it has become self-perpetuating and fights any attempt to shrink it to reasonable proportions.

"Want to visit the other six drifts?" Morrie asked.

"Are they the same as this?"

"Pretty much."

"Naw, one does me fine," I said. "Time for me to get back on patrol anyway."

"One more thing," Morrie said. "I want to show you something."

I followed him into a short side tunnel, blocked halfway through by a massive and rusty old iron door. With a key he undid a heavy Yale padlock and pulled the door open, its hinges sighing smoothly. They had been recently oiled. I followed Morrie inside and he shut the door.

"This drift doesn't go in very far—about a hundred yards in, the roof collapsed long ago," he said. "We sometimes use it to store stuff and we sometimes use it to educate folks."

"About what?" I asked.

In response Morrie reached up on the wall and flicked off the light switch.

Think of the blackest black you have ever been in, and multiply it a hundred times. When you can see absolutely nothing, not even the tiniest glow of light—my shirtsleeve blanketed the luminous dial of my watch—you slowly become confused, unable to tell which way is up. In all my life I had experienced that disorientation only once, having flown through thick fog when the airplane's vacuum system failed and the attitude indicator, the artificial horizon on the instrument panel, tumbled crazily. Fortunately the flight instructor who was teaching me instrument flying pointed to the electric turn-and-bank indicator and the altimeter, and by keeping the wings level with the first and the altitude constant with the second I was able to fly the airplane straight and true despite a seat-of-the-pants sensation that falsely told me the plane was diving. Now that clammy, long-forgotten sensation came back to me. Involuntarily I put my hand on the jagged rock wall to recapture my faltering balance.

"Wow," I said. Words always failed me at times like that.

"Yeah," Morrie said with a sly chuckle. "Now think of the millions and millions of tons of rock above your head and what would happen if that tunnel roof failed some more."

I am not ordinarily claustrophobic, but beads of sweat broke out on my forehead and my bowels churned as I contemplated that possibility, which seemed to grow less unlikely by the second. I began to breathe heavily.

Suddenly Morrie flicked on the light. I took in a deep

slug of air.

"You're a fairy, it seems," he said.

Despite my discomfort I bristled.

"Relax. Fairies are what a lot of miners in these parts used to call folks who don't like going deep into the earth," Morrie said with a broad grin. "Nothing to do with the other meaning. Fairies live in the trees, you see. Trolls — miners — dwell underground. Those terms go back to the old Cornish miners who used to work the Venture. Pretty apt, huh?"

"Okay, now let's troll right out of here, do you mind?" I said, trying to keep my voice light.

Morrie laughed. "C'mon. But don't be embarrassed. Your reaction's quite normal."

In a few minutes, at the entry to the drift as we waited for the skip to pick us up, I noticed a rubber-clad electrical cable the size of a man's thigh dipping down into the hoist pit below. It looked as if it could handle billions of watts.

And I said so. "What's that thing for?"

"Those sump pumps take a lot of juice," Morrie said. "Gotta overengineer to be absolutely safe."

At almost the same moment the skip ground to a stop, and we climbed aboard, the cable forgotten.

In a few minutes I stepped gratefully out of the hoist house, suffering from what I can describe only as delayed panic, and inhaled a deep breath of fresh fairyland air under the friendly sun. I could never have made a living as a troll.

"Thanks, Morrie," I said as I climbed into the Explorer. "For lunch and for the tour."

"Good to get to know you, Steve," he said. Don't be a stranger."

"Won't," I called back.

"Steve!" Morrie suddenly shouted.

"Yeah?"

"I'm going out in my boat with a couple of friends tomorrow morning for lake trout. Be delighted if you'd come. Bring a guest. Whattaya say?"

I needed less than a tenth of a second to make the weighty decision. It had been a long time since I'd gone lake fishing. Most of my angling outings are up the rivers and creeks for rainbow trout in the spring, before they've deserted the streams for the cooler water of Lake Superior in the summer, and for walleyes in Lake Gogebic at the southern end of Porcupine County. And Morrie Weinstein's *Lucky Six* was a big, comfortable cruiser, the kind for kicking back under a warm sun.

"Sure! What time?"

"We'll meet at the marina at five-thirty and be out on the lake by six."

Some days end better than others, don't they?

ELEVEN

And that one sure did.

In the evening I told Ginny about my visit to the Venture Mine, my nonkosher lunch with Morrie Weinstein, and his invitation for Saturday. She listened with considerable interest to my description of the interior of the mine and eagerly accepted the rare chance to go fishing. About the lunch with Morrie, however, she was unimpressed.

"That's not so surprising. Morrie's mother was a Catholic, too. All the Holdermans were. For most Jews, except those in the Reform movement, Jewish identity is handed down through the mother, not the father. One wouldn't necessarily have expected Morrie to be a practicing Jew even if his father had been."

"Still," I said, "I can understand how he feels, being one thing while looking like another. He was pretty open about that. It's hard not to like the guy."

Ginny nodded with deep understanding but not a whole lot of sympathy. She'd heard me on the subject all too many times. She thought I should grow up and accept things I couldn't change. She was of course right, but it's sometimes hard to shake a lifetime of resentment at the cards circumstance had dealt.

I sighed and shrugged. "He's quite a fellow," I said "Like you he's put a lot of financial capital as well as emotional investment into Porcupine County."

Ginny, who as the widow of an Eastern industrial magnate had inherited a pile only a little smaller than that at Fort Knox, spreads much of her wealth around the county where she was born without letting anybody know where the money came from. Many, if not most, of the grants she writes for the Historical Society she runs, as well as other needy Porcupine County institutions — such as the nursing home, the Little League team and the historical society she heads — are sent to her own foundation, headquartered in Detroit. She never wants anyone to judge her by the accident of her wealth and keeps it carefully under wraps. I am probably the only person outside her foundation director and her lawyer who knows the truth about her money, and I have no idea how much she is worth. I am not sure she does, either. Her fortune is the kind that fluctuates by six and sometimes seven figures a day, depending on the mood of the stock market.

"I don't think Morrie makes a lot of money out of that mine," I added. "Maybe not yet. Maybe not ever. Maybe it's just a labor of love."

"That," said Ginny, "is hardly surprising. People up here care."

They do indeed. Porcupine County is not an easy place to make a living, but it is an attractive place to live. The woods, the wildlife, the fishing, the lake, the astonishingly neighborly people who remain here are powerful magnets for someone like me, who has always searched for a welcoming home. As jobs have dwindled so has the population, and perhaps to slow down the exodus, those who remain behind try to take care of each other, even if it's only donating labor for a new roof on a needy family's house or repairing an ancient pickup truck for free. One finds altruism in surprising places, and so it stood to reason that Ginny was not Porcupine County's only wealthy benefactor. Morrie Weinstein was probably a close second. He loved theatrical groups and generously supported the Northwoods Playhouse in Porcupine City.

"Good old Morrie," I said. "Good old Ginny."

She crooked an amused eyebrow. "Thank you. Now let's tuck in."

We sat down to a leg of lamb I'd grilled over charcoal,

slathering it with mint jelly Ginny had put up from the herb garden she raised in the sandy soil between her house and the beach. She puts up a lot of jelly each year, for the mint she had planted a few years before had spread like kudzu, even in these cool northern climes. At Christmas seemingly everybody in Porcupine County gets a jar of Ginny's mint jelly with hand-lettered labels. Sometimes I tease her about the jelly, once suggesting she put up a sign where her driveway meets the lakefront highway and selling it to passersby, the way many people who live up here augment their meager incomes by selling eggs to locals and firewood to campers in the Wolverines.

"Experiencing the life of a poorer resident," I once suggested in a moment of blind self-righteousness, "might make you a truer Porky."

"Except I don't have to do it," she replied. "They do. I wouldn't insult them that way."

And she was right. I can be *so* dumb.

Rounding out the feast was a plate of buttered fresh asparagus I'd picked up in Rhinelander and a tureen of wild rice the Ojibwe had harvested from inland lake shallows on their reservation near Baraga fifty miles east of Porcupine County. We washed it all down with a inexpensive and unpretentious but excellent Australian merlot I'd found in an Eagle River liquor store, returning several times to stock up on it. Home cooking in the remote North Woods doesn't get better than mine, I will immodestly admit.

After an hour I said regretfully, "Can't stay the night. Got to get my tackle ready for tomorrow."

"Getting old, eh?" Ginny replied slyly.

"Hey! No fair!"

"Just kidding. We'll need our sleep."

"See you at five-fifteen."

I kissed her good-bye and drove home.

TWELVE

At a quarter to five I arose in pitch dark, quickly donning heavy sweatshirt and sweatpants over T-shirt and cargo shorts against the morning chill, rounding out my wardrobe with a pair of Docksiders. By ten o'clock the sun would warm the day, but this far north even a summer dawn almost always broke in the low fifties. A quick splash of coffee and I was almost ready to go. But first I popped into a knapsack a bag of one of Upper Michigan's best-kept secrets — *korppu*, the flavorsome hard cinnamon toast Finnish loggers once carried into the woods for their midmorning coffee breaks. The most-sought-after *korppu* is also called "Trenary toast" for a celebrated bakery at Trenary, a tiny town in the waist of Upper Michigan between Marquette and Escanaba. Every day the toast is baked fresh and shipped to cafes and supermarkets all over the Upper Peninsula and to mail-order customers, most of them exiled Yoopers, in every state of the nation. *Korppu* looks like overgrown zwieback and amounts to something like the hardtack biscuits sailors used to eat during long voyages, but is much, much tastier. A little *korppu* slathered with butter and softened by hot coffee gives one a jolt of energy that easily lasts until lunch.

I selected a seven-foot medium-action spinning rod — the *Lucky Six* would carry plenty of specialized lake trout gear, but like the true Yooper I wanted to be someday, I preferred familiar old tools — then saddled up the Jeep and in ten minutes was at Ginny's place five miles east on the lakefront highway. Ginny, bless her heart, is a woman who believes in being prompt. I have never had to cool my heels while she pulls herself together to go out, dabbing on lipstick and visiting the bathroom for one last time to brush her teeth. She stood waiting outside her door, rod in one hand, kit bag on a shoulder, and a gorgeous smile on her face, ready to go. My heart, as it always does when I see her for the first time every day, did a little lub-de-bub-dup.

At five-thirty on the dot we arrived at the Porcupine City Municipal Marina a few hundred yards up the Porcupine River from the rock-lined channel to the lake. A dozen or so automobiles, pickups and minivans occupied the large asphalt parking lot, their owners doing boat things under half a dozen powerful floodlights that illuminated the thirty-eight-slip marina. Almost all the boats aft tied up there were sixteen- to twenty-foot runabouts with big outboard motors. Most local yachtsmen are not rich, and Morrie Weinstein's forty-foot *Lucky Six*, moored at the end of the single pier where the water was deepest, the burbling exhausts of its two powerful engines raising foam at the stern, overshadowed all other boats.

I started in surprise. Under a floodlight at the entrance to the slip, holding a duffel in one hand and the elbow of Mary Ellen Garrigan in the other, loomed big Chad Garrow, grinning from ear to ear.

"Hi, Steve!" Chad shouted gaily. "Ready to go for a big one?"

I glanced at Ginny. A small smile played on her lovely countenance, threatening to break out into a huge amused grin, but she won the fight with her face.

"Ginny, this is —," I began.

"We've met," Ginny said, in a friendly way. "Nice to see you, Chad, Mary Ellen."

One of Ginny's talents is something I will never master in a lifetime: the ability to greet people with just-folks ease and a chummy disposition, no matter who they are or what the circumstances. Everybody always feels comfortable entering her presence.

Not necessarily mine. "Hello," I said to my brother

officer and his companion. In my consternation that was all I could think of to say.

"Steve!" Mary Ellen called gaily, so loudly that heads snapped up all over the marina. "So good to see you again!" She took a deep breath, her ample chest nearly bursting her thick alpaca turtleneck sweater. She looked me in the eye, as if to declare that our unpleasant little encounter at George's was only the opening skirmish in a patient campaign to get me into her bed. I couldn't see it, but I knew Ginny's left eyebrow was rising in barely concealed amusement. She was comfortable in her own beauty and not the sort to feel threatened by another knockout of a woman. And I had not told her about the scene at George's. It hadn't mattered.

"Mrs. Garrigan," I responded politely.

"Mary Ellen," she said in an insistent tone.

"Okay," I said, although it was not okay.

Chad, who is not much smoother than I am socially, just stood rooted to the spot, like a huge oaf with a thatched red roof and an expanse of teeth that spread from east to west as if he were showing off a record catch on the dock at Key West.

"Hiya," he said brilliantly.

Morrie Weinstein broke the moment with a bellow from *Lucky Six*. "Right on time!" he shouted. "We're ready to go!"

Down the slip we scrambled, then leaped onto the big fiberglass boat, Mary Ellen's shapely round rump, outlined in tight stretch jeans, preceding us aboard. On the boat's broad stern was painted its name in flamboyant white script, FORT LAUDERDALE in smaller Roman capitals underneath. A short and wiry fellow in a hooded blue sweatshirt waved to us from his perch high on the flying bridge, the glow of a cigarette barely lighting his face, obscured by the hood. A long ski-jump nose protruded over the cigarette.

"This is Mike Anderson, the skipper," Morrie said, making introductions all around as he cast off the stern line.

As the boat drifted away from the slip in the slight current, Anderson opened the throttles gently and swung the wheel to its starboard stop, swiveling the big boat almost in its own length to enter the Porcupine River from the marina, a rectangular pond carved from the riverbank just west of the village. I knew enough about boats to recognize the maneuver as an expert though unflashy piece of seamanship. Anderson clearly knew his stuff, and I felt better. Lake Superior can be fatally treacherous, a fast-moving squall churning a gentle chop into six-foot whitecaps in just a matter of minutes. This was no Sunday captain of the sort I sometimes had to go searching for out on the lake in the sheriff's Cessna.

As we headed around into the river the skipper loosed a blast from the boat's horn, and a hundred yards away the lights of the low swing bridge over M-64 carved a slow horizontal arc through the night as the highway deck pivoted to open a clear passage for the *Lucky Six.* The span, a much-repaired relic of the Depression and the last operating swing bridge in all of Michigan, required a full-time bridgetender during the boating season. The state highway department had scheduled it to be torn down the following year when M-64 was rerouted just upriver from the marina. A new stationary concrete bridge would go up high above the river, and it would need no human attendant. Another job would be lost to Porcupine County.

On the other hand, sometimes during hot August weather the steel in the old bridge expands and the swiveling span binds shut. Often cold river water has to be hosed onto the rusty, swollen metal to shrink it and free the span. All the same, I was fond of this battered old piece of early-twentieth-century engineering. Steel swing bridges have grown as rare as wooden Kentucky covered bridges and carry the same nostalgic appeal for those who like old machinery.

As *Lucky Six* entered the turning pool just before the two-hundred-yard-long steel-and-stone channel jutting from the shoreline, she lurched slightly to starboard, then port. The lake outside lay almost calm, slow, whale-like swells breaking gently on the beach, but a nasty chop roiled the channel.

Some years before I came to Porcupine City, the Army Corps of Engineers had reinforced the rock riprap that made up the channel breakwaters, in its infinite wisdom lining the channel with huge corrugated steel sheets driven into the bottom. The steel would hold back the lake for a century, the soldiers said, and no doubt it will. But they're army, and they're engineers — they're not sailors. The corps had no idea that instead of breaking up the waves as did the rough rock riprap, the vertical steel walls would magnify them. The rollers ricocheted their way upstream and created a turbulent hazard for small boats. It is not for nothing that Porcupine County natives take a dim view of the munificence of outside government. Federal and state bureaucrats never listen to the advice of the locals.

Mike, however, steered the *Lucky Six* expertly through the turbulence as Ginny and I sat on a bench in the stern, huddled together for warmth and because we just like huddling together. Presently the boat chugged past the lights at the ends of the breakwaters and out into the open lake, the insistent pounding of the hull replaced by gentle rolling. Mary Ellen and Chad sat opposite us, lost in each other as well, his huge arm around her shoulders. Barely half a mile out the eastern sky began to lighten. Ginny and I faced the sun as it slowly rose from the horizon, flooding the sky with light, its rays reddening the high cirrus that floated down from the north and outlining in stark green relief the slowly receding forested shoreline. Fifteen miles to the west we could see rising from the tree line the mountains the Indians who once crossed these waters in war canoes called the Wolverines, after the shape of the animal they saw on the horizon. The huge wilderness state park named for the mountains marked the western boundary of my jurisdiction.

"C'mon up here," called Morrie, who had stood shoulder to shoulder with his skipper on the bridge just above us as Anderson conned the boat out into the lake. I climbed up the half-dozen steps onto the bridge under its canvas awning and looked about. Though I am not a sailor, modern electronic equipment always interests a pilot, and the *Lucky Six* was as well-equipped a sportfisher as I'd ever seen. On one side of the cockpit coaming lay a marine radio set to the distress channel, two big electronic fish locators and a depth finder. A large monitor built into the center of the coaming displayed a rotating green line, the visible return from the radar antenna high above the bridge as it swept the empty lake for miles ahead. Another screen, fed by a global positioning satellite receiver, displayed the *Lucky Six*'s latitude and longitude within half a dozen feet, the numbers slowly changing as the boat churned farther north. An older readout from loran ground radio stations displayed an almost identical position. I approve highly of redundancy in navigational equipment. If we should sink, we'd know exactly where we went down at the very moment we did, as if that were any comfort. But we'd never lose our bearings on the open water far from the sight of land.

Over the windshield a scoped Remington rifle lay cradled in wooden pegs, lashings keeping it secure to the bulkhead. That was odd. Why would a sailor need a deer rifle out on the lake?

"Cool, eh?" Morrie said, breaking my reverie.

"Why the rifle?"

Morrie glanced at it. "Protection, of course."

"Against what?"

"Pirates."

"*Pirates?*"

"Not here on Lake Superior. The Caribbean. In the fall and winter we charter the *Lucky Six* out of Fort Lauderdale, and sometimes outside American territorial waters Colombian crooks lie in wait to snatch charter boats and use them to run drugs up from South America. When they're done with a run they scuttle 'em and go back to hijack some more."

"I'll be damned." I was mollified, although a stray thought struggled unsuccessfully to reach the surface of my brain.

"This sure is a hunk of pleasure boat," I said after a moment. "It must cost an arm and a leg to keep up."

"Yeah," Morrie said. "We charter her a lot to help pay the bills. That's why I've got Mike. He lives aboard and runs the charters. I often go down to Florida in early May to help him bring the boat up the St. Lawrence Seaway and through the Soo. Takes a couple of weeks. Mike's just back from a charter in Lake Huron with half a dozen fellows from Chicago. He cleared the Soo two days ago and got in just last night."

I looked at Anderson, who had pulled back his sweatshirt hood as the sun warmed the day. Under his long-billed sailor's ball cap his beak thrust forward like an old underslung nineteenth century battleship prow, but that was not his most striking feature. He was a fairly young man—mid-thirties, I guessed—but I had never seen anyone so leathery, seams and wrinkles crisscrossing his deep brown face like the hide of an old sea turtle. But this was not just a man who had spent a lifetime at sea. Anderson looked almost reptilian, glittering black eyes sunk under prominent brows, lips pushed forward by prognathous teeth already yellowed by the cigarettes he smoked constantly. It must have been hellish to go through life looking like that. He had barely said a word since we came aboard.

"Where'd you learn about boats?" I asked, just to be polite.

"Navy," he said after a long beat.

"Sailor?"

"Petty officer." His response also took longer than needed.

I had done time in the military, and I knew that the noncommissioned naval rank of petty officer could have covered a thousand specialties in the modern service, from coxswain to nuclear technician. But I didn't press the subject. No point in poking a reticent fellow with a sharp stick. And anyway, he needed to pay attention to his job. All the same, his manner seemed appropriate to his looks. He creeped me out.

Three miles offshore Morrie climbed down from the bridge and shouted "Time to fish!" He had been chatting soliticiously with Ginny, playing the genial host while Chad and Mary Ellen stared hand in hand out over the lake, no doubt anticipating their upcoming evening. Chad glanced at Mary Ellen frequently, almost in disbelief, as if he could not understand why this gorgeous and — at least to him — elegant creature had taken up (if that is the word) with a rough-hewn clodhopper like him. I could have lectured him about notches on bedposts, but young men of his age aren't inclined to listen to the wisdom of their elders. It was none of my business anyway.

"Do you really, really need to catch lake trout today?" Morrie asked nobody in particular. "If so, we can use the high-tech stuff, the fish finders and all, and go out real far and real deep. We do that on charters so that the customers are all but guaranteed to go home with a fish or two. But if you want to give 'em a sporting chance, we can just use basic tackle, a ball downrigger and ten-pound test, and the depth finder."

"Fine by me," said Chad, immediately raising my estimation of him by a notch. It usually takes a young guy much longer to learn that hunting and fishing are not just about the quarry, but also the adventure. He must have spent time with wise men at deer camp in his boyhood.

"Fine by me," I echoed.

"Sure," Ginny said.

"You go right ahead," said Mary Ellen. "I'm going up front to catch some sun."

As Morrie took the helm Mike climbed down and swiftly prepared the starboard downrigger tackle. A simple downrigger is nothing more than a heavy iron ball weighing five to ten pounds, attached to the end of a braided wire line dropped over the stern from a stiff rod, four feet long, jutting over the gunwale. The other end of the line is attached to a winch, the bigger ones driven by an electric motor, as Morrie's were. On the heavy-duty models like those aboard the *Lucky Six*, a dial on the winch tells how far down the iron ball is running as the boat trolls it astern, and a digital readout reveals the water temperature at the ball. Far down on the cable a few feet above the iron ball, a quick-release clasp holds ordinary monofilament fishing line trailed from an ordinary fishing rod. At the end of the monofilament is a standard steel leader to which is affixed the bait.

"Wimps use minnows," Morrie had said. "Real men use spoons." Those are large silvery steel fingerlings, shaped like long, skinny serving spoons, with sharp hooks on the business end. Dragged through the water, a spoon wiggles and flutters sexily and, in theory at least and in practice often enough to keep people using it, is simply irresistible to lake trout. Once a fish strikes, the clasp on the cable releases the monofilament so the fish can be played with the rod and, if the angler is lucky, brought to the surface and taken home for dinner.

"Ladies first," called Morrie from the bridge.

Ginny took up the rod and watched as the iron ball slowly sank below the surface. Swiftly and wordlessly Anderson readied the port side downrigger. He looked up at me. I nodded to Chad. "Youth before age," I said.

The lad didn't even hesitate in deference to a superior, let alone an elder, but eagerly grasped the rod, his thumb on the reel. I chuckled inwardly. That was me once.

"We'll let the rigs down to about eighty feet," Morrie said. The bottom's at ninety all along this stretch, and as we go on it'll fall to about a hundred twenty feet, where the big ones are." Leaving one engine throttled back, he opened up the other slowly, pushing the boat ahead at a bare three or four miles per hour. The downrigger cable hummed insistently, the water strumming it like a huge bass fiddle string.

Time passed, Ginny and Chad at their rods, fingers lightly touching monofilament, feeling for a strike. Onward the *Lucky Six* trolled, Mike paying out downrigger cable as the bottom slowly fell away. An hour went by without a strike. Presently I broke out the coffee and *korppu* – both Ginny and Chad were too absorbed in their quest to accept any. Morrie, the genial host, sat with me, and we munched and chatted about anything and nothing as the boat chugged slowly ahead and the sun rose higher. Just as I thought we'd be skunked – not that that made much difference to me – Ginny shouted. "Got one!"

Her rod bent almost double as the fish struck the spoon and ran to starboard.

"Reel!" Morrie shouted. "Reel it in now!"

Soundlessly as always, Anderson knelt by Ginny, ready to snatch the rod from her if she spooked or tired. She didn't. It was easy to tell that she'd grown up around boats and fishing, just as she'd spent large parts of her youth in hunting camps. She is not a frail little thing, but tall and strong, with wide shoulders and hips, and she carries plenty of well-shaped but lean meat on her bones. She chops her own firewood and shovels her own snow. Now and then she shoots a deer during hunting season and stocks her freezer with venison. For all her wealth and education Ginny Fitzgerald is a true "Yooper Woman," an accolade that is not lightly bestowed.

"This is a good-sized trout," she said unnecessarily. "Not a monster, but it'll feed quite a few people."

"Going to take it home if you get it in?"

"Absolutely. Without a doubt. Now stand back."

To make a long story short, Ginny expertly played the trout for ten minutes, letting it exhaust itself by running out and back, then slowly reeled it in. With a long-handled net Anderson scooped the fish from the water, letting it flop on the deck as the life leaked out of it. When it was still he removed it and hung it by the gills from a fish scale.

"Nineteen pounds," Morrie said. "Not bad."

All the while Chad had watched with one eye, paying attention to his own rig with the other. He wasn't a greenhorn. He grinned at Ginny, generously happy for her, totally undisappointed in his lack of luck. There's hope for the lad yet, I thought, as I looked at my watch. It was eleven, well past the best feeding time for lake trout, and the sun was nearing its zenith in the sky.

"If we go out farther and deeper, we might get lucky again," said Morrie, himself delighted in his guests' pleasure. "But chances are we won't. What say we go home?"

"Sure," I said.

"Right," Ginny said.

"Okay," Chad said.

Mary Ellen said nothing. We hadn't seen or heard her for the last hour, and simultaneously we all stood and looked toward the bow.

She lay supine atop the forward deck, taking the sun, her head cradled on Chad's big duffel. Cotton balls covered her eyes. A black wisp too skinny to be called a thong covered her womanhood. Nothing covered her breasts. Chad's eyes covered all of her. Before I could avert mine Ginny punched me in the ribs, but she giggled softly. Morrie grinned at me from the bridge. Next to him Anderson stared stonily astern, as if he had seen it all before, more often than he cared to count. Charter-boat skippers are like the old Pullman porters of a hundred years ago—faceless servants that are just part of the furniture with which a luxury traveling conveyance is equipped. Aboard trains and boats many adventurous and conscienceless passengers indulge in indiscretions they'd never commit at home, confident that they'll never see the crew again.

Most of the way home I stared astern too, chatting casually with Ginny while Chad sat up forward beside his girl friend, at least fifteen and maybe twenty years older than he, enjoying the view. Morrie and Anderson stood on the bridge, their heads together, talking quietly, paying no attention to the flesh-colored scenery on the deck a few feet in front of them. From time to time Ginny glanced at me and giggled.

Just before we entered the channel Morrie dropped down from the bridge.

"Ginny," he said, "has anybody volunteered to fund the new wing?"

The previous year the Historical Museum had hired an architect— paid for, of course, by a foundation Ginny secretly funded with her widow's wealth—to design a new wing devoted to Porcupine County's mining history. The museum owned a great deal of old mining equipment donated over the decades, including huge winches, hoists, skips and tram cars, but was unable to display most of it for lack of room inside the old former supermarket building downtown. The architect had suggested taking up part of the parking lot, never half filled by vehicles even at the museum's busiest times, for the extension. A specialist would be hired from Eastern Michigan University to sift through the relics and design an authentic historical display. But the total cost would approach six figures, and Ginny hesitated to write herself another grant, for fear the size might attract attention.

"Not yet," she said.

"I've been thinking about it," Morrie said. "The Venture's begun to do well enough so that we can put some money back into the county. How much do you need?"

Ginny told him. Morrie's expression didn't change.

"I think we can cover that," he said. "How about I come down to the museum sometime soon and talk about it?"

Ginny nodded, delighted. "That's very generous of you, Morrie. Of course we could name it for you."

"No. How about the Gordon Holderman Wing? My grandpa would have loved that."

"It's a deal."

At Ginny's house that night, as we ate the trout—

slathered with lemon and butter and broiled over charcoal —
Ginny did not mention Mary Ellen. Many women would
have, some of them shrilly, until they had discussed,
criticized, dismantled and condemned every physical and
moral defect of their subject. Not Ginny, whose self-
confidence had grown boundlessly during our months
together. She was a hell of a woman and she knew it. Much
later that night, she let me know she knew.

Afterward, just before falling asleep, I thought about
Morrie Weinstein, my new friend and fishing companion, and
his understanding, his generosity, his geniality, and his all-
around good-eggedness. "Too good to be true," I told myself
quietly as sleep began to enfold me, but I also thought I was
just being Steve Martinez, Lakota off the reservation, fish out
of water, a stranger in a strange land, unable to appreciate a
gift freely offered.

THIRTEEN

On the southern shore of Lake Superior in upper Michigan, the shank of an August evening is the best time of year to sit out on the beach in a folding lawn chair, feet up on a big old log, and contemplate one's world. Often the lowering sun reddens the sky through a scrim of high cirrus into subtle shades of vermilion. The onshore wind that kicked up a chirp of wavelets on the beach all day usually has settled into a slight breeze just enough to shoo the mosquitoes inside the tree line. The sigh of grass on the sand is interrupted now and then by squawks of geese and calls from loons. From time to time an eagle that often perches on a snag just down the beach will soar low over the water, hoping to snatch a minnow feeding close to the surface in the shallows. If I'm lucky a doe and her fawn, or perhaps a small black bear, might emerge from the woods by Quarterline Creek a hundred yards or so up the beach to the west and take a sip from the lake.

I could investigate many more interesting cases and make a lot more money as a detective in Duluth or Wausau or any of the small cities half a day's drive from Porcupine County, but the boondocks routine and subsistence salary of a country deputy does me just fine for now. I don't miss the crash and yammer, the snarl and snipe of daily combat on urban battlegrounds. Been there, done that, thank you. Of course sometimes I need better brain food than rustic life can provide, but though the Joffrey Ballet and the Chicago Symphony never come to town, we've still got itinerant musicians, community theater, arts colonies, PBS, Minnesota

---

Public Radio, C-SPAN, and the Internet. We're not exactly isolated from the rest of American cultural life, although sometimes it can seem that way when a racist yahoo shatters a beer bottle in a roadside bar and threatens a dark-skinned visitor. But that happens in the big cities, too.

If one has enough food and shelter, the comfortable routine of the North Woods can be gratifying and by no means boring. For the unexpected sometimes happens in Porcupine County.

In the far distance toward the east I saw a figure walking down the beach in my direction and, figuring him to be a local looking for agates, glanced away and lost myself again in my reverie.

"Hello," said a soft and cultivated voice.

I peered upward. A small, slight and brown-skinned man about my age stood on the sand, squinting into the sun. He wore faded jeans — the genuine old-fashioned kind, not the artificial stone-washed stuff beloved of mall marketers — and a cast-off military khaki shirt, its flap pockets bulging. A lumpy blanket bedroll hung from one shoulder on a rope that bound both edges, in the old frontier style. Modern moccasins with rubber soles clad his feet. He wore his rich black hair long, in double braids resting on his chest in traditional Indian fashion. A leather medicine pouch dangled from his neck. His face was broad, his eyes sparkling and intelligent, and a gentle smile played upon his lips.

"Hi," I replied. "What can I do for you?"

"Sir, I need something to eat and a place to sleep," he said casually, as if remarking upon the weather. His relaxed manner suggested that if I said no, he would simply nod politely and say, "Just asking," and continue on up the beach. And if I said yes, he would simply nod politely and say, "Thank you."

"Well," I said noncommittally, "who are you and where are you bound?"

The lake shore is mostly lonely and deserted, except on

summer days when residents sun themselves and take dips, sometimes exercising by walking a mile or two in either direction and back. Once in a long while a long-distance hiker with backpack and bedroll will break the routine, returning my wave from the cabin if I'm at home. Now and then one tarries a bit for a chat and, if he or she seems interesting, I will offer a cup of coffee. One Sunday, shortly after I had settled into the cabin and long before I met Ginny, a beautiful blonde graduate student in sociology from Helsinki who had been visiting her American kin in Porcupine City had stopped by. I offered her lunch and, to make a long and complicated but sweet story short, we hit it off. On the last morning before she returned to Finland I woke up to find her pillow next to mine empty, but with a lovely good-bye note and a fresh daisy plucked from the roadside. Itinerants like these, I knew, were only temporary visitors to the wilderness. They had homes and careers to go back to.

Instantly I knew that the man standing in front of me was no stranger to the Upper Peninsula.

"I'm Anishinabe," he said, using the Ojibwe word for Ojibwe—it means "Original People," and some Anishinabe include all Native Americans in the term—and holding out his hand. His grasp was dry and strong. "My name's Edmund Sixkiller, I'm a medicine man, or shaman as some say, and I'm heading for the reservation at the Lake in the Woods. Call me Ed."

"I'm Steve Martinez. Wow, that's a long way. What is it, about three hundred miles?"

"Something like that."

"We don't get too many folks like you on this beach," I said. "Most everybody else is a local just going up and down for a bit."

"Men and women must take long journeys," Ed said "Otherwise, what's the point? You haven't found truth unless your feet hurt." He grinned, sat on the log and faced me.

"Medicine man, eh?" I said. "Tell me about your job."

"It's not really a job," he said. "It's a calling, like the ministry or the priesthood. It chooses you, you don't choose it."

"Exactly what does an Anishinabe medicine man do?"

"Depends. Some of us are full-service healers that will take care of your body as well as your soul, but let's face it, the calling has changed and modernized for all tribes and nations. Many of us are specialists now. The specialty I'm working toward is helping troubled souls become grounded with Mother Earth again."

He cocked his head and gazed at me with the same narrow-eyed, professionally interested expression Doc Miller has when he's giving me a physical at Porcupine County Hospital.

"Do I look troubled to you?" I said, only half seriously.

"Everybody's troubled. It's the times."

I chuckled. "What's your diagnosis?"

"My guess is that you were born Indian and brought up white." His eyes twinkled, but he did not laugh.

"Now how would you know that? I've never seen you before!"

"Sheriff, everybody in this small part of the world knows about you. Even we Anishinabe take notice of a Lakota cousin who has made his mark on the world."

"Well, I'll be—"

The medicine man grinned widely.

"And I'm a deputy, not a sheriff."

"If you say so."

I changed the subject and made a decision. "All right. Stay for supper. You can sleep on the couch."

"Thank you." Ed said casually, as if his request was rarely turned down.

"Anishinabe medicine men don't ordinarily depend on charity, do they?" I asked.

"This one does. But I've had a lot of practice at being a mendicant. I used to be a Franciscan friar."

"Really?"

"Yes. I grew up on the Baraga reservation and was educated by the Black Robes — that's what we called the Jesuits long ago — and I thought I had found my calling as a monk. But one morning not too long ago I woke up and decided the Catholics didn't have all the answers, at least for me. So I decided to return to the blood and become a traditional Anishinabe."

"That must have been difficult, given your Jesuit education."

"All belief systems and creation myths are based on revealed truth. One man's religion is no more outlandish than another's."

"But the Franciscans must have given you something," I said.

"Indeed they did. Among other things, their vows of poverty taught me how to live without owning anything except what I can carry on my back. What you see is what I've got. That's a mark of the traditional Anishinabe, by the way. We believe that people should own nothing. Traveling light allows a medicine man to bear heavy spiritual burdens, his own as well as those of others. And you never have to worry about feeding the Internal Revenue Service."

"Hmm."

"Sheriff, I don't mean to be rude," Ed said, "but I'm hungry."

"Deputy," I said again. "So am I."

We dined in my cabin on broiled whitefish and new potatoes sprinkled with basil and parsley. I had a little shiraz, but Ed declined the wine. "It's not that we're just denying ourselves something pleasant," he said. "Anishinabe religious tradition holds that alcohol causes people to lose control of themselves. And that is what has happened to Anishinabeg everywhere. Whites, too, of course."

"Do you think alcohol should be banned on the reservations?"

"It is in many places, but prohibition never works. Anishinabeg who want to drink will find liquor. What we need to do is teach Anishinabeg to disdain alcohol, to find solace and self-control in our religion. It must come from within, not without."

On into the night we talked about that and about the Ghost Dance, the mystical nineteenth century revival that had brought together Indian tribes from all over North America and badly frightened the whites. We talked about the central belief of Indian religions — the sanctity of Mother Earth — and the latter-day Native American Church. We also talked about the casinos — Ed hated them, for he believed gambling as dangerous as alcohol to an Indian's sense of self — and about a million other social problems facing the Native American in "the twenty-first century of the Common Era," as Ed put it. We talked about the Packers (Ed favored them) and the Vikings (I'm a fan) and the Lions (both of us disdained them). We talked about the best places to buy wild rice. We talked about the *midewewin,* the Grand Medicine Society of the Anishinabeg that Ed hoped to be invited to join someday. "It practices a strict code of ethics," Ed said. "It has eight stages, or degrees, on the road to spiritual knowledge, and I'm just what you would call a postulant. My first language, like yours, was English, and I'm still learning *Ojibwemowin,* as we call our tongue. I have a long way to go."

And we talked about the Venture Mine. I told Ed about my visit and my delight that an old copper mine was being used to grow plants to benefit humanity as well as provide jobs for half a hundred Porkies.

"Did you know that traditional Indians believe modern mining rapes the earth?" he asked. "Drilling deep violates its sanctity, and wresting precious metal from its ribs robs it of nourishment."

"But Indians also mined copper in the old days, didn't they?"

"Yes, but they merely scratched a small bit from the

94

surface, knowing that Mother Earth would eventually heal the scars in her skin. That was considerably different from the white man's drilling, crushing and refining ore and scattering the tailings over acres and acres, poisoning the water table. And America has used most of its copper not to make bowls to feed people and decorations to delight them but for munitions of war to kill other human beings."

I nodded. "But now, perhaps, growing medicinal plants in the mines can change that view?" The Ojibwe are famous for their knowledge of such plants.

"I don't know. Great harm has been done to Mother Earth for a long time. Can a small good heal it? I have my doubts."

It was well past midnight when we hit the sack, I in my bedroom and Ed on the old leather couch. He refused my offer of a coverlet, preferring his woolen blanket. "Hudson's Bay," he said, "woven by Indians. Tight and warm, and it also makes a good shelter from the rain."

Just before he lay down he patted my laptop computer, sitting on a small desk next to the couch. "*Wiindibaanens.* That translates literally as 'little brain machine.' *Ojibwemowin* is a wonderfully supple language. It evolves with the times."

I expected him to disappear before dawn, as that Finnish student had done years ago, maybe leaving a pleasant little bread-and-butter note behind. But shortly after sunup I awoke to a soft sound from the beach. Ed sat cross-legged on the sand, chanting not in *Ojibwemowin* but in some other language over the glassy lake toward the rising sun.

As I approached I heard these words:

"Pater noster qui in caelis es, sanctificetur nomen tuum. Adveniat regnum tuum, fiat voluntas tua sicut in caelo et in terra."

I remembered enough Latin from my schoolboy classes to recognize the Lord's Prayer. "Matins?" I asked in open-mouthed astonishment.

"Lauds, actually," Ed said. "Matins are sung at three in the morning, lauds at dawn."

"Why? I thought you'd become a traditionalist Ojibwe."

"You can take the boy out of the Franciscans," Ed said with a chuckle, "but you can't take the Franciscans out of the boy. Don't look so surprised, Sheriff."

"Deputy. It was just the notion of an Ojibwe medicine man reciting a Catholic prayer that startled me."

"No religion, no tradition, is pure and unchanging," Ed said. "Early Christianity was greatly influenced by the pagans it overwhelmed. Indian beliefs changed when Christianity swept the Americas, and I daresay American Christianity has been and is being influenced by Indian spirituality, too. Remember, I was educated in the Western tradition, as you were. It is a strong and appealing intellectual heritage, but North American Indian wisdom is also powerful. Western culture engages the mind, but Indian spirituality touches the heart. They need not war against each other, as perhaps they are inside you, Sheriff. You can accept them both. I have, and I am the more content for it."

To that I had no response, although Ed's words made sense to me. We went inside for breakfast—juice, eggs, *korppu* and coffee.

"Where did you get this swill?" Ed demanded, tapping the coffee pot.

"Hey, that's good French roast from Starbuck's." I'd bought several bags there on my last foray to Rhinelander.

"Nonsense. You want pure Colombian. And not from a designer chain but the grocery store."

"Opinionated, are we?" I said with a laugh.

Ed laughed, too. "About some things. Like everybody else."

After breakfast he stood up and said formally, "Thank you. Now I must bless your house for the charity it has given me."

He took the medicine bag from his neck and opened the pouch, shaking a few bits of tobacco into his palm. Into the four corners of my living room he tossed a few grains, chanting softly in Ojibwe as he did so.

"An offering to the *manitou*, the spirit, of the house," he said. "It's analogous to the sprinkling of holy water and the wafting of incense. It may make good things happen here."

"I hope so," I said.

He peered into the pouch. "Have any cigarettes?"

"I don't smoke."

"I'm getting short of tobacco. I'll have to ask as I go down the beach."

"You use cigarette tobacco for medicine?"

"Sure. Priests make holy water of ordinary water by sanctifying it with a blessing. We medicine men don't exactly sanctify tobacco, though. The spirits like it just as it is. Of course, aromatic pipe tobacco is the best kind, but that's because it smells so good in the medicine pouch. When we can't get it we'll field-strip cigarettes."

Swiftly Ed bound his extra clothes into his blanket bedroll, tied it with the rope and slung it over his shoulder. I followed him out on the beach.

"Any parting advice for me?" I said.

He drew himself straight and peered out over the lake.

"Sheriff, the central belief of any Indian tradition is to look at yourself as not what circumstance has made you but what you have done with your life," he said. "The songs in your memory will celebrate what you leave behind." After a beat, he added: "The Christian Bible has something to say about that, too. 'What good is it, my brothers, if a man claims to have faith but has no deeds?' That's James, chapter two, verse fourteen."

After a moment of shared silence I said, "I guess this is good-bye."

"Anishinabeg don't say good-bye. That's too abrupt, too final. We say 'Gigaa-wabamin,' which means 'I'll see you again.'" He thrust out his hand in farewell. "Gigaa-wabamin, sheriff."

I didn't bother to correct him, but watched him shrink into the distance as he strode down the beach and finally disappeared around a rocky promontory.

FOURTEEN

Ginny eats slowly and daintily, like the cultivated Wellesley graduate she is. For no good reason I tend to bolt my food like a starving dog. I always have, despite my adoptive mother's efforts to rein in my headlong appetite. My adoptive father was no help. All his life he had too many things to do and too many people to see to regard the dining table as anything other than a brief and necessary fuel stop. Much as I love the taste of good food, I was sadly influenced, and boyhood habits are hard to break once they've become ingrained. Lectures about slowing down to enjoy the taste make good sense, but about eating I have never been sensible.

Ginny and I finally reached a truce after several months of hissing at each other across the tablecloth: "It's not a race!" and "You're the president of the Slow Eaters of America!" And so I sat patiently waiting for her to finish her lamb chop in an upscale lodge restaurant in Eagle River, where we'd escaped for a little midweek rest and recreation. It was late and the place was nearly empty, but we spoke in hushed tones, as if the walls hung on every word we said.

Almost immediately after I told her about the visit from the Ojibwe medicine man, Ginny quietly dropped the bomb she had carried all the way down from Porcupine City.

"I'd like a child," she said casually, as if she were telling me what she'd prefer for dessert.

An iceberg of panic suddenly calved from the walls of my stomach. Only once before had that glacial feeling enveloped me. It happened the night my childhood sweetheart told me she was pregnant.

"You would?"

"Yes."

Thank God I didn't say "Why?" But consternation must have been written all over my face, for Ginny took my hand in hers and gazed calmly into my eyes.

"I'm not getting any younger," she said, "and neither are you."

"I don't know if I— "

For a couple of years now Ginny and I had been keeping company, as the old-timers still called relationships like ours. We still lived in our own cabins several miles apart on the lake shore, but had settled into a comfortable routine of weekends at each other's places, content to enjoy the present without dwelling on the future. I could have gone on for years more, basking in the love of a beautiful woman while making her happy in small, everyday ways. Sooner or later, I knew somewhere in the unvisited nooks and crannies of my mind, things would have to change. It was the natural order of life. But I was hardly ready for that, even though, like Ginny, I had reached my early forties.

"But aren't you—"

"Too old?" she said. "Yes, for a natural child. I know the risk is small these days, but I dont want to take it. I want to adopt."

Her use of the first person startled me. "You?" I said dumbly.

She arched a pretty eyebrow and gazed at me steadily.

"Don't you mean we?" I said.

"Perhaps." Her eyes fastened on mine like lasers.

"I—"

"Stevie Two Crow, you are having trouble finishing your sentences."

"This is so— "

"Sudden?" she said after a long beat.

I nodded and looked at the table, then the far wall, then the ceiling, anywhere but into her eyes.

"I need time to get used to the idea," I stammered.

"Obviously." Ginny's smile was warm and amused, but maybe not as warm and amused as it could have been.

For a few moments we sat silent. Then she rolled another grenade down the aisle.

"I'd like to adopt an Indian child."

My jaw dropped as a rush of memories blindsided me.

The Reverend Carl Martinez, the white Methodist missionary who with his wife had adopted me, loved me. In the manner of so many public men, however, he was incapable of showing it with those closest to him, though he was generous and demonstrative with God's love for his flock. To an immature lad like me it seemed that to me he could express only anger, infrequent but often accompanied by a slap or whack of limber birch. I loved and hated him at the same time, as sons will. I learned the truth about Dad's feelings only long after he and Mother were killed at the hands of a drunken driver. He was proud of the child he had rescued from the pagans to bring up as a highly achieving, although brown-skinned, Christian schoolboy and athlete. Deep down I had always known Dad cared, but by then it was too late. I had left his church. Not for me his piously selfish certainty that Jesus was the only true path to salvation.

I was glad, however, that he was not around to learn that my girlfriend had become pregnant. I doubted that the generosity of his Christian forgiveness would have extended that far. He just would have been too disappointed that the youth in whose bright future he had expended so much hope and energy had turned out to be like everyone else, tasting forbidden fruit before marriage—even though we had planned to wed as soon as I returned from Desert Storm. I doubted that Dad would have thought to console me after I learned one dark night in Iraq that my sweetheart was pregnant not by me but by the close friend who had been part of our inseparable neighborhood triumvirate when we were growing up in Troy. Nor would he have approved of the impulsive, self-lacerating leap I then made, resigning my lieutenant's commission as soon as I could and running away to hide as an ill-paid deputy in an obscure Upper Michigan backwoods sheriff's department. Of course I had come to believe that that hasty act was the smartest thing I had ever done, for it had led eventually into the heart and arms of Virginia Anttila Fitzgerald as well as roots in a part of the country I had also fallen in love with.

But now I began to resist Ginny's plan. "You know it's not necessarily a good idea for whites to adopt nonwhite children," I said. "I know something about that, after all."

"Indeed?" said Ginny. "And what if there aren't enough good Indian homes for Indian orphans? Should they be left to grow up in pinched and crowded orphanages with only meager bits of love from overworked caregivers?"

"No, but—"

"But?"

She had me there, and I couldn't argue with what she said next.

"Steve, times have changed since your adoption. No matter what minority a kid belongs to, the thinking today is that his adoptive parents, whatever they are, should ground him solidly in the culture of his birth parents. Everybody recognizes that the problem you had—and you *still* have—is a problem and has to be dealt with."

And then she drove home the lance. "Besides, Steve, what better adoptive parent could an Indian child have than you?"

Involuntarily I sucked in my breath. The word "marriage" had never been mentioned in our relationship. Someday, sure, I had thought many times, Ginny and I might marry, but "someday" seemed to be a vague time a long way ahead. But did "parent" mean, to Ginny, "husband" or "partner" or "lover" or something else?

"You're thinking Lakota?" I said to cover my confusion.

"Why not Ojibwe?" she said. "The tribespeople of

Upper Michigan almost all belong to that nation."

"I don't know much about being an Ojibwe," I protested.

"Do you know much about being a Lakota?" Ginny countered.

During the 1870s, I knew, the Lakota sent a spearhead of warriors farther west to Wyoming to win glory with Sitting Bull and Crazy Horse and their Cheyenne allies at the Battle of the Little Bighorn. Like a fifth-generation Boston Irishman singing the praises of Cuchulainn, I was proud of the Indians' victory over Custer and his men and would often relive their brilliant military tactics over the dinner table, but that didn't make me a cultural Lakota, only a genetic one. What could I say? Everything I knew about my native people—which wasn't much—came from books and from a brief and unsuccessful visit to Pine Ridge when I was in college to see if I could locate my birth parents. And from yesterday's visit from an Ojibwe medicine man.

"No," I admitted, trying to keep the grudging edge out of my voice.

"It would be a new journey for you, Steve, learning how to be an Indian at the same time you're teaching your son how to be one." Ginny, like me, preferred the old word to "Native American," a term invented by a bureaucrat in the United States Department of the Interior and instantly adopted by white professors. I think "Native American" smacks of academic condescension, though I won't argue with anybody who uses it. Many Indians do, though others simply want to be known by the names of their tribes. Identity politics is complicated and more shape-shifting than a Navajo skinwalker.

"I'm just—" I couldn't think of anything more. I stared dumbly out the window into the night, hoping the stars would tell me what to say.

"Not ready to commit," Ginny finished.

I shrugged mutely. Maybe I was and maybe I wasn't.

Damn it, a man needs time to get used to a new idea. It's in our nature. Some of us take longer to come around than others, and I am one of the slowpokes. Deep down I knew that I wanted to be a father someday, and deep down I knew that I would love an adopted child as much as a natural one. But I didn't know it yet.

Silently Ginny slid the bill toward me. We usually went Dutch. I couldn't afford fancy restaurant meals for two on a deputy's salary, but Ginny refused to rub my nose in my poverty by offering to pick up the checks. Tonight, I knew, I had disappointed her with my lack of enthusiasm, and she was making me pay for it.

We drove back to Porcupine City in silence, both of Ginny's hands in her lap rather than one on my leg provocatively. At her house she did not invite me inside, as I had eagerly anticipated earlier in the evening, but instead gave me a cool kiss on the cheek and a pat on the shoulder.

"Good night, Steve," she said. "Think on it a bit."

"I will," I said, and drove home to my cabin and a lonely bed.

FIFTEEN

By noon the next day I was feeling better, having spent a long morning in the shallows repairing one of my two cribs, twenty-four-foot-long, eight-foot-wide log-and-stone jetties jutting into the lake like beached wooden bargeloads of rocks the size of basketballs. Well into the nineteen-sixties, owners of beachfront property on Lake Superior constructed the cribs to protect their shorelines from savage winter tempests, but the truth was that they mostly just caused sand to pile up on one side of the crib or the other, depending on the direction of the waves. Whether or not storms ate away a sandy beach depended more on the fluctuating levels of Lake Superior than on any human intervention. Mother Nature was more powerful than any but the most aggressive concrete fortifications thrown up by the Army Corps of Engineers, and the soldiers had to spend considerable time, as I did, to keep their structures in good repair. And now new cribs were forbidden because they upset the natural course of the currents, or so the feds claimed. They were probably right, although no true Porky would admit such a thing.

I suspected that many cribs were originally cobbled together not only to protect the shoreline but also to give their wealthy out-of-town owners something to occupy their time during the summer in a place that has no theme parks or shopping malls. Out of a perhaps misguided sense of respect for the late Milton Browne, a Wisconsin businessman who had a Finnish craftsman build my four-room cedar log cabin and its cribs shortly after World War II, I kept both in good repair. Log structures are as high-maintenance as Victoria's Secret models and a good deal less exciting to look at. Winters are hard on wooden edifices in Upper Michigan, and to keep ahead of rack and ruin people must spend many days, even weeks, fixing them. Over the decade since I'd bought the cabin from Browne's estate shortly after my arrival in Porcupine County, I'd replaced the roof and several windows, re-chinked the logs and fought rot with hammer, chisel and epoxy wood filler. The summer before, I'd had to have a decayed bottom log in the cabin replaced with masonry, a job I left to the Metrovich brothers, skilled mill hands and bachelor woodsmen who live on their own lakefront land near Porcupine City. They hadn't charged much, just what I could afford with a small bank loan.

I could probably have let the lake slowly pound away the cribs—it would take decades, so solidly built were they—without jeopardizing my beachfront, but inasmuch as the cabin lay dangerously close to the water right on the tree line, I wanted to take no chances, feds or no feds. Hence I spend several weekends each summer repairing storm damage that is usually slight but if ignored will eat away the cribs bit by bit. Mostly I have to wrestle massive stones, hurled by huge waves, back into the log-enclosed structures, sometimes needing block and tackle for a hundred-pound boulder, now and then shoring a broken side log with concrete. Every couple of years a big log needs replacing, and for that I enlist the help of the Metrovichs. We find twenty-foot white pines uprooted by winter storms floating close to shore, trim off the branches, notch the ends and nail things home with yard-long steel spikes and heavy iron sledges. I love watching the Metroviches work. They both are chainsaw sculptors who can scoop out log ends solely by eye, without measuring, and drop them into place over their neighbors for a perfect fit.

Repairing cribs not only helps keep me in shape, but the sweat lubricates my mind, helping me deal with problems that have nothing to do with property maintenance. Each stone heaved back into the crib is a step closer to truth. And so, rock by rock, I was coming to terms with Ginny's dream. Yes, it was time, time to settle down, marry her and start a family. That's not exactly an unexpected milestone for a man, but sometimes a guy has to be blindsided into facing it head on. We give up our carefree old lives only grudgingly. If this was what it took to keep the heart of a treasure like Ginny, so be it. She was right. Marriage and an instant family would be a challenge, but today I felt quite up to it. And so I was going to tell her that evening, for she hadn't broken our supper date at her house.

I had been working in the shallow water bare-chested in soaked jeans and neoprene canoer's shoes to protect my feet from sharp stones. A gentle onshore breeze was clearing the beach of sand flies and mosquitoes, allowing me to work shirtless. Suddenly I felt a familiar yen. My beachfront is isolated, and Sheila Carnahan, I knew, had gone away for the weekend. So had the couple from Arizona who occupy the beach house to the west. And the temperature of the inshore water had crept well into the seventies under the summer sun.

Yes, Lake Superior is cold — fishermen often chill their beer over the gunwales of their boats — but by mid-July the inshore water temperature can climb into the upper sixties, warm enough for comfortable swimming once one gets over the initial shock of immersion. Later in the month and all through August and the middle of September, gentle onshore winds often blow warmer surface water into the shallows, sometimes raising the temperature into the low seventies. Today was one of those days, and it would have been a crime not to glory in it.

Shucking my jeans, briefs and canoe shoes and laying them atop the crib, I dove naked into the water, stroking briskly over the pebbly bottom to a sandbar seventy-five yards out. There the water was shoulder-high, and I could feel a colder layer below my knees. I began swimming laps parallel to the shore, counting two hundred strokes each way and navigating with the edge of the sandbar below through the glass-clear water. Rounded stones lay scattered in piles among the smooth, clean sand, and now and then a minnow darted away in panic as I splashed by. As I swam I exulted quietly in the unfettered stream of water past my flanks, the truest glory of skinnydipping. This must be what it feels like to be a dolphin. I am not a naturist—there are few in Upper Michigan, because of the intense fogs of mosquitoes and blackflies the only sizable American region that has no commercial nudist camps—but I can still appreciate unclad closeness to nature.

Especially in the splendid isolation of these parts. The low growl of an outboard carried over the water from half a mile away, and the only other sign of life was a sail far in the distance, hull below the horizon. Probably a yacht harbored at the Porcupine City marina. Floating on my back in waist-deep water, I let the warm swells rock me gently as the sun flushed my face and belly. In a minute or so I had been lulled into a semi-doze of sensual contentment, and my thoughts drifted to Ginny. She would, I felt sure, be happy about the decision I had made, and would reward me not only with a splendid dinner but also a lovely—ah—dessert far into the night. That mental image, helped along by the warm kiss of the sun, stirred the center of my being. There I felt twitches of anticipation that slowly grew firmer as I lost myself in lustful thoughts. And then a strange hand grasped me.

I looked up into the eyes of Mary Ellen Garrigan.

"God *damn!*" I bellowed. She was as naked as I.

"Thought I'd surprise you, Steve," she said, laughing, her face colored by a concupiscent leer, the kind often seen on the faces of people to whom sex is a contact sport.

I backed away from her in consternation, eyes fixed on her body. It was impossible not to look. Even without her usual encrustation of gold and diamonds she was a traffic-stopper, her tanned flanks doubtless sculpted by hours of work at the Nautilus as well as nips, tucks and shoves by a distinguished and very expensive plastic surgeon. As I'd seen aboard the *Lucky Six,* her boob job looked almost natural instead of resembling hard grapefruits tucked under the skin, and if her breasts had swayed a little more I'd have been fooled. She'd had a butt tuck, too, I was certain. And she was shaven. A wet dream for porn addicts.

Despite my deepening anger at the woman's arrogance—I am, goddamnit, just too proud to allow my Indian identity to be used for cheap thrills—I am a healthy male with a normal autonomous nervous system and normal physiological reactions, and my body was now fully awakened. Despite that I stood and strode furiously through the now knee-deep water across the pebbled bottom toward the beach, ignoring the painful crunch of rough stones under the soles of my feet.

"Let's!" Mary Ellen called breathily. "Right here in the water! Nobody will see!"

I stopped and turned to her, fighting to keep my composure. "I'm not interested, Mrs. Garrigan," I said from between clenched teeth.

"What a sorry, sorry asshole you are!" she replied as I strode onto the beach next to the crib. She followed me out of the water, lunging and reaching for me, laughing. I quickly stepped back out of range.

"You want me, Martinez, but you're a coward!" Scorn stained the leer on her face.

I glanced down at myself, dismayed by my still-attentive state, and hid it with my jeans. "Please go home, Mrs. Garrigan," I said. "You are on my property, and I do not want you here." It took all my willpower not to call the scheming bitch a scheming bitch.

Just as she turned and strode to the pile of clothes she had left on the beach, a car door slammed. I peered into the woods. The brown Ford van belonging to the Historical Society that Ginny drove every day fishtailed violently, throwing gravel, as it sped away up my dirt driveway to the highway beyond the forest. My heart sank, and so did the rest of me.

SIXTEEN

Long before we met and shortly before she returned to Porcupine County, Ginny, then a young widow in Manhattan, had very nearly lost her heart—and her considerable portfolio—to an unscrupulous, much-married fortune hunter who had also betrayed many other wealthy women in order to fund the charitable enterprise that had made him famous. She discovered his treachery in time, but her recovery from the betrayal took many years and a change of scenery from glittering New York City to rustic Porcupine County, where she had grown up, daughter of a mining engineer who sent her to Wellesley. I'd been recovering from the shock of my sweetheart's perfidy, too, and Ginny and I had slowly healed our wounds together. Now she thought I had turned on her. Her newfound, hard-earned confidence was probably shattered. Persuading her otherwise was going to be difficult. Very difficult. She had seen what she had seen, and the truth would just sound lame.

I pulled on my jeans and shirt and, not bothering to comb my hair, leaped into my Jeep and tore after her. But when I knocked on her door, she called out the kitchen window, "Please go. I don't want to talk to you."

"But, Ginny—" I said, ashamed of the pleading I could not keep out of my voice.

"Go."

I left. What else could I do?

I wrested the Jeep back onto the highway and drove home, flooring the accelerator, the rusty old heap's transmission protesting as it slowly crept up to its top speed, seventy-five miles an hour. There would be no cop to run me down, for I was the cop who caught speeders on Highway M-64 along the lakeshore.

On my way to work the next morning I pulled up at the Historical Society, an old supermarket building in Porcupine City slathered with donated purple paint, and strode inside.

"She called twenty minutes ago," said Nancy Aho, the sweet blue-haired docent in charge, "and said she had to go away for a while, but that she'd be in touch. Is anything wrong?"

"No," I said, ashamed of the lie, trying to keep my voice normal. "Just checking."

"I'm sorry, Steve," Nancy said. "But I'm sure everything will be all right. Is this your first fight?"

Shit. It's impossible to conceal a secret of the heart from the good ladies of Porcupine County. They generally don't make other people's sex lives their business, but they're extraordinarily observant about them. And, there not being a lot else to occupy their minds besides hunting, fishing, moving snow and making love, as the old Yooper joke has it, they gossip. A lot. Before nightfall every woman in the county and many in the neighboring ones would know that the Lakota deputy and his sweetheart were on the outs. And so, by the time supper was done, would the men.

I tried Ginny's cell phone from the Jeep but she either wasn't answering or was out of range, for few places in the Upper Peninsula are hospitable to wireless calls. With a sinking heart I guessed where she had gone. She was on her way to Detroit and the comfort and counsel of her lawyer and accountant. It would take her almost eleven hours to get there, for she had to drive due east to the Mackinac Bridge, then south by southeast down the middle of Lower Michigan.

I knew the number of her lawyer — she had entrusted me with it just in case something untoward happened to her — but knew that he would take his client's side against mine. That's a lawyer's job. It was pointless to call.

I drove back to Ginny's cabin and scrawled a note.

"Dearest," it said, "it's not what you think. Please call. My deepest love. Steve."

Banal as these words are, they were all I could think of, and I knew they would not move her.

But I slipped the note inside an envelope and left it inside her screen door, hoping it would be the first thing she saw when she returned.

SEVENTEEN

Before I had finished dressing the next morning, my heart a cast-iron lump in my chest, the radio on my kitchen table crackled. It was Joe Koski.

"Steve?"

"Here. Still at home." As I listened I buckled on my gunbelt, from which dangled a tooled leather holster cradling a well-oiled .357 Combat Magnum, an old-fashioned six-shot revolver the other deputies, who carried up-to-date 9mm Beretta semi-automatics, liked to make fun of. But I preferred tried-and-true old tools. Though it was unlikely, a high-tech nine-shot Beretta still could jam. A revolver never would.

"It's Sam Williamson and Steve Turner," Joe said.

"Oh no," I said. I knew what that meant.

"Yes," Joe said. "Steve is in the woods outside Sam's place and they're shooting at each other," he said. "With hunting rifles. Neighbor heard the gunfire and said he saw Steve behind a tree shooting cedar shakes off Sam's house."

"Jeez."

Williamson and Turner, two elderly and fierce Porkies, occupied opposing sides of an issue that recently had inflamed the more politically engaged segments of the county: the return of timber wolves to the western Upper Peninsula. The wolf had been eradicated from the state early in the twentieth century along with the passenger pigeon, grayling trout, caribou, fisher, wolverine and moose. Over the last few years a couple of wolf packs from Canada had traveled south and east around Lake Superior through Canada and upper Wisconsin, seeking *lebensraum* — room to live — and food. Wilderness had returned to the old cut-over logging and mining lands where the population of deer, their favorite prey, had exploded. The wolves were migrants, not hopeful reintroductions of rare species by human hands but a natural event. And they had begun to multiply, splitting off into new packs as their numbers grew.

Most Upper Peninsulans have welcomed the return of the wolf as well as the fisher, the big martenlike weasel now legally trapped for its fur. Eagles abound. Young moose now wander through downtowns and have to be shooed back into the woods. The cougar is back, too, many Yoopers will tell you, although the DNR steadfastly denies its presence in Upper Michigan. It's too easy, say the rangers, to mistake a fleeting sight of another animal, perhaps a lynx, for the big tawny cat. Still, most folks who say they have seen them don't strike me as the kind to be fooled easily.

All the same, the return of once vanished animals warms the hearts of people who love the wilderness and all its wonders, as it does mine. More than once I've spotted one or two wolves trotting along highway verges. I have pulled off the road to watch them, and they have stopped, turned and stared at me confidently, as to say, "Keep out of our way, and we'll keep out of yours." They're beautiful, proud animals, and, like any Ojibwe or Lakota, I'm happy to share the territory with them. They call out to me from the heart of a land they lived in for many millennia before human beings arrived. "We were Native Americans long before you," their piercing golden eyes seem to say, "and we belong to this country as much as you do."

But in some places, Johnny-come-lately wolf haters are almost as plentiful as wolf lovers. Driven by emotion and irrationality, they condemn the animals as wasteful and indiscriminate, preying on domestic dogs and cattle and killing for sport, not for survival. The nuttier among them claim anti-hunting organizations have encouraged government efforts to reintroduce the wolf, even though it has come back on its own, absolutely unaided by humans. They say elderly berry pickers can no longer walk the woods confidently, for the wolves will kill them and drag them to their lairs for supper. The very nuttiest perceive wolves as a sign of the Devil, as if their fur were emblazoned with the number "666."

Sam Williamson is one of those, and no amount of argument from the opposite side would sway him as wolf sightings increased in the last few months. No wild wolf has ever attacked a human in the entire state of Michigan. Wolves do take the occasional calf, but the Michigan Department of Natural Resources reimburses farmers for their losses. Wolves do prey on deer, but prefer old, sick and catchable specimens, leaving more browse available for strong bucks and does. Wolves do kill dogs running loose as well as those tied out overnight in their owners' yards. A breeder of Karelian bear dogs had been repeatedly warned by the Forest Service not to release his animals in a particular stretch of the Ottawa National Forest where a wolf pack had been sighted, but scoffed and did so anyway. In a single day the pack killed all four of his dogs, and the breeder shouted that his right to use public lands had been violated.

Sam, who is an educated man—he grew up in Porcupine County, graduated from the University of Michigan, and spent forty years as a certified public accountant in Lansing before retiring to his home county—took up the breeder's case, writing furious letters to the *Porcupine County Herald* that spurred furious counter-letters. For weeks the letters-to-the-editor page roiled with rage, and readers couldn't wait for *The Herald* to appear in the supermarkets on Wednesday morning to see who had taken up the cudgels.

Steve Turner was one of these, and though he had the facts on his side so far as I was concerned, he was as hotheaded as Sam, who had been his closest friend in high school. Like Sam, Steve had left home after high school, made a living as a plumber in the Chicago area and, when he reached retirement age, had come back to Porcupine County to live. Not for nothing do some Porkies call their home the world's largest retirement village.

Twice Steve and Sam had been thrown out of Hobbs' Bar, Grill and Northwoods Museum downtown after coming to blows over the subject of wolves, and the second time I arrested them, drove them to jail, and clapped them into separate cells to sleep it off. The next morning we didn't bother with charges—if we did that we'd have to triple the size of the jail to accommodate all the drunken Saturday-night score-settlers we pick up—but the undersheriff had threatened to skin them and nail their hides to his wall if they went at it again.

Gil's tough love had done no good. Slowly the dispute had escalated. Now Sam had threatened to take his rifle from his cabin in the woods off Norwich Road—he is an expert deer hunter, like Steve—and kill every wolf he could find, and Steve had vowed to shoot him before he could carry out his threat.

"They're liquored up, too," Joe cut in, almost as an afterthought. Surprise.

If Porcupine County had been a big city, SWAT teams swiftly would have been called out and the subjects immediately isolated and perhaps picked off by black-clad sharpshooters before they could threaten the lives of others. There is a plan for sheriff's departments and state police posts to come to the aid of any Upper Michigan jurisdiction that needs such a show of force, but Sam and Steve were likely to kill each other before reinforcements could arrive.

I keyed the radio. "Chad?" I asked.

"On the way," he replied immediately. "I'm at Matchwood. I can be at Sam's cabin in ten minutes." That was on State Highway M-28, the main east-west road in the southern part of the county, about seven miles south of Sam's cabin on Norwich Road. Though Chad's voice was brisk and professional, that did not make me feel better. Inexperience often trumps courage. Though Chad hardly lacked grit, he had almost no seasoning.

"Trooper with you," crackled the gravelly voice of Sergeant Alex Kolehmainen. "I'm at Ewen." That was five miles southwest of Matchwood on M-28. If Alex and I started now, we both knew, we'd get to Sam's about the same time. Chad, being closest, would arrive first, and I hoped he wouldn't do anything stupid and heroic.

"Chad?"

"Yes, Steve?"

"When you get there, wait for us."

"Yes sir!"

I perform my highway patrols in the department's Explorer. Much of my work takes me into the woods on old logging tracks, and a sturdy four-wheel-drive is much better than the old Ford police cruisers the other deputies use. The Explorer is fast enough, but it still took nearly fifteen minutes to slalom around the potholes down Norwich Road to Sam's cabin. When I pulled up, Chad's cruiser and a beefed-up state police Tahoe Alex had lately been driving stood cheek by jowl on what passed for Sam's lawn. They had come in silently, as I had, without siren or flashers. No reason to announce our arrival with fanfare and spook our targets into wasting bullets in our direction.

"They're not here," Alex said. "Neighbor said Sam ran into the woods with his rifle and Steve followed. They've gone north."

Alex glanced at me. Though we shared the jurisdiction, troopers outrank deputies. But Alex is not a rank-puller. And he respected me and I him. Slowly our relationship had become collegial, then friendly. He knows forensics better than I do, I know nature better than he does, and we divide tasks according to our talents.

"What think?" he said.

I pulled out a topographical hiker's map and pointed to a faint dashed line representing the North Country Trail.

That's a little-known transcontinental work-in-progress nominally headed by the National Park Service but administered by local hiker's groups. Some seventeen hundred miles of a planned four-thousand-mile trail so far has been carved from east to west across the United States. The existing path stretches from the Appalachian Trail in eastern New York State to the middle of North Dakota. It is not unbroken, but the gaps are slowly being filled in. In western Upper Michigan, the trail has been well established with blazes, wooden footbridges, lean-tos and campgrounds for 140 miles from Baraga to the Wolverines, and it draws hundreds of serious hikers every summer. The rugged track is gorgeous, traversing hardwood and conifer forests, lakes, bogs, rivers, beaver ponds, waterfalls, and high cliffs with spectacular views. Ginny and I had trekked much of it one October when the bugs lay dormant and the nip of oncoming winter rustled the falling leaves.

"See where the trail crosses Norwich Road and enters the woods, right there? Sam and Steve probably took it. They're old guys and they won't be moving fast. They'll stop now and then to fire at each other and keep at it until one hits the other or they run out of ammo."

As if to punctuate my words a muffled rifle shot rang through the woods, followed by another, not quite as loud. Sam and Steve both were packing powerful rifles that could easily drop a deer or a man. I hoped we could catch up to them before one did in the other. I also hoped drink would spoil their aim.

"Maybe we should split up," I suggested. "One of us can follow the trail while the other two go through the woods twenty or thirty yards away on either side and a little bit behind. We'll be able to cover each other better that way. And if Sam or Steve uses us for targets, we won't be bunched up."

"Good idea," Alex said. He had been in the military, too, and knew infantry tactics. "You take the lead, Steve, and Chad and I will cover the flanks."

We set off, each armed according to our preference. Chad and Alex carried lightweight AR-15 military rifles, and I a police riot shotgun, an excellent weapon for close combat. I hoped mightily that none of us would need to use them. While neither Sam nor Steve was a particular friend of mine, neither were they truly bad guys, only impassioned hotheads who had suddenly lost what remained of their good sense, if they ever had any in the first place. That's what's tough about law enforcement in this part of the world. We're not dealing with simple clashes between good and evil, but the petty imperfections of human beings. Big-city cops separate themselves from the people they arrest by calling most of them "assholes," but we country deputies just call ours "idiots."

That part of Porcupine County is world-class rugged, the rocky trail dipping into bramble-choked gullies and climbing up bare, slippery escarpments. The going was slow. The temperature had climbed into the nineties, as it often does in late August. Blackflies and no-see-ums assaulted every square inch of bare skin. I tried to breathe shallowly, hoping not to inhale the fiery midges. And, following the trail, I had the best of it. Chad and Alex had to fight their way through the brush. Neither man made much noise, except now and then the crack of a dry twig or the scrabble of loose rock.

A shot rang out nearby, immediately followed by an answer. If they were still trading gunfire, Sam and Steve had not killed each other yet. At such moments I grasp for the obvious.

"Steve!" Chad yelled. He crouched only a few yards west of me, but I couldn't see him through the brush.

"Which one?" I yelled back. A common name can be most inconvenient when both hunter and hunted share it.

"You! Not him!"

"Well, thanks!" I shouted. "Call me Martinez, for Chrissake!"

"Martinez! Turner's coming your way!"

At the same moment I spotted the other Steve twenty yards up the trail, shambling toward me in a crouch. He wore hunting camouflage and no signal orange. That was evidence of premeditation. It might mean a rap for attempted murder.

Turner whirled, knelt and fired in the opposite direction. A heavier report answered, and a bullet neatly decapitated an inch-thick sapling six feet from my head. I dropped to my belly and thrust the riot gun in front of me, taking a bead on Turner's broad back. At this range a spread of buckshot couldn't miss. It probably wouldn't be fatal, but the heavy shot would tear him up some.

"Turner!" I yelled. "Police! Drop the rifle right now!"

He had the good sense to stop in his tracks, toss the rifle to the side, and fall to both knees, his hands up.

"Don't let Sam shoot me!" he called. "I'm out of ammo!"

"Well, shit," Williamson shouted whiskily from behind a stump on higher ground. "So am I! Ain't this your lucky day?"

"Shut up, Sam," Alex called.

"Steve, lie down on your belly and put your hands behind your back!"

"Who zat?" Sam said.

"Sheriff's department," I called back. "State police. We've taken Turner. Put your rifle down and walk toward us slowly and keep your hands in sight."

Slowly Sam lurched into view, grinning sheepishly.

"The son of a bitch tried to kill me," he said righteously.

"Yes, yes," I said. "Never mind. You're coming with us till we get this all sorted out."

Alex stepped out from the shelter of a thick tree trunk and swiftly cuffed Sam's hands behind him. Sam did not protest. All the vinegar had whooshed out of him, whether from the exertion of the chase or the sudden realization that his cause had very nearly gotten him killed, I didn't know.

As Alex covered Turner, facedown in the leaves, I knelt, one knee in the small of his back, and clapped my own set of cuffs on him, wrinkling my nose against a cloud of cheap rye. Before I pulled him to his feet I fished the Miranda card from my shirt pocket and read him his rights.

Almost before I finished, a crackle of branches and a thud echoed from close by "Shit! Damn!"Chad bellowed.

"Chad, are you all right?"

"Yeah. Slipped down a creek bank. I'm okay. . . . Holy Mary, mother of God!"

"What's wrong?" I shouted.

"Aagh," he replied.

In a moment Chad had climbed back up the muddy bank, his uniform stained with mud, his face white. With a trembling hand he held toward me what appeared to be a small brown horseshoe.

It was a human mandible.

EIGHTEEN

The jaw, stained by decades in the muddy bank of the forest creek, looked almost ancient, maybe a century old. Yellowed teeth still clung to its sockets.

We scrambled down the bank, rising the height of a man above the pebbly trickle of a creek, and braced our feet on roots jutting from the ground. As he skidded down the steep slope, Chad had reached out to catch himself, and his hand had unwittingly plucked the mandible out of the moist earth. The skull to which it had once been attached protruded from the rocky loam.

"This," said Alex, "is a crime scene."

"How?"

"See that?" He pointed a latex-clad finger at the large triangular hole on the back of the skull. "Dollars to doughnuts that was made with a miner's pickaxe."

We had frog-marched the two woozy miscreants back to Sam's cabin, where Undersheriff O'Brien and Sheriff Garrow had rolled up shortly before in the sheriff's nearly new Crown Victoria cruiser, the one a jailhouse trusty washed once a day and waxed once a week. They and Chad had transported Sam and Steve to the lockup at Porcupine City, where Sam faced a stern lecture from the undersheriff and Steve a felony charge that probably would send him to prison long enough to douse his political fires. Afterward Gil, his ranks always understaffed, had ordered Chad back on patrol. I wished he were still on the scene. Like the aftermath of the discovery of Frank Saarinen's body, what happened next would have been instructive for a green young police officer.

Alex opened his crime-scene kit, fished out his digital

camera and examined the bare creek bank before him. "That's a hand," he said. "And there's a boot."

The body protruded from the bank a good four feet below the surface of the forest floor. It had been buried away from the creek, which over the decades had slowly carved its way through the earth toward the body until its bones lay exposed.

Carefully Alex troweled out every bone and bit of moldered clothing he could find after photographing it *in situ*. The job took several hours because the stained skeleton was mostly disarticulated, though a few remaining thews and sinews bound together an arm and a hand here, the spine and pelvis there. Alex lay everything on a plastic tarp in more or less the same arrangement it had enjoyed in life.

"Good thing the anthropologists aren't here," Alex said halfway through. "They'd want to do things their way, and that'd take days and even weeks."

University scientists set up tents over their sites and uncover artifacts layer by layer, pebble by pebble, capturing everything as it lies, amassing mountains of data to sort out in their labs and workrooms. Cops have crooks to catch and prosecute and just don't have the time to enjoy the details of history. This is not to say that good cops are careless about their crime scenes. They try hard to preserve and record anything and everything that might convict a perp.

"But this is no archaeological dig," Alex continued. The scene isn't that old."

"Yeah."

"Steve, this guy was probably a miner. It's not just the hole in the skull. Look at that boot."

The thick rubber sole dangling from a crushed ankle-high boot, its leather falling in tatters, was the sort miners of a hundred years ago favored to cushion their feet against the rocky floors of mine drifts.

"Figures," I said. "We're almost on the site of the old Norwich mine, and the Venture is just a couple of miles away."

"Aha!" Alex said as he troweled a greenish round lump from beneath a tattered leather belt. "Here's a pocket watch!" With a paintbrush he whisked away the damp soil. "Look."

The legend A. CARMICHAEL 1889 loomed faintly through the mold and verdigris.

"This is probably the name of our victim," Alex said, unconsciously adopting the tone of a schoolmaster, as he usually does in such situations. "And what else does that tell you?"

"That he most likely wasn't killed in a robbery," I said. "The perp or perps would've taken everything, even a cheap two-dollar brass pocket watch that had come from a general store."

"Right," Alex said. Those conclusions were obvious to both of us, but voicing them put them out in the open where we could use them as a point of departure.

"Whoever killed this guy didn't want him to be found," Alex added. "Even with six inches or so of new leaf mold laid down over seventy-five or a hundred years, this grave was at least three feet deep. That would've kept animals from getting at the body."

"And if it had been an honest burial, which it wasn't," I said, "the hole would have been the traditional six feet deep. There always have been plenty of cemeteries around here. No reason to bury a loved one alone in the woods." Like most rural people, Upper Michiganders favor community for death as well as survival.

Alex daintily fished a rusty clasp knife from the grave. "Look, there are a few coins, too. Here's a silver dollar."

Finished, Alex folded the tarp carefully around its contents and clambered up the bank.

"I'll ship this stuff to Lansing," he said, "but we may never hear a thing about it. The forensic guys have enough to do without worrying about a murder so old the perps are long gone."

"I'll see if I can find out who A. Carmichael was," I said.

"Why bother?"

"Never can tell."

"Suit yourself," Alex said with a grunt, but his tone wasn't derisive. He knew a little dogwork in old archives could sometimes turn up surprising clues. Like me, he'd solved crimes that way. And like me, he took a deep interest in the history of his jurisdiction. In the Upper Peninsula of Michigan, one can sometimes find motives for latter-day murder in resentments buried so long and so deep that everyone but victim and villain have forgotten them.

"Let's take a look around," I said. "Cover a bit of ground, see what we can turn up."

We trudged along the North Country Trail over the creek and through the woods west along the ridge that, I knew from my study of old maps, marked the limit of the Norwich Mine. Over a rise we heard the grinding hum of a wood chipper, and in a few moments we entered a large clearing in the forest. On one side rose a ridge four hundred feet high. On the opposite side of the ridge lay the Venture Mine.

Two eighteen-wheelers with big open box vans stood on a gravel road along the ridge. The steel spout of a wood chipper, its machinery turned off, curved high into the top of one of the trailers. A nearly new galvanized steel building, thirty feet by forty, fetched up against the ridge. Before it stood three men, rough and unshaven woods types clad in soiled canvas jackets and pants. They stared at us suspiciously as we emerged from the brush. One held a rifle loosely in his hands.

"Why the weapon?" I said, hand on my holster.

The man relaxed slightly and glanced away. He was a stranger, as were the other two. "Heard shots a couple hours ago," he said laconically. "Didn't know what was going on. Just wanted to be careful."

I wondered if he ever used the first person singular. People who avoid "I" usually avoid your eyes, too. They're a little short on personality.

"Well, it's okay now," I said. "You can put that away."

Carefully he cranked back the rifle's bolt, extracted the cartridge from its chamber, and laid the weapon against the chipper, but his stony expression remained.

"Just a couple of drunks shooting at each other," Alex said, reducing a complex story to a sentence fragment. "We sorted that out. Nobody hurt here, right?"

They nodded silently, still tense. That was odd. Most woodsmen would have relaxed visibly, maybe made a little joke.

"Who you working for?" I asked, nodding at the chipper.

"Weinstein," said the oldest of the three.

"Ah, yeah," I said. "This is Venture Mine property." Morrie Weinstein liked to maximize his income, even though the money his property earned from the sale of shredded pulpwood couldn't have covered much more than the cost of its labor. "Where do you sell the chips?" I asked, just to be conversational.

"Wisconsin."

I didn't ask "Where in Wisconsin?" because there was no reason to. But I did think it curious that Morrie, who was such a Porcupine County booster, wasn't selling the chips to the paper mill in his adopted hometown. I grunted.

Alex had picked up on my suspicion. "Let's have a look at the trucks," he said.

The three men stiffened. But they didn't protest as Alex swung up the ladder on the side of one open trailer box and peered inside.

"Looks full," he said. "You must be ready to make tracks."

"Yeah," said the oldest of the men.

None of them had anything to add, and neither did we.

"Take care," Alex said. "Stay out of trouble." He was subtly warning the men that the cops had their eye on them. Law-abiding citizens will resent such a suggestion, but you can sometimes get a rise out of crooked ones with it.

Both Alex and I spotted the quick, furtive glances the men shot at each other.

We disappeared into the woods and made our way through whippy saplings and grasping underbrush back to the old trail. Out of earshot Alex stopped and turned.

"Those guys are up to no good. Those wood chips were almost pure aspen. No hardwood at all." Paper mills prefer hardwood chips, which bring a much greater yield of pulp per cord—a ton and a half per cord—than aspen at eighty-five hundredths of a ton. No real woodsman, unless he were desperate, would cut only aspen. He would also throw in as much low-quality scrub hardwood as he could find, leaving the good stuff to grow, as the law demanded. Otherwise the return for his heavy labor would be absurdly low, like collecting thousands of soda and beer cans for the nickel deposit.

"Agreed," I said. "But what?"

"I don't know," he said. "What's there for criminals to do out here in the woods? Poach? Maybe they have some deer carcasses buried in those chips."

"Nah. There are easier ways to transport poached deer."

"Maybe they're just idiots."

"Probably."

Neither of us really thought so.

NINETEEN

Less than forty-eight hours had elapsed since the unpleasant scene on my beach, and I was missing Ginny mightily. The whole town now knew that the quiet pool of our relationship had been roiled by a huge rock, although no one had any idea of the stone's shape or size. At the sheriff's department that morning, nobody offered a word to me but carefully made sure not to cross my path. Even Gil, a martinet born to stare daggers through underlings, avoided my gaze. Only the gossipy Joe Koski, who had never in his life been at a loss for words, said anything.

The dumpy little dispatcher slipped off the stool at his counter in the front of the office and patted me on the shoulder. "Want to talk about it?" he asked solicitously. Everyone's jaw dropped in astonishment. Even for Joe, a man who had absolutely no self-awareness, that was presumptuous. Gil scurried into his office and shut his door. Chad clapped on his hat and shambled out the door, his big hip catching an oak swivel chair and spinning it madly. Riley Pearson, another deputy at his desk, found something to do in the lockup. Only Joe and I were left in the room.

I sighed. Joe is really a good fellow, even if he matches Chad's gorilla-in-a-china-shop clumsiness with folks' feelings.

"I don't think so, Joe," I said, trying not to sound irritated but failing.

"It'll be okay," he replied confidently. "Uncle Joe knows." He patted my shoulder.

"See you, Joe," I said. "I'm heading for the archives to see if I can identify that body we found yesterday."

I quickly thrust back my chair and stalked out, winning

the battle against slamming the door as I departed.

On the short drive to the courthouse, where the county's archives are stored, I realized that the chances of discovering the identity of A. Carmichael were not open and shut. The watch presumably had come into his possession in 1889, but the sheriff's department had burned to the ground in 1896, when a forest fire from the south ignited nearly the entire village of Porcupine City, the holocaust fueled by the superdry tinder of the Diamond Match Company mill in the center of town. If Carmichael had been killed before then, no official trace of him might exist. After the great Porcupine City fire, however, the county had carefully stored its records in the most fireproof manner it could, and today's nearly new courthouse was a shining example.

I wasn't a stranger to the records department, and Julie Boudreau, the birdlike little French Canadian clerk in charge, seemed to think me one of her more interesting patrons. Ginny's eager tales about Porcupine County had whetted my curiosity about the place's history, and once I had asked Julie to help me research famous old murders in Porcupine County for a little slide lecture for a dinner meeting of the historical society.

But the interest Julie showed that day had nothing to do with smoking out obscure old facts. She looked up with sad, concerned eyes from her desk and said simply, "Hello, Steve." I was glad she neither offered condolences nor pretended perkily that everything was fine and isn't it a nice day.

"Need the sheriff's archive beginning in 1896," I said.

"Trying to identify the body you found yesterday?" Julie said. "I've already got the boxes lined up."

I wasn't the least bit surprised. News travels fast even in these parts, over the forest telegraph network—CB and police radios, scanners, cell phones and landlines, even e-mail and the Web. When a county's lifeblood is slowly leaking away, the survivors stay afloat by paying close attention to each other, as if lashing together their life rings. That's annoying and gratifying at the same time. You can't change your brand of toothpaste without everyone knowing about it. And mounting a quiet investigation out of sight and out of mind? Ho-ho.

Julie led me to the back of the fireproof storeroom, its walls constructed of painted concrete blocks, and sat me at a long low table among a dozen large white cardboard boxes. She removed the lid to the box marked "1896-97" and handed me a pair of soft cotton gloves. The records, I knew, would be of considerable historical value someday, and Julie was taking very good care of them.

"Be real careful, Steve," Julie said.

"Will," I said.

As she turned to leave, she solicitously patted me on the back. I sighed.

The old sheriffs, I saw, had been meticulous at their recordkeeping. The closed cases were arranged in separate files marked ascending order of gravity—"Incidents," "Papers served," "Misdemeanors" and various felonies all the way up to "Homicides." But it was the open case files I was looking for, and in a few moments of rummaging I fished out the "Disappearances" folder for the pertinent years. It was surprisingly thick.

In those days many men disappeared every year into the forest or out onto the lake. The late nineteenth century was a violent time in Upper Michigan, for the territory marked the northern frontier of the United States. It didn't have cowboys and horses, but it had tough, rowdy, hard-drinking miners and loggers. From time to time, as the years rolled by through the files, I'd spot a dry, brown and crumbling "Missing" or "Information Sought" clipping from the Porcupine County Herald attached to a missing-persons sheet. Arthur Kempainen, Toivo Karttunen, Michael Welch, Ronald Aho, William Mazurek, Guy Paulsen and John Kucinich all were being hunted by their wives and sometimes their children, too. Some of them had wandered drunkenly out of gin mills and passed out in the woods or out on the frozen lake, and in the spring a few bodies would turn up in the forest or wash up on the shore. For the most part nothing ever was heard again about the men (and a few women) who had vanished.

And then, in the box marked "1909," I finally found what I was looking for—the sheet headed with the name of my quarry and a cutting of a classified ad, just a few lines in the "Personals," in *The Herald* of April 12, 1909:

MISSING

Information sought on the whereabouts of Andrew Carmichael of Porcupine City, last seen at his place of employment at the Venture Mine, Norwich Road, Porcupine County, last March 6. Reward. Write Mrs. Mary Carmichael, 312 Lead Street, Porcupine City. Your wife and children long for your return.

A faded photograph of a square-jawed, heavy-browed man was clipped to the missing-persons sheet, together with a description of the clothes Carmichael had been wearing and the possessions he had been known to carry—including a "brass Parker & Ives pocket watch engraved with the subject's name and the date 1889."

That nailed it. I'd send copies of the sheet, the clipping and the photo to the state police forensics lab in Marquette, and if the pathologists had time—which I doubted—they'd compare the photo to the skull and officially identify the bones in the folded blue tarp. Probably the case would get shunted aside, victim of tight budgets and more pressing latter-day investigations. I kept on reading to see if there had been a follow-up, perhaps an obituary or a death notice, though I didn't expect to see a funeral announcement for a body that had never been found—until yesterday.

A shadow loomed over my shoulder. "What do you got, Stevie boy?" it said.

He was Horace Wright, *The Herald*'s only reporter, a

retired Milwaukee newspaperman who ten years before had moved to the Upper Peninsula and gone to work part-time as a proofreader for the weekly. Slowly the job had expanded and he had returned to his old street-reporter specialty full-time. It kept Horace, now pushing eighty, alert and active. He was the only man in Porcupine County who, day in and day out, wore a suit and bow tie, usually with deliberately clashing color and design, underneath a wild gray walrus mustache that set off his plump, reddish face. "Got to be noticed some way," he once had confided. All that was missing was a fedora with a press card in the hatband. Horace usually went hatless, except when the winter wind chill approached absolute zero. Then he'd don a bright red plaid woolen Elmer Fudd hat, carefully tying the earflaps under his chin.

I marveled at the broad ground Horace covered in the Herald every week, reporting on the meetings of the village commission, the county board and a score more official bodies. Horace's reports on governmental meetings were narratives, not news stories that presented the important stuff first and worked their way down through lesser details to trivialities. Like official minutes, every one of them began at the beginning, following Robert's Rules of Order from first gavel and the reading of old business and including every parliamentary detail, comment, aside, and, I could swear, fart and burp. This method made for long, long articles, but Herald readers are not busy-busy urban types and have plenty of time to devote to them. Horace said he believed in letting his readers make up their own minds about the importance of items of county business, not filtered through the biased brain of a journalist. From time to time, however, he would let drop a jaundiced editorial aside if he felt strongly about a subject. "Horacisms," we called them, and we could recognize them for what they were, although some readers resented Horace's interjection of opinion in news stories.

Horace also exercised his considerable prose skills in

the pungent right-wing opinion pieces he "contributed" to the
Herald in the guise of letters to the editor. During Bill
Clinton's presidency he had expounded almost weekly on the
character flaws of "Slick Willie," and the discovery of
Monica's semen-stained dress had brought forth stern and
doom-laden flourishes that startled even the most ardent
conservatives of Porcupine County. A couple of evangelical
preachers had asked Horace to tone things down. But
enthusiastic demonization was the mark of a true Horacism,
and he continued to load his pen with vitriol. Lately he had
been teeing off on "the homosexuals" and was calling for a
constitutional amendment against not only gay marriage but
also civil partnership.

Liberal readers — and there are quite a few of them in
this conservative but not monolithic rural county — may have
scorned Horace's political ideas, but they still liked the man.
Although cops and reporters are natural enemies, I respected
Horace. He was nosy and noisy, but he was also bright, quick
and mostly accurate. I liked the guy, too. He was cordial
company at the dinners of the Historical Society, full of
rollicking cop stories from his younger days in Madison and
Milwaukee. And, despite his printed fulminations against
"alternative lifestyles," Horace included Billy Bissell, a large,
muscular and flamboyantly gay local plumber, among his
poker-table friends. "Hate the sin, love the sinner," Horace
said grandiloquently when anyone pointed out this apparent
contradiction. Billy was good-natured and forgiving enough
to put up with Horace's unconscious patronizing.

"You know perfectly well what I've got, Horace," I
said. I shot a resigned glance at Julie, who was trying hard to
look studious and innocent at her desk across the room. I
knew she had called Horace as soon as she saw I had found
what I was looking for. She was one of his best sources. He
took her out to dinner frequently.

"May I see?"

They were public records and as a citizen Horace had a

perfect right to examine and copy them.

"Okay," I said without rancor, standing back as Horace donned cotton gloves. Horace can be a colorful writer, and I have to admit I looked forward to the story and photo that would appear on the Herald's front page the following Wednesday. I wouldn't be surprised if Horace also turned up a Carmichael descendant or two for comment. He had once been an investigative reporter, and he was as much a digger as he was a political bomb-thrower.

"Would you say Carmichael had been murdered?" Horace asked.

"Fishing for a headline, are you, Horace?" I said with a laugh. "No, I won't. It's not my job to do that. But you can draw your own conclusions."

Horace grinned.

"Julie, can you scan in this stuff and print out three copies of it?" I asked. "One for me, one for Horace and one for the forensics lab?"

"Sure thing." Swiftly Julie ran the documents and photograph through her scanner, producing the results on a big laser printer and slipping them into three folders.

"Don't forget to bill The Herald for Horace's copies," I said. The cost was trivial, two dollars a sheet, a dollar for the folder, but economy is economy, especially in Porcupine County.

"Cheapskate," Horace shot back as he sauntered out with his folder.

Afterward I pushed back the chair and sank into a cloud of contemplation. Frank Saarinen, Roy Schweikert, and now Andrew Carmichael. Three dead men, all employees of the Venture Mine. Add a perhaps overly chummy Venture Mine owner, his creepy yacht skipper, and an unfriendly trio of woodsmen near the mine. What did all that mean?

Maybe something. Maybe nothing.

TWENTY

"What do you think?" I asked Alex a day later in Anthony's, a diner at Bergland at the junction of Highways M-64 and M-28 in the southwest corner of the county, hard by Lake Gogebic and its first-class walleye fishing. I'd asked him to meet me for a late lunch there, and we sat at a booth in the back, well away from curious ears.

Donna, the overstuffed and overcurious owner-baker-waitress who presided over Anthony's the way Gil O'Brien directed the sheriff's department, tried to find things to do at nearby tables, but Alex and I just stopped talking as she approached and gave her big toothy smiles to encourage her to go away and let us be. She waddled back to the front, mopped the counter and shot furious "you're-up-to-something-and-I-have-a-right-to-know-what-it-is" glances at us. But Alex and I were adamant. That pay phone on the wall behind Donna was a direct link to the rest of Porcupine County.

"I hate to admit it," said Alex, "but I think you're right. Something is going on around the Venture. Those three guys in the clearing yesterday sure had pickles up their asses. There's more going on than having just a hard-on against cops. I sure would like to know what they're up to. As for Saarinen and Schweikert and that old corpse, that's *probably* just coincidence."

The stress on the word said Alex, for all his doubts, was keeping an open mind on the facts.

"We can't just go poke around in back of the mine and that building without a warrant," I said. To mount a legal search, we needed the owner's consent, or probable cause that a crime was being committed or had been committed, and that evidence of said crime would be found there. A puzzling encounter with three silent and hostile woodsmen with two truckloads of almost pure aspen pulpwood wasn't probable cause. If we simply traipsed around on private property looking for evidence, found the loggers up to no good and busted them, Judge Rantala would throw out the case. That's what Eli and Gil would tell me if I informed them of my suspicions. And they'd also tell me to lay off the Venture. Don't piss off Morrie, they'd say. He's too important to the county. Go serve subpoenas, douse domestic fires and catch speeders. That's your job.

They'd be right. And Alex's superiors would tell him much the same thing. They don't like independent investigations. Brass hats everywhere hate loose-cannon cops who operate on their own.

But we will anyway if we think we can get away with it. And sometimes we do.

"I have an idea," I said. "Can you get hold of a night-vision video camera? Without the brass asking questions?"

"Sure," Alex said, his dark eyebrows rising at the prospect of performing old-fashioned police work with cutting-edge tools. A wide smile suddenly enlivened his narrow, mournful and blue-jawed face. He looked almost handsome in his ugliness, like a young Abraham Lincoln. For some reason I cannot understand, women find that attractive—even Ginny does—and Alex, a confirmed and dedicated bachelor, makes the most of it. "I can call in a marker at the aviation division. I'm going downstate tomorrow anyway. What have you got in mind?"

For drug-hunting over vast rural expanses, wooded and open, the Michigan State Police headquarters at Lansing equips its helicopters with night eyes and infrared heat-seeking equipment so sensitive it can spot a live Bunsen burner in a meth lab deep inside somebody's basement, although the Supreme Court has ruled that an illegal search. Night-vision gear is too expensive for a country sheriff's department. Our application for a federal grant for some hadn't yet been approved. I often wish we had a pair of goggles or two for night searches in the sheriff's old four-seater Cessna, but those things have to be left to the big boys with bigger budgets.

"A night flight," I said. "We can't go in and look on the ground, but we can go over and look from the air," I said. "Whatever we find, if we find anything, we can always say we were hunting for drugs. And who knows, maybe we'll find some." Search-and-seizure laws are written to protect a citizen's privacy, but sometimes are much harsher where drugs are concerned.

"Right you are!" A smile wreathed Alex's face as the idea sank in.

"How long will it take you to get the stuff?"

"Two, three days," Alex said. "This isn't the sort of equipment you can just put in a overnight chit for. But I'll get it."

"Great." We got up to leave. Donna stirred crankily by the cash register, still miffed at having been shut out of our conversation.

"But." Alex's expression had suddenly turned dubious.

"But what?"

"Won't they hear us?" The roar from airplane engines carries at night, and even a small single-engine Cessna can be heard from miles away.

"You leave that to me. How much do you weigh?"

"One-eighty-two. Why?"

"You'll see."

"I'm afraid I will."

TWENTY-ONE

Even throttled back to idle, the single 160-horsepower engine of a vintage Cessna 172 burbles loudly enough to be heard from more than a thousand feet up, and the still air of a quiet summer night would magnify the noise. But I knew there was a way around that obstacle—a kind of poor man's stealth technology. Basically, Alex and I would take the sheriff's airplane to an altitude high enough and far enough away from the clearing where we had met the three suspicious characters so that I could turn off the engine, kill the airplane's lights, and glide invisibly and noiselessly—or almost so— until we were upon the target we wanted to reconnoiter. Then we'd peer down at the clearing through night-vision equipment, seeing whatever there was to see.

That sounds like a no-brainer, but the details of the plan would need to be carefully thought out and rehearsed, for gliding without power at night over a dark forest is not a casual stroll in the woods. Most pilots like to know exactly where they are over the ground so that if anything goes wrong with the engine they can glide to a safe landing in a field or on a highway if they can't reach an airport. And when they can't see the ground in the dark of night, they get nervous. Still it could be done, and I was confident Alex and I could get away with the stunt.

First, I'd have to work out a plan on paper, drawing a course from Point A to Point B over the midsection of Porcupine County. Then I'd have to roll out the sheriff's airplane and make a casual daylight flight to scope out the course and locate the waypoints I'd need to mark on the chart to tell me where I was. I'd traverse the county at an altitude high enough so that nobody on the ground would think I was on a search, whether for malefactors or the missing.

Back at my cabin I unfolded a topographical hiker's chart and spread it on the dining table. All of Porcupine County, and much of the rest of western Upper Michigan, is visible on the chart, whose scale is about three miles to the inch, detail sufficient for my purpose. First I drew a straight line from the Bergland lookout tower on a bearing of 095 degrees to the ridge in whose shadow the Venture Mine nestled, the clearing I wanted to reconnoiter lying on the other side of the hill. I measured the line with a ruler, then compared it with the map's scale. Almost exactly ten miles from Point A to Point B.

Then I started on the calculations. A fully loaded Cessna 172, engine at idle, set up for its best glide speed—70 miles per hour—glides for slightly more than a mile and a quarter while losing 1,000 feet of altitude. Let's see now. The top of the Venture Mine hill is 1,100 feet above sea level. I'd need to arrive above the hill about 500 feet higher. That'd put me on a collision course for the 1,600-foot Norwich lookout tower directly ahead, a little too close for comfort. Hmm. Tinker, tinker, mutter, mutter. Don't forget the drag of a stopped propeller. Better allow for a little wind in either direction. Night air isn't always still. I filled several sheets of paper with scratched-out sums.

At last I had a plan. I'd climb to 8,000 feet above sea level right over Point A, the U.S. Forest Service lookout tower at Bergland, ten miles from the clearing. Then I'd point the plane slightly east by southeast, cut the engine, douse the navigation and strobe lights, and put the nose down until the airspeed indicator read 120 miles per hour. She'd glide almost noiselessly, the rush of wind over her wings and tail barely audible on the ground. Those with sharp ears directly under the flight path might think they'd heard an eagle or a large owl after its prey. The plane would steadily lose altitude over that 10 miles until it reached 1,400 feet above sea level, just 500 feet above the ground at Point B, a little to the left of the clearing Alex and I had our eye on. The course would carry the plane well clear of the Norwich lookout tower.

As we swept by the clearing, we could take a look through night eyes at the place, then sneak away unheard as I lifted the plane's nose and turned southeast, turning the extra glide speed into a few hundred feet of altitude and giving me a couple of miles' room to soar out of earshot before I restarted the engine. Whoever was committing anything naughty on the ground would have no idea that they'd been spied upon.

But we were going to do this in the black of night, without lights or power. If I couldn't restart the engine at the end of the run, we would be in deep diddly indeed. In my mind's ear Ginny berated me for risking my beloved neck.

Beloved? Maybe not any more. A pang shot through my heart. I missed her, more than I could say. Forming the plan had helped make my loss more bearable, but again blood oozed from the cut of my loneliness.

I shook my head against the heartsickness. I'd have to practice by day, to make sure my calculations were accurate and to see if there wasn't something I hadn't thought of. Unexpected events can spoil a pilot's day.

One of my tasks as a deputy with a pilot's certificate is to fly the sheriff's airplane for an hour once a week, to keep the engine rust-free, the control systems limber, and everything ready for business. It would be easy to camouflage my trial run in the logbooks by declaring it a maintenance hop and writing in the real trip as a training flight to maintain my night proficiency. I make a night flight every three months to satisfy Federal Aviation Administration requirements.

And so two afternoons later I pulled up in my Jeep at the ramshackle hangar at Porcupine County Airport where we stored the old Cessna. A breeze blowing no more than three miles an hour wisped up from the south. It wouldn't throw off my figures by much. After preflighting the plane, checking to make sure all parts were present and accounted for and that they worked as intended, I measured the level of gas in the tanks, then at the pumps added a few gallons more fuel to reach the one-quarter mark I had calculated I needed for the flight. To the weight of the gas I added that of Alex. Bang on. To stretch the long power-off glide I proposed to make, I didn't want to carry any more weight than necessary. And, in case we got into trouble, I wanted an emergency reserve of a little more gas than I had calculated the Cessna would burn on the entire flight. The FAA wants forty-five minutes of reserve fuel, but I settled for fifteen minutes. I had had enough experience in the air to know exactly how many gallons that engine would burn under a variety of conditions. Good pilots leave as little to chance as they can. And I tried hard to be a good pilot. There are old pilots, the saying goes, and there are bold pilots, but there are no old, bold pilots.

After warmup I took off on the northbound runway, clearing the tall birches at the far end with plenty of room to spare, and arched out over the bright blue lake before banking left and heading fourteen miles southwest to Norwich lookout tower, which guarded the Ottawa National Forest against wildfires. The Cessna knifed smoothly through the air, soaring upward through light, almost imperceptible turbulence, the song of its Lycoming engine filling my ears. In flight I feel most connected to my Lakota ancestors, for they, too, must have soared with eagles as their war ponies raced into battle. Climbing away is an exultant time. Ask any pilot—not just an Indian one.

At three thousand feet I leveled off. In a few minutes the sights I was looking for came into view below—the Norwich tower, the Venture Mine hoist house against the high ridge, and finally the clearing beyond it. I banked the plane right and peered at the clearing with seven-by-fifty Bushnells, marking its location on my handheld GPS. That would be my aiming point on the money flight. Two eighteen-wheelers sat in the center, not at the edge, of the clearing. If those were the same trucks Alex and I had seen, they should have left for Wisconsin days before. Men—at least six of them—lolled about on crates and tarps. There seemed to be no activity. And that was curious all by itself. I wanted to circle a thousand feet lower to get a better view. I was too high for them to identify the airplane, and Cessna 172s are ubiquitous everywhere, the Chevrolets of the sky. But if I went in low and circled, they might wonder why and take a hard look at the Cessna, noting its registration number, looking it up on the Internet and making it as the sheriff's airplane.

So I banked to the left, heading southeast, and examined the terrain. It was mostly thick second-growth forest, hundred-year-old white pines beginning to tower over copses of birch and aspen and singleton hardwood trees, but here and there old gravel logging roads, their verges cut back several yards on either side, appeared. Having driven them in my Jeep many times, I knew they would make adequate emergency landing strips. I was leaving nothing to chance. I marked their locations on the GPS. If need be, I could steer to them with the GPS and locate them even in pitch dark. But it wasn't necessarily going to be pitch dark. There might even be what pilots used to call a bomber's moon, a bright, full moon that enabled attacking aircrews of the Second World War to follow unfamiliar terrain on night flights to their targets.

One more task to do before making the dry run from Bergland Tower: see if I could restart the airplane's engine after turning it off. Some aero engines are difficult to restart when hot after an hour or so of flight. A bit of fussing with throttle and primer—and anywhere from a few minutes to half an hour of patience—often is necessary to get the cylinders firing again. I'd been temporarily stranded on an airport many times after refueling, waiting for the engine to cool down enough to get started again. But never in the sheriff's 172. Its sturdy four-cylinder Lycoming always roared to life on the first crank of the starter, no matter how little time had elapsed since it had been shut down. At any rate, high up the rush of cooling air past the engine would hurry its temperature down to a tractable level.

Just to be safe I arrived over the Porcupine City airport at a point three thousand feet above the ground, giving me plenty of maneuvering altitude for a dead-stick landing in case the engine failed to catch. First looking all about for traffic — even if there are only a few small airplanes in the far north, they always seem to blunder into your airspace when other things occupy your attention — I snaked back the throttle and the mixture knob. Quickly the engine, starved of fuel, coughed and died. The propeller stopped.

As I expected, the propeller, at first stationary but then spinning slowly as the airspeed increased, caused a great deal of drag, steepening the airplane's angle of glide. In barely three minutes the Cessna lost a thousand feet of altitude, at which point I closed the mixture, opened the throttle and turned the ignition key. Immediately and without a cough the engine burst into song and the whirling propeller swiftly carried the airplane away from the airport. I set course for Bergland tower, climbing all the way.

The airplane spiraled upward above the tower until it had reached the target altitude of eight thousand feet. Then I again killed the engine and banked eastward at a diving glide at 120 miles an hour onto a course that would take me within half a mile of the clearing, but far enough away to make it unlikely I would be seen and heard. Slowly the airplane dropped until, just abeam the clearing, I checked the altimeter. One hundred feet too low, but not bad. I pulled back the yoke gently. The plane rose almost five hundred feet until the altimeter needle stopped, a good two miles southeast of the clearing. Quickly I started the engine and went home.

It was a workable plan. Plans are always workable when you rehearse them.

TWENTY-TWO

In my cabin that evening I sat alone at the dining table picking at a pasty I'd bought at the supermarket on my way home. Normally I have to ration myself with that Upper Michigan specialty, a portable pot pie stuffed with diced beef, potatoes, carrots, rutabagas and onions. About the size and shape of a softball and four times heavier, the pasty was brought to America by miners from Cornwall who unwrapped theirs and lunched on them deep in the copper mines, still hot inside their thick pastry hides. Pasties are are as caloric as they're tasty, and for the sake of my arteries I don't have them more than once a week.

But loneliness had taken the edge off my appetite. It had been a week since Ginny had disappeared.

The phone rang.

"Steve?" said a familiar voice. "Nancy Aho."

The kindly docent at the Historical Society. I sat upright so quickly the silverware rattled. "Yes?"

"Ginny's back. She arrived from Detroit this afternoon and went right into her office."

"Is she all right?" I blurted.

"Yes. But something's on her mind. She's been furiously digging into boxes in the back room. She asked that we hold all her calls."

"I'll go over right away," I said, forgetting that this was none of Nancy's business and that she had no good reason to call me. But I was glad she had. The human concern country people often show for each other sometimes can match their nosiness, and this was one of those times.

"I wouldn't," Nancy said, her voice full of warning.

"She still needs time."

Something told me that Nancy knew exactly what she was talking about. Embarrassed at the public nature of my predicament, gratified that Nancy cared enough to try to help and annoyed that she had, I fell silent.

"Come around in a couple of days," Nancy said helpfully. "She might not see you at home but she has to open her office door to the authorities."

I closed my eyes. This was too much. "Yes, Mom," I said, trying to sound sarcastic but failing. Nancy was right.

She chuckled. "Everything will be okay. You be patient."

The sweet little old busybody hung up.

I sat slumped in the chair, wrestling with my emotions. Ginny was home. She was safe. She was back at work. And she still hated my guts.

As much to forget my predicament, I reached for the phone and dialed Alex at home.

"Commence," he said briskly. No "hello" or "howdy" or even "yeah?" for Alex Kolehmainen is a superefficient man who hates to waste words, even to identify himself on the phone.

"Hello, Mr. Clements," I said. "Could you put Sergeant Kolehmainen on?"

Alex recognized my voice and grunted.

"That's why you're still a bachelor," I said nastily. "You don't know the meaning of foreplay."

"What's on your mind, Steve?" Alex was unruffled.

"Got the night vision stuff?"

"Yeah."

"Tomorrow good for you? The forecast's for a clear sky with a full moon."

"Sure," Alex said. "Time to ride!"

His voice wasn't as enthusiastic as his words. Alex hates flying and always stiffens into a bundle of tension the minute he boards even a jumbo jet. Small planes and helicopters greatly spook him. But he is a brave and tenacious fellow, and even makes fun of his own fear, calling the state police's aviation fleet "the Michigan White Knuckle Airways." He calls the sheriff's battered old Cessna "that piece of flying crap."

"Midnight at the airport?" I asked.

"Sure." I could hear Alex's mainspring commencing to wind tight.

"See you then."

TWENTY-THREE

Before dawn the next morning I drove into Porcupine City, passing the Historical Society on River Street, the main drag, on my way to the cop shop. Though first light was only just beginning to fill the sky, Ginny's van already occupied its slot in the parking lot. The sight both gladdened and saddened me. So close, yet so far. I carried my maudlin mood into the sheriff's department. As usual, everyone looked my way and then away, but this time their unspoken curiosity clouded the air like bloodthirst at a dogfight. They all knew Ginny had returned and something was soon to happen. It doesn't take much to entertain Yoopers.

I spent the day at my usual routine, chasing speeders on M-64, lurking in driveways just out of sight with the radar gun switched on. Almost all the idiots I busted were from outside the county and in my grey mood I didn't give any of them a break, like knocking a few miles an hour off the actual offense and reducing the fine they'd pay. Only once did I let someone off with a warning. He was a familiar face, an old-timer with a weak bladder. He was doing eighty miles an hour in his ancient pickup, whose color was that of overcooked asparagus shot through with rust, twenty-five miles an hour over the limit and twenty more than was reasonably safe in such a wobbly old beater.

"Deputy, I've got to go real bad," he wailed as I walked up alongside.

"Give me your license and registration and proof of insurance and go off into the bushes while I check them out," I said.

Gratefully he opened the pickup door and skittered

into the woods. His license and record were clean. I was sterner than I needed to be but let him off just the same. Old men can't help it. When they need to go, they need to go.

And then just outside Porcupine City, a nearly new Grand Cherokee pulling out of the marina on the opposite side of the highway had slowed almost imperceptibly, its driver swiveling his head to check for traffic, before blowing the stop sign and accelerating toward town. I flicked on siren and flashers, swung the Explorer around and in a few hundred yards pulled the offender to a stop like a cowboy roping a calf. I parked behind the Cherokee and, as I always do, radioed the location and plate number to Joe Koski before I dismounted and walked up to the vehicle, hand on gun butt, a precautionary act. No telling what drivers will do.

But this one kept both hands on the wheel where I could see them. On his left bicep, bared by a sleeveless T-shirt, was tattooed a large fouled anchor. As I saw his hooded eyes I recognized him as the skipper of the *Lucky Six*.

"Good afternoon, Mr. Anderson," I said gravely. "License, registration and proof of insurance, please." A traffic bust is an official event, and I use formal address with the busted.

Slowly, as I watched, Anderson reached into the glove compartment and fished out the vehicle's Michigan registration card.

"License in my wallet," he said. He was no stranger to traffic stops. I nodded for him to reach behind and pull the wallet from his hip. Slowly he did so. As he proffered the Illinois driver's license I relaxed and removed my hand from the holster.

"What did I do, Steve?" They are all *so* disingenuous.

"That was quite a California stop you pulled back there at the stop sign."

"I thought I slowed enough."

"No," I said. "The law says *full* stop."

"Oh. I didn't know." They are all *so* shameless.

"Sit there. I'll be right back."

Back in the Explorer I copied the license and registration numbers and radioed Joe again. I heard the clacking of his keyboard as he plugged his computer into LEIN, the Law Enforcement Intelligence Network, linked to all fifty states and Canada. If I had been a big-city cop or a state trooper, I could have done the job myself from a laptop attached to the dash, but that equipment is too expensive for a boondocks cop shop on a tight budget. Within seconds Joe had the answers. The Cherokee hadn't been used in a crime, nor had it been reported stolen. Owner, Morris Weinstein, 2 Hazel Street, Porcupine City, Michigan. No surprise there.

As for Michael Anderson, 1440 North Lake Shore Drive, Chicago, Illinois—my eyebrows rose at the upscale address on Chicago's Gold Coast—he had a perfect driving record, with two years to go before his license needed renewal. A poster child for a warning ticket for a violation that wasn't terribly reckless. I made a decision.

I wrote out a citation and walked back to the Cherokee. Anderson gazed without expression at me, like a motionless stone lizard taking in the summer sun. I kept my voice civil and professional.

"Mr. Anderson, you have a clean record. I saw you slow down and I saw you look for traffic, so you might argue that your violation isn't necessarily a dangerous one. But you need to obey the law. I'm going to give you this citation. You may pay the fine by mail. The amount is ninety dollars. Maybe this will help you to remember to come to a full stop at every stop sign in Porcupine County."

"All right, Steve." He spoke quietly, almost lazily, but did not glance away from my eyes. He held my gaze almost insolently. I stifled my irritation at his deliberate use of my first name. Familiarity isn't a violation of the law, although in this case it was a small but definite challenge of my authority. For that reason I had jotted down not only Anderson's address but also his Social Security number. You never know when those things might come in handy, and I have notebooks full of them.

"Be careful now." I walked back to the Explorer and Anderson drove away.

I had given him the ticket not only because he gave me the creeps but because he had pissed me off.

TWENTY-FOUR

An hour before midnight I rolled off the couch after a brief sleep and turned on my laptop. The thick web of the Internet sprawls even way up here in the North Woods. Some homes along the highway even enjoy fast broadband service — cable television arrived in the Upper Peninsula long ago — but a deputy sheriff's pay won't finance more than a dialup connection. It didn't matter. The weather forecast service funded by the FAA wasn't bandwidth-heavy with fancy graphics. I punched up the service and typed away. No need to feed in the information for a flight plan. It wasn't required, and in any case I didn't want anybody knowing what I was up to, not only to keep things quiet but also because I would be breaking a goodly number of federal aviation regulations.

In a few seconds the data from the closest weather station, at Houghton fifty miles to the northeast, unrolled down the PC screen. I skimmed the lines of code until I found the important stuff: 36003KT 10 SM CLR. That, in aviation weather parlance, meant that right now the wind was blowing from magnetic north at a gentle three knots, and that I'd be able to see at least 10 statute miles ahead in clear weather. The forecast for the next three hours was FM 0600 VRB03KT P6SM CLR. Decoded, the line told me that from 0600 hours Zulu — two o'clock in the morning Eastern Daylight Time — the wind would continue to swirl about at a negligible three knots, with the visibility six miles plus, and the skies cloudless and clear. Finally, the winds aloft at 3,000 and 6,000 feet were reported at "9900," meaning no wind at all. I wouldn't have to redo my figures.

"It doesn't get better than that," I exulted to myself as I

hopped into the Jeep and headed for the airport.

Alex was waiting by the sheriff's hangar when I arrived. Like me, he was dressed in civvies, Michigan State sweatshirt over faded jeans. If anyone was around, we'd just be a couple of old buddies going for a night flight. But even by light of day the Porcupine County airport is usually deserted. In the summer a few wealthy pilots bring their Bonanzas and Mooneys up from Detroit, Chicago, and Milwaukee, and a local farmer's half-century-old Piper Tri-Pacer, its fabric covering streaked and faded, occupies a ramp tie-down all year round. But most of the time I encounter only Doc Miller, chief of medicine at the Porcupine County Hospital, in his hangar working on the cranky engine of his Bird Dog, a Korean War-vintage spotter plane a little bigger than the sheriff's Cessna. At midnight he was home in bed, like every sensible pilot I knew.

"Got the thing?" I asked.

Alex held up the trophy of his expedition to Lansing. It looked like a super-8 video camera with a few extra lumps and knobs. "Gallium arsenide!" he chortled. "Generation three image intensifier, mil-spec stuff. Ten power zoom. Four gigs of digital memory."

"Could you put that into English?"

"All you need to know is that with this baby you can spot an ant at a thousand yards in starlight, and capture it forever. It's cutting edge, the very latest thing. The Army hasn't deployed it yet, but the DEA and the flying coppers are already having fun with it."

Swiftly I reviewed the plan with Alex.

"I've detached the stop bracket on the passenger side window," I said, showing Alex. "When it comes time to point the camera out of the plane, you unlatch the window carefully and keep hold of the handle until the slipstream pulls the window up underneath the wing. The air pressure will hold it there no-hands."

Then I came to the money issue.

"You're going to turn off the *engine*?" he said, his grimace etched in horror.

"Yup. Practiced it the other day. Should work fine."

"If you say so." He looked more than dubious.

"All right, let's saddle up."

Together we rolled the Cessna out of the hangar and I swiftly completed the preflight ritual. Alex folded his skinny frame into the right seat and I climbed into the left.

"Steve." Alex sat rigidly, staring forward. His voice was desperate. His anti-aviation funk had enveloped him.

"Is this going to be *safe*?"

"As houses."

"You sure?"

"Trust me."

"Okay," he said resignedly. "Let's get it done."

"One thing."

"Yes?"

"Would you mind removing your feet from the rudder pedals? I can't drive the airplane that way."

"Oh, sorry." Alex unlocked his rigid legs and stepped away from the pedals. I hoped he wouldn't freeze in panic on the controls once we were in the air.

"I'll be all right," he said, as if reading my mind.

He sat quietly, hands cradling the camera, as I started the engine, fiddled with knobs and switches and dials and checked the magnetos during the run-up before takeoff.

"Ready?"

"As I'll ever be," his voice crackled through the intercom. At least he kept a sense of humor. That meant he was in control of himself.

"Away we go then."

After climbout I set course for the Bergland fire tower, its coordinates captured on my GPS, but the light from the new moon was so bright that I saw the dim outline of the tower on its rocky knob miles before flying over the spot and banking into a gentle upward spiral.

Just as the plane leveled out at 8,500 feet—I decided to add a little more height, just to be sure—I decided that a little hackneyed pilot humor might relax Alex and help him to get through the ordeal of the next ten minutes.

"Know what a propeller is for?"

"What?"

"To keep the passengers cool."

"You're kidding."

"No. Turn it off and watch 'em sweat." I chuckled.

Alex shot me a dirty look. "All right, all right."

Pointing the nose of the airplane toward Norwich Tower, I pulled back the throttle, then the mixture knob, and switched off the ignition key. That turned out to be a mistake.

The engine choked and died and the propeller stopped. I flicked off the airplane's navigation lights and strobe. We now swooped silent and dark through the night, like a great horned owl on the prowl.

The rush of wind increased as I dropped the nose slightly until the airspeed indicator needle touched the 120 miles per hour mark. The propeller began to windmill slowly. My ears popped and Alex gulped audibly, pinching his nose and blowing slightly to clear the pressure. The good old Valsalva maneuver.

"Open the window," I said. "We'll be over the spot in three and a half minutes."

Ahead I could see the line of ridges snaking across the midsection of Porcupine County like the backbone of a great gray sea monster. Every few seconds I checked airspeed and altimeter and made tiny, almost imperceptible course and speed corrections. As the high ridge under Norwich Tower appeared ahead, I turned slightly to the left, so that Alex would have a clear view of our target clearing just below and to the right.

"There it is!" I said.

"Got it!" Alex said as he opened the window on his side and let the slipstream press it up against the wing. Wind roared into the cockpit and swirled small bits of paper and dust around our heads. Alex bent to the camera's eyepiece. I banked the plane slightly to the right to give him a better view of the clearing. Suddenly we were alongside our target.

"Buncha guys," Alex said. "Two trucks. They're carrying stuff from the building to the trucks."

Then we shot away from the clearing and I gently pulled back the yoke, zooming the airplane upward and away from the tower, at the same time banking to the right. On the other side of the ridge I'd have a thousand feet of altitude to restart the engine.

"They see us?" I asked as I reached for the ignition key.

"No. They never looked up. We got clean away."

There was no key in the ignition. *Damn. It must have fallen on the floor.* Quickly I unhooked my shoulder belt, bent over and groped around on the floor. Nothing.

"Looks like we'll have to go to Plan B," I said, trying to keep my voice calm. We were losing altitude rapidly, though the airplane was gliding at optimum speed, seventy miles an hour.

I didn't need the GPS to locate the road below that I'd reconnoitered two days earlier. It loomed ahead, a long tan stripe against the dark forest.

"I'll put her down just up there."

I snapped on the landing lights just to be sure I had seen what I thought I had, then turned them off again to save the battery.

"Why'd you do that?"

"If you don't know what's under you," I said, keeping my voice as casual as I could, "you turn on the landing lights. If you don't like what you see, you turn 'em off." Another hoary old pilot joke.

"*Shit.*" Alex wasn't amused.

We were a little high. To bleed off speed, I put the airplane into a slip—a maneuver in which the pilot banks the airplane in one direction while turning the rudder the other way. The plane crabs forward, one wing low, nose pointing to the side, increasing drag as the side of the fuselage meets the airflow. A slip helps an airplane lose altitude quickly. It's one of the first maneuvers a student pilot learns. But slips scare hell out of uninformed passengers. They think the plane is falling out of control.

"*Son of a bitch!*" Alex cried.

"Relax. We'll be down in a second."

I turned the landing lights back on. The road rushed up at us. The old Cessna's wheels gently kissed the ruts, then bounced sharply over the uneven gravel and within fifteen seconds rolled to a stop. Just to be safe, immediately before touchdown I had killed all the electric switches and closed the fuel valves as well.

We sat silently for a moment as our adrenaline levels sank back to normal. I took a deep breath. I didn't tell Alex that was the first time I'd ever made a genuine emergency landing at night, though I'd done plenty of simulated ones. I took a Maglite from its clip and played it around on the floor of the cockpit. "Where the hell is that key?" I said.

"It's hanging from your sleeve," Alex said, pointing.

A cuff button on my shirt had come partly undone, dangling just enough to snag the large ring hanging from the ignition key and pull it out as I maneuvered the airplane in the darkness.

"Well well well," I said. "Let that be a lesson to me. Never hang up an airplane ignition key on a ring that could catch on anything. In my two thousand hours of flying, that's never happened before."

I kicked myself mentally. I didn't tell Alex, but a pilot does not need to turn the ignition key to OFF to kill his engine. Simply cutting off the mixture does the job. Had I left the key turned to ON, it would have been locked in the ignition and ready to be turned to the right for the restart, like that of an automobile.

"That's nice to know," Alex said. His sarcasm meant he

had come back down to earth in more ways than one. "Now how are we going to get home? And aren't you going to radio for help?"

"We're not going to let anybody know we're here," I said. "With the key the engine will start just fine. We'll take off at dawn."

"Why wait until then?"

"Don't want to risk a takeoff down an unfamiliar road in the dark. That wouldn't be safe."

"*Safe? Safe?*" Alex yelled. "What the hell, do you think what we just did was safe? You said it was going to be safe!"

I looked at him pityingly. "We got down, didn't we? Have we got a scratch on us?" Sometimes cops bicker like old couples. After a moment of silence I patted the night-vision camera in Alex's hands and added, "Now, what have we got?"

Alex stopped grumbling and opened the camera's folding video screen.

"Later we'll look at this on a big monitor," he said, "but I think this will show us all we need to know." He flicked a switch.

Dim green shapes materialized on the tiny screen, then sharpened into absolute clarity, as if we were watching the scene in broad daylight. Half a dozen men moved about, one driving a forklift piled high with unidentifiable flat boxes. The wide door to the building stood open, as did the rear doors of the trucks. Scurrying green figures hoisted boxes into the empty interiors. But the open tops showed full loads of pulpwood chips. In a few seconds the picture was gone. None of the men glanced up at the airplane as it ghosted by.

"Got away with it!" Alex chortled. "Clever, no? False tops under a shallow layer of wood chips. I don't know what's inside those trucks but I'm willing to bet you next year's salary it's illegal. Why, it might even be . . . drugs."

We looked happily at each other. We now had probable cause, reason enough to go to the prosecuting attorney for a warrant to present to Judge Rantala, requesting permission to enter private property and open up that steel building to see what was inside. Whatever it was, the possibility, however slim, that narcotics were involved would instantly unlimber the stern judge's pen.

Alex and I dozed in our seats the rest of the night, awkwardly elbowing each other like an old couple in a tiny guest-room bed. Just before dawn I climbed out of the airplane and brewed coffee from its small survival kit. We sat silently on logs, shivering against the morning chill and munching chunks of the *korppu* I had tucked into my flight bag, washing it down with the coffee.

As daylight broke we climbed back aboard. This time the engine started smoothly, and in a few minutes we lifted off the gravel road. No one, I felt sure, saw our takeoff.

At the airport no one saw us land, either. After I had pulled down the hangar door, I extended my hand to Alex. "We done good, sarge," I said.

"By God," Alex said, relaxing for the first time in seven hours. "Fighting crime is fun."

TWENTY-FIVE

"And so, at my request, Deputy Martinez made the department's aircraft and himself available for the search," Alex said in a lofty tone. During the meeting in the sheriff's office, in which we had screened the video from our previous night's mission, he had pointedly and frequently reminded us that as a state police sergeant he perched above sheriffs, undersheriffs and deputies on the law enforcement totem pole. "I congratulate your department on its excellent co-operation."

Eli, who really had no idea what we had done, beamed. Gil, who did, grimaced. "That was a risky thing to do, wasn't it?" the undersheriff asked, a skeptical eye on me. I tried hard to look innocent and nonchalant, leaning back in the chair and hooking my feet around the legs.

"Not at all," Alex said. "Deputy Martinez is an outstanding pilot and at no time during the flight did I have any doubt of the outcome." I stifled a chuckle.

We had not told Eli or Gil of the night emergency landing, nor had I committed it to either my pilot's logbook or deputy's daily report. Why ask for trouble?

"All right," Gil said, unable to keep the disbelief out of his voice. "The state police, of course, will reimburse the county for the cost of the flight."

"Send me the chit," Alex said. "I'll make sure Lansing gets it."

I smiled inwardly. Alex would simply make sure the request for reimbursement—just a couple of hundred dollars—got lost, and sooner or later Gil would give up asking about it. As undersheriff he may have to pinch pennies, but he knows when a cause is futile. And Alex's lieutenant would remain blissfully unaware of his sergeant's unauthorized mission. Everybody wins.

"Eli, to save time I'd like to ask you to join me in requesting a search warrant from Judge Rantala so that we may go back to that clearing today and toss that building for drugs," Alex said. "It'll take another few hours if we make the request from the state police post at Wakefield. And I'd also like to request that Deputy Martinez accompany me on the search. Is that all right?"

"Yes, sir," Eli said, ever the helpful old pol. "Steve's your man."

Gil raised a finger. "Please be careful. We can't afford any errors."

Cops do make mistakes. When evidence is circumstantial and causes are vague, fixating on one idea at the expense of others is dangerous, and that single-mindedness often grips police and prosecutors. If we can't admit we might be wrong, our judgment becomes cloudy. We exaggerate soft evidence and ignore harder facts. Too often the innocent are punished, in extreme cases sometimes by execution, and the guilty escape. Things are a little easier in Michigan, which has no death penalty.

Exactly the opposite had seized my mind about Morrie Weinstein. I just could not believe that he was something I very much wanted him not to be. But nagging clues, like three dead men, kept getting in the way. I couldn't write him off until I'd found out more. But the time had arrived to take the case to my bosses before it turned into a rogue investigation. I had thought that maybe with their superior experience they'd view the situation through different eyes.

At the beginning of the meeting they hadn't wanted to see it at all.

"Jesus Christ, Steve," the sheriff had moaned when Alex told him who we were investigating. "Morrie Weinstein is the second biggest employer in Porcupine County. We can't go after him with what you've got!"

"Can you spell 'c-i-r-c-u-m-s-t-a-n-t-i-a-l'?" said Gil nastily.

But now that we had laid out what we had seen the night before, Eli and Gil admitted that very likely something was going on.

"We'll be very careful," Alex promised.

"How are you going to conduct the search?"

"We'll drive to the site, proffer our identifications if we see anyone, and request that the building be opened. If there is any resistance, we'll show the subject or subjects the warrant. If no one is there, we'll open the door and effect a search." When he wants to, Alex can speak police bureaucratese with the best of them.

We, in other words, would do things by the book. Except we wouldn't.

As we drove to the courthouse in the Explorer I turned and said admiringly, "Alex, you are full of shit."

"It's all that summer stock I've done." Two years before, Alex had played a supernumerary in a single performance of "The Mikado" at the Ironwood Playhouse when a cast member fell ill. His dramatic role had been to shut up, sit still, and look scenic.

"You do all the talking," Alex said as we climbed out at the courthouse. "It's mostly your case anyway. I'll back you up."

That surprised me. Alex was not the sort to hide his light under a bushel. He had done a good job of intimidating Eli and Gil in the sheriff's office. Why should he suddenly take on the role of second fiddle? Before I could ask him to explain, we had arrived in the office of Garner Armstrong, the county prosecutor.

Garner is the nephew of Geoffrey Armstrong, the Upper Peninsula's longtime and only congressman, and is as different from his uncle as can be. Geoffrey is a caricature of a politician, a man who bends with the wind more than he needs to in order to stay in office. I can't stand him. But I like and respect Garner, a tall, skinny and handsome fellow who looks like James Stewart and has something of that actor's deceptively diffident personality. But Garner is highly ambitious, and sooner or later, everyone thinks, he will oppose his uncle at the polls. He is the unchallenged leader of the Democratic Party in Porcupine County. Few argue with him when he has made up his mind.

Garner listened carefully as I presented the case, Alex nodding sagely as I made each point.

"Okay," the prosecutor said without hesitation or questioning. "Let's do it." He called in his secretary and in a few minutes she had typed up the warrant.

"Walk with me," Garner said.

Down the hall we strode to the chambers of the district judge, General Rantala, a bald-headed, big-eared squirt of a man with all the prickly personality of Judge Judy, the television figure. Judge Rantala's first name really is General, inflicted upon him (or so the rumor goes) by a father embittered by his failure to rise higher than buck private in the Army during World War II. Every time the judge makes a restaurant reservation in a city where he isn't known he says in a commanding tone, "This is General Rantala. I'd like your best table at eight o'clock. Carry on." And the maitre d' always replies, "Yes, *sir!*" The snap of a salute is almost audible.

Behind his back we call the judge "The General," although he never rose higher than second lieutenant as a motor pool commander in the National Guard. He is stern and authoritarian, the DEA's best ally in all of Upper Michigan. He complained mightily when the legislature relaxed the state's minimum sentencing laws for drug offenses — once the toughest in the nation — and gave judges more leeway to be lenient. In my opinion, mandatory sentences of twenty years for simple possession were cruel, unusual, and harmful to society, and I would have held the judge in pitying contempt if he had not otherwise handled his courtroom expertly and fairly. Prosecutors and defense attorneys alike always appear before him as well prepared as they can be. His cases are rarely overturned on appeal.

The judge read the warrant carefully and without asking questions, and almost as soon as he encountered the first mention of drugs, he picked up a pen and quickly signed it with a flourish.

"Bring them to me," he growled. "I'll throw their ass in jail. If they're guilty, of course."

"Thank you, Your Honor," Alex and I said simultaneously, bringing a small smile to Garner's face.

As we left the judge's office Garner leaned toward me and said quietly, "You going to be home tonight, Steve?"

"Yes," I said, surprised.

"Mind if I come by for a minute or two? I'd like to talk to you about something."

"Well, sure," I said, utterly puzzled. What private business would the county prosecutor want to lay upon a lowly deputy sheriff?

As Garner returned to his own office I stole a glance at Alex.

"What do you suppose that's all about?"

A cherubic smile played around the corners of his mouth. "Beats me." He shrugged, a little too elaborately. Then he said, "Let's ride."

We headed through town—yes, Ginny's van occupied its space outside the Historical Society, sending a dagger through my chest—and out Norwich Road. Halfway there Alex said, "We going to drive all the way to that clearing, Steve?"

"Nah."

"Nah," Alex echoed.

We were simply employing good military tactics. First reconnoiter in the air, then on the ground, then destroy the target—if the intelligence supports an attack. If anything was going on, we'd surprise our quarry in the act. If not, we'd withdraw and regroup.

We parked Alex's cruiser off a Forest Service track a mile from the clearing and the mine. "In the old days," Alex said, "snipers would put on war paint and gillie suits and go in on their bellies. We're too old for that now." While I was herding captured Iraqi prisoners in the first Gulf war, Alex had been an Abrams tank commander chasing the enemy toward Baghdad.

At that "war paint" I shot a suspicious glance at him but he meant camouflage greasepaint, not Indian ochre. Relax, I told myself.

With sidearms and binoculars we set off through the woods on a deer track I knew skirted the mine from the west and climbed the ridge in back of it. The going was rugged, as it always is in this part of Porcupine County, and the bugs didn't help. Mosquitoes slithered under my uniform collar and probed through my epidermis, taking deep draughts of my being. As soon as I slapped one, another came to take its place. Deerflies buzzed around our heads and now and then one bit painfully, sometimes on the exposed backs of our necks and sometimes on the exposed backs of our hands. Wherever skin showed, it was assaulted. Bug dope, the industrial-strength insect repellent Yoopers use in the woods, barely slowed the creatures.

As he swatted the bugs Alex issued a faint growl, barely audible, that would have reminded me of the soft chant of a Lakota war chief but for the words: "Shit . . . goddam . . . shit . . . shit . . . little bastards . . . shitass*rat*fuck," over and over. Maybe, I wondered, that's what the warriors said in Lakota when they went into battle. Maybe the bugs drove them nuts, too.

"Soft white man," I whispered. "What a wuss."

"Why did I ever let you rope me into this?" Alex whined.

"Shh. There it is."

We emerged onto a shelf of bare rock overlooking the

clearing, fifty yards away and the same distance below. With two fingers Alex pointed to his eyes, then with one finger pointed to the clearing. Crouching out of sight, we slowly traversed the scree down to the forest floor, careful to place our feet on solid rock. A small avalanche of pebbles would spook anyone in the clearing.

In a few minutes Alex and I squatted at the edge of the clearing, five or six feet inside the tree line, screened by leaves and branches. Two men, one holding a heavy military rifle loosely on his chest, hand on trigger, muzzle downward, emerged from the steel structure. As one swung the heavy door shut and clapped a softball-sized padlock on its hasp, the rifleman scanned the tree line all across the clearing. I unlimbered my Bushnells and peered at him.

The reptilian eyes of Mike Anderson met mine, seeming to hold them for an instant, then swept away toward the other side of the clearing.

The two men took another quick look around, then climbed into a dusty Expedition and bounced away down the gravel track that led to Norwich Road. As the big SUV disappeared, I turned to Alex and said, "I recognized the guy with the rifle. He's the captain of Morrie Weinstein's boat."

Alex's eyes widened. "Five will get you ten Morrie is involved in this, too," he said.

"Whatever it is," I said.

"Yes. Well, maybe something inside that building will tell us."

We crept around the edge of the clearing, staying carefully inside the tree and brush line, concealing ourselves from any sentry who might spot us from the ridge above. At the front of the galvanized steel building we examined the lock. Large as it was, it was an old hollow barn padlock that wasn't as strong as it looked.

"Easy to break," I said, "but do we want the bad guys knowing we were here?"

"Easier to pick," replied Alex, fishing from his shirt

pocket a small plastic box and opening it. "Here, hold this."

He selected a thin steel rod with angled ends from the assortment of lock picks. In a few seconds Alex swung free the hasp.

"Where'd you learn that?" I said, astonished.

"Once I escorted a second-story man to prison on a train from New Jersey to Lansing. To pass the time he taught me to pick locks. Never forgot how."

The door swung open noiselessly on well-oiled hinges. Inside the windowless, cavernous building, its interior warmed by the sun steadily beating down on the steel roof, was strewn a shambles of chainsaws, axes, shovels, sawhorses and lumber peaveys—the typical equipage of woodsmen who make a living in the forest any way they can. In the corners lay a big wood- chipping machine, an old Farmall tractor missing a wheel, and the forklift we had seen from the air. In one corner squatted a chemical toilet. I opened the lid. Yuck.

I played my flashlight around the single room. The building had been constructed right up against the escarpment. A wide latticework of steel shelving spanned half the back wall from top to bottom, a few hand tools occupying part of one shelf, but the rest lay utterly bare. I waved my hand over the empty shelves.

"What's all this for?"

"Beats me," Alex said.

We had half expected to find the paraphernalia of a meth or cat lab inside, but everything we saw suggested a much older and more rugged way of making a living. It didn't make sense. What was being loaded onto those trucks in the dead of night?

For nearly an hour we carefully examined everything we could see, returning every item to its place exactly as it had been. Alex snapped photo after photo with a digital camera. In all that time we turned up nothing interesting except a small Baggie of pot, hardly worth busting anyone for. Alex pocketed it.

" I'll take this bag to the lab," Alex said. "Otherwise we're skunked."

"Maybe not. Let's see where Mike Anderson's trail leads us."

Alex and I glanced at each other at the same instant. Great minds and all that.

"Didn't you say the *Lucky Six* was in Lake Huron when we found that stiff on the beach last month?" Alex said.

"Yeah."

"I've got an old buddy in Customs at the Soo who owes me one. Let me drop a dime on him, see if I can find out the dates the boat went through the locks."

"You do that. I've got Anderson's numbers. I'll run them down in Chicago. I busted him the other day for running a stop sign."

We replaced the lock on the shed door and hiked back to the cruiser, rousting a cloud of no-see-ums and releasing another round of soft invective from Alex, and drove back to Porcupine City.

"Call you tomorrow," Alex said when we pulled up at the cop shop. It was way past quitting time, but I stopped inside before picking up the Explorer to report to Gil what we had found—or, rather, hadn't found.

"All that trouble for a goose egg?" said Gil, who hates wasting time and effort, let alone meager resources.

"Something's going on," I said. "We just haven't found it yet."

Gil grunted. "Will you ever?"

I didn't tell him about Mike Anderson. It wasn't time yet.

When I drove through town on the way home, Ginny's van still stood in its spot outside the Historical Society. I started to turn into the lot, then caught myself.

For that it wasn't time yet, either. It was time to withdraw and regroup.

TWENTY-SIX

I had just washed the single dish I'd used to nuke a
Lean Cuisine—convenience food doesn't thrill my taste buds,
but I also dislike cooking only for myself—when Garner
Armstrong's Grand Cherokee rolled into the driveway, Alex's
Chevy pickup close behind. Riding with Garner was Jack
Kemppainen, the wispy Tru-Value hardware store proprietor
who was chairman of the county commissioners. Shoulder to
shoulder they strode onto my porch and knocked. I opened
the door.

"Hello, gentlemen," I said, baffled. What could they
want with me?

"Isn't it a splendid evening?" Garner said. "Shall we go
sit out on the beach and enjoy it?"

I don't have much patience with social foreplay, but
one doesn't get shirty when two powerful county politicians
and a state police sergeant come to call.

"Beer?" I asked.

The three nodded, and we carried our Molsons and
folding chairs out to the beach. It *was* a splendid evening, the
temperature hanging in the comfortable low eighties, a light
bugsweeper of a breeze clearing the sand. Wispy stratus
wreathed the sun, still high in the western sky. It would be
more than an hour before it settled into the lake, and the thin
clouds promised another spectacularly multicolored sunset.

After a few minutes of idle North Woods chitchat about
deer and bear and fishing, I could control myself no longer.
"Why are you guys here?" I demanded as politely as I could.

Garner chuckled. "Softening you up," he said.

"For what?"

Jack patted me on the shoulder. "You know, Steve," he said gravely, "Eli is getting on in years, and it's time for him to retire."

"But he said just the other day he planned to file for re-election," I said.

"Yes," Jack said. "We asked him not to. But he's a proud and stubborn old bastard."

Eli Garrow had once been as good a sheriff as Porcupine County ever had. He had come up through the ranks as a sworn deputy and served as undersheriff before running against and beating the incumbent in his first election. Short and bald, Eli is in his seventies, a sawed-off big man whose luxuriant handlebar mustache, accompanied by an unfeigned folksiness, delights widows and small children. Women find him charming and men like him instantly. Once I did, too, and worried for him when he hired his own wife as jail matron and used a brand-new all-terrain vehicle belonging to the county for deer hunting, much to the outrage of Porkies who couldn't afford that kind of useful but expensive tool. But that was as far as scandal ever colored his long career.

But now Eli had become more of a self-serving politician, devoted more to keeping himself in office than doing his job as a hardworking public servant. He held forth on the rubber-chicken circuit as amusingly as ever, but he rarely showed up at the office, preferring to let Gil O'Brien run things while he tooled around in the department's newest cruiser, the only expensive, purpose-built beefed-up Ford police car it owned. And Eli's behavior was growing ever more worrisome. He was drinking more than he should, and he was starting to become forgetful.

Late one snowy night the previous winter, returning from a liquid evening at a friend's house, he had spun out at speed on a patch of ice, his cruiser ending up in a ditch along M-64. Fortunately, a short while later while driving home from Ginny's, I spotted the vehicle before the snow covered it and blended it into the background. Immediately I stopped and pulled Eli, unhurt but confused and reeking of Wild Turkey, from his cruiser and put him into my Jeep. I drove him home and called Bill Gleason, a local mechanic, who winched the cruiser out of the ditch and towed it to his garage to repair a broken tie rod and replace the smashed muffler. I swore Bill to secrecy — not very difficult, since he owed me a couple of favors — and at my suggestion he had sent the bill to Garner, who paid it out of petty cash instead of submitting it to a vote of the commissioners at an open meeting, where Eli's folly would have been revealed. Thus scandal was avoided and no one ever heard what had happened.

Eli never thanked me for saving his hide. In fact, he had never acknowledged the incident in any way. I suspected he simply did not remember it, that he had suffered an alcoholic blackout. He was guzzling that much about once a week, though most of the time he could hold his liquor without seeming drunk.

"I understand what you mean," I told Jack. "But isn't Gil next in line?"

Traditionally, when a Porcupine County sheriff retires, the undersheriff — if he has the stomach for politics — runs for his boss' old office. Occasionally, as Eli had, he even runs against his boss.

"Gil is a great undersheriff," Grant said, popping his second Molson's, "but he's no politician. Just hasn't got the temperament. Can you imagine him kissing babies?"

As an administrator Gil O'Brien was superefficient, running a tight ship, holding down costs — important in a county whose straitened finances had been stretched even tighter by the loss of federal funds, thanks to a parsimonious White House — and handling arrestees and prisoners so meticulously that judges and juries rarely found Porcupine County law enforcement at fault.

But this transplant from Nebraska, a decorated veteran of two hitches in the Army, was a dour and irascible man who held to the Hobbesian view that life was nasty, brutish and short and that all men were irredeemable sinners, most particularly the deputies who worked for him. He was unmarried, lived alone in a small house in town, and seemed to have no private life of any kind. No one had ever seen him smile. Joe Koski claimed to have spotted a grin once, but I thought the dispatcher was just putting us on. I could not imagine Gil campaigning for office of any kind.

Up here in the wilderness, local politics is low-key. Compared to the nasty knock-down-drag-out campaigns in most of the rest of the United States, Porcupine County political warfare tends to be outwardly genteel, the candidates publicly stressing their own positives rather than focusing on the negatives of their rivals. No matter what hopefuls might say privately about their opposition, they keep their public comments clean.

And they run their campaigns on a shoestring. They press the flesh at church suppers, display their faces at every public event they can, buy and post signs, walk door to door, hand out buttons and brochures and buy ads in *The Herald*. If their modest war chests—fed by meager donations—are large enough, they might purchase a little airtime on the local radio station. On Election Day they'll also work the polling places just outside the one-hundred-foot boundary, campaigning to the very last minute. They have to. They're not millionaires who can spend their way into office like wealthy Chicagoans and New Yorkers and wait out the events of Election Day in swanky hotel rooms.

The Democratic Party all but owns the Upper Peninsula, so Republicans rarely bother to field a candidate. Often there's no competition for clerk, treasurer or prosecutor, but once in a while two names will run for sheriff. The only other candidate for sheriff besides Eli in recent years had been Benny Kramer, a "Finndian"—half Finnish, half Ojibwe—who had been a Porcupine County deputy, but after Eli's landslide victory quit the department and became a tribal cop on the Lac Vieux Desert reservation at Watersmeet in Gogebic

County, just to the south.

Our pols are not necessarily saintlier than others — it's just that Porcupine County is so poor and budget-strained every nickel is accounted for and voted upon at the county board meetings. There's nothing to loot, no extra money for nest-feathering. Our political scandals run on human frailty, not corruption.

Still, behind the scenes of any contested campaign, even in Porcupine County, a certain amount of sniping and logrolling goes on. During the campaign when Eli first won the sheriff's office, the incumbent attempted to intimidate the then nonunionized deputies into supporting him publicly, threatening to fire them if they refused. Things were tense in the sheriff's department when both candidates occupied their offices off the squadroom — the incumbent refused to speak to his challenger or even acknowledge him in any way — and the deputies found reasons to be elsewhere.

The man Eli vanquished had taken his defeat personally, refusing to come to the office even once during the eight weeks between Election Day and the swearing in of the new sheriff. But when the old sheriff belatedly discovered that he was a couple of weeks short of qualifying for a full pension, Eli magnanimously hired him as a desk officer for the few shifts he needed. People noticed that.

The idea of running for office in Porcupine County did not exactly repel me now that the subject had been broached. But I had never thought much about it, having preferred to consign that event, like fatherhood, to some vague time in the future. And now that prospect, as fatherhood had been just a short time ago, had suddenly been dropped in my lap. Again I didn't know if I could handle it.

"Is Gil going to run?" I asked.

"Don't know," Garner said. "We haven't approached him and we don't plan to."

"But what makes you think I can beat Eli? He may not be what he used to be, but he's still very popular with the voters."

"So are you, Steve. You're a personable guy. People like you. And they respect you, too. We know you're a first-class cop. You have a hell of a record."

"But I'm only a deputy," I protested. "What makes you think I can run a whole department?"

"Let's not hide behind false modesty," Garner said. "You were a first lieutenant in charge of a military police company during Desert Storm. That's good enough for us."

"What if Gil runs?"

"That could be a problem. He wouldn't stand a chance against Eli alone in the primary. But if you and Gil both run against Eli, Eli would be likely to get a plurality while you and Gil divided up the rest of the votes. If it's you against Eli alone, you've got a good chance. And if it's you against Gil alone, the people will vote for the more likeable guy, and we both know who that is."

"But I'm an Indian."

"Is that a liability?"

"It could be. I'm not saying that Porkies as a whole are prejudiced, but there are more than a few who don't care for people who look like me. They might make the difference in a tight election."

"Only one way to find out," Jack said.

"Look," I said. "I've just lost my girlfriend, and I'm not sure I can handle a campaign on top of that." That public admission of vulnerability discomfited me, but it didn't seem to surprise the three other men on the beach.

"Those things have a way of working themselves out," Garner said. "I wouldn't worry about that. Every man here has been in that fix at some time in his life."

I sighed. "Could I get back to you on this? I've got some crooks to catch first."

"And a girlfriend to make up with," Jack said.

I didn't bother to shoot him a none-of-your-business look. The truth is that the men's proposal had affected me deeply. In spite of having been a Porky for a decade, in spite of setting down roots at the cabin I owned, in spite of having fallen in love with a native, I had always carried a burden of unease — a feeling of not quite belonging. Being half one thing and half another will do that to a guy. But Garner and Jack, in suggesting I run for office, were telling me they considered me a true Porky, and I was not going to argue.

"Can you wait for an answer?" I asked.

"Take your time. Still got months to file the petition." Garner and Jack stood up and gravely shook my hand. They folded their chairs and as we walked through the sand back to my cabin I realized that Alex had not said a word during the entire evening.

"What's Alex got to do with all this?" I said.

"Oh, not much," Garner said, chuckling. "He put us up to it. It was his idea. And a very good one, I might add."

"You bastard," I told Alex.

"Yup," Alex said, laying a long arm across my shoulders. "That I am."

Grant and Jack grinned. And so did I, for the first time in a week.

TWENTY-SEVEN

The next morning I phoned the building manager at 1440 North Lake Shore Drive in Chicago. I called from home, not wanting Joe or Gil to know — yet — that I was trying to scare up dirt on an employee of Morris Weinstein. For all our labors, Alex and I hadn't yet come up with persuasive evidence of wrongdoing at the Venture Mine, and the undersheriff would have taken a dim view of a uniformed loose cannon rolling around gundecks he didn't belong on. But sometimes poking a pile of clothes with a stick stirs up something useful.

"Not here," the building manager said brusquely.

"Moved, maybe?"

"Never heard of a Mike or Michael Anderson at this address. And I've been here thirty years."

"Thanks anyway," I said. Then I dialed the Chicago Police Department.

"Criminal records."

I identified myself and gave my star number. A flurry of keyclicks and the clerk had my bona fides. "What can we do for you, Deputy?"

"Hunting a suspect." I offered name, address, driver's license number and Social Security number, all jotted down the day I stopped Anderson on the highway outside the marina.

"We have no sheet on a Michael Anderson with that Social Security number. The Secretary of State driver's license records does show that name at that address."

"Apparently a fake."

"Not surprising. This is Illinois, after all. Driver's

licenses are bought and sold every day." Her voice was weary and cynical. The State of Illinois' driver's license system is notorious for corruption. A former governor who had been secretary of state in charge of the system had recently been indicted by the feds.

"Mm. Thanks all the same." I hung up and pondered my next move. Aboard the *Lucky Six*, Anderson had said he'd learned his seamanship in the navy. I thought of calling Joe Koski and asking him to look up the number of the Naval Criminal Investigative Service in Washington. He'd find it in a trice in the computer directories. But Joe would wonder aloud, no doubt with Gil in earshot, why a country deputy was calling the feds.

I snapped my fingers. The Internet. Everybody's on the Internet, including the NCIS. In a couple of seconds I fished half a dozen hotline numbers from its Web site, and called the one reserved for naval affairs. A clerk answered, and after a couple of handoffs, I reached the records office.

"Senior Chief Tom Clark here. What can I do for you?" The voice was professional and polite.

"Deputy Steve Martinez, sheriff's department, Porcupine County, Michigan," I said. "I'm investigating a possible drug case." Then I took a deep breath and added, "Not sure, but homicide might be involved, too." There. For the first time I'd expressed my suspicions aloud.

A few swift keyclicks later the chief responded. "Okay, Deputy, what can you tell me?"

Name, address, Social Security number.

Tap-tap-tap.

"We don't have anyone by that name or address in our system. But we do have the Social Security number."

"Who owns it?"

"Algis Petrauskas. P-E-T-R-A-U-S-K-A-S. He's a former sailor."

"He have a record?"

"Does he ever."

"Can you share it with me?"

"There seems to be a Chicago mob connection, though it was never proved in court," the chief said. "Otherwise a clean record there. But Petrauskas did five years at Naval Consolidated Brig Miramar for smuggling several kilos of marijuana from Tijuana and selling it in the naval barracks on the base at San Diego. Beat a couple of charges of aggravated assault. He was a mean one with a knife. Suspected of having killed a fellow prisoner in Miramar. But nobody would testify. The guards were damned glad to see him go."

"Physical description?"

"Five-five, hundred forty-five pounds. Six-inch fouled anchor tattooed on his left arm. Pretty ugly guy, too, judging by his photo."

"Sounds like my man. Can you scan his jacket and email it to me?"

"Sure. It'll take just half an hour."

"One more thing. Why do you suppose he didn't change his Social Security number to a fake one when he took the alias of Michael Anderson? He could have had the number left off his driver's license. Illinois allows that option to help people protect their privacy."

"You never can tell with criminals, even the smart ones," the chief said. "In the back of their minds a lot of 'em think keeping a Social Security number means they'll eventually get a full pension from the government. They buy and sell drugs for hundreds of thousands of bucks on the street, and they're worried about chicken feed in their old age? Go figure. As for the option of omitting the number from the Illinois license, either the guy got careless or it's a fake number."

Thirty-three minutes later my computer beeped. I opened the message and scanned the contents. The flattened, snakelike muzzle of the man I knew as Mike Anderson stared out at me from the photograph on the computer screen.

Before his drug arrest, conviction and incarceration in

one of the military's toughest maximum-security prisons, Algis Petrauskas had served a three-year hitch aboard the frigate USS *McClusky*, rising to petty officer third class as a bosun's mate as well as earning a commendation for skillful small boat handling. He had been busted back to seaman twice, once for a barroom brawl on shore in Seattle and again for three days' absence without leave after too enthusiastic a liberty at San Diego. Needless to say, after serving his sentence he had been sent packing with a dishonorable discharge.

It was his hometown that intrigued me the most. Petrauskas had grown up in Winnetka, Illinois, and had graduated from New Trier High School. That wealthy lake shore suburb of Chicago, with its famous high school, is not the kind of place the usual violent thug comes from. Mary Ellen Garrigan lived in Winnetka during the winter. Just a coincidence? Maybe not.

I dialed Alex.

"Commence."

"I don't want Clements," I said for the tenth time. "I want Sergeant Kolehmainen."

Alex whooped.

"Got something," I told him. "Mike Anderson, Weinstein's boat skipper, one of the guys we saw in that spot behind the mine yesterday? He's got a heavy record." I spelled it out for Alex. "Navy says there seems to be a Chicago mob connection, too."

"Doesn't surprise me a bit," he said. "Got something for you, too. This morning I called that friend in Customs at the Soo Locks. Asked him to check the transit records back in June and see when the *Lucky Six* sailed through from Huron. He gave me a little la-de-da about national security but I just blackmailed him. Never mind what I had on him. It was good enough."

"Don't keep me on tenterhooks."

"The *Lucky Six* cleared the Soo and entered Lake

Superior on June 18. That was five days before the stiff washed up on the beach."

"Aha!" I said.

"Weinstein lied. The *Lucky Six* wasn't in Lake Huron when he said it was."

A boat whose captain had a drug conviction and maybe was connected to the Chicago mob. A dead Chicago hood who had been a drug runner. The link wasn't open and shut, but only an idiot couldn't see its potential. "This sure is worth following up on," I said unnecessarily.

Everything we had still was circumstantial, nowhere near enough to pick up Anderson and interrogate him, let alone call his boss on the carpet. Morrie Weinstein was still a hot potato we'd have to handle carefully. We needed to scare up one or two more solid leads before informing Eli and Gil and Lieutenant Jim Card, Alex's boss at the Wakefield post, of what we had found so far, and maybe really getting down to business.

"Go to it," said Alex.

I drummed my fingers on the kitchen table. But where could I start?

TWENTY-EIGHT

Mary Ellen Garrigan. Algis Petrauskas alias Mike Anderson. I'd shake that tree and see what fell out. And the best place to start was Chad Garrow, who, so far as I knew, was as familiar with Mary Ellen—in more than one way— as well as anybody else in Porcupine County.

After patrol the following day, as we turned in our traffic stop copies, summons sheets and other products of the paperless society at the sheriff's department, I stopped Chad on the way out. "Buy you a beer at Hobbs'?" I offered.

Chad didn't hesitate. In my experience, next to newspaper journalists, cops are the easiest people on earth to seduce with a freebie. But I knew I'd have to play him carefully, partly out of respect for a brother officer and partly to avoid spooking a naïve young man infatuated with an older woman.

For a while at the tavern, full of quitting-time drinkers, we talked about everything and nothing: the girls' high-school basketball team, the peewee hockey teams, the cost of grooming snowmobile trails, whether Eli would stand for re-election, whether Gil might challenge him, the relative merits of Winchester and Browning shotguns, which restaurant had the best pasties, the Farmers' Almanac snow depth prediction for the following winter, whether the flashing red light at the intersection of U.S. 45 and M-64 ought to be replaced with a true stoplight, the Vikings and the Packers, the hot young kindergarten teacher, what would become of the abandoned boat works and half a hundred more everyday topics that occupy the minds of working Porkies. Two Buds had disappeared down Chad's commodious gullet and thoroughly relaxed him before I made my move.

"Speaking of women," I said casually, nibbling on a bartop pretzel, "that Mary Ellen Garrigan is a knockout, isn't she?" I carefully watched Chad's expression. It did not change. That meant no one knew what had happened on my beach the week before. Only Ginny had witnessed the tail end of the encounter, and she was not the sort to confide such details to her friends — only her lawyer, and I wondered if she had done even that.

Chad's brows rose, his eyes widened and a stupid grin crept up his chubby cheeks. I had to stifle my own smile. But the lad offered no details of intimate activities, as many immature and self-absorbed louts eagerly would have in order to pump up their reputations among the boys. Young as he was, green as he was, clumsy — even oafish — as he could be, Chad Garrow respected women.

He straightened, his smile giving way to a grave expression. "You know, Steve, she's a little older'n me." A *little*? Chad, I knew, had just turned twenty-four, and Mary Ellen had to be in her mid-forties, though the miracle of cosmetic surgery had shaved a decade off the truth. "I'm not sure she's right for me."

"Well, I don't think the time you've spent with her has been wasted," I said. "She's an interesting person, isn't she?"

"Damn right. Interested, too. Allus wants to know what we do up here in the sheriff's department. Loves all the yarns about crooks and weirdoes and stuff. So easy to talk to. So different from the girls up here. Always wants to know what I'm doing."

Like many backwoods Yoopers, Chad often speaks a foreshortened language of sentence fragments, and sometimes a listener needs to guess at their subjects, though the verbs and objects are perfectly clear.

Mary Ellen sounded like a cop groupie, I thought. I'd had experience with those.

"She must be a bright lady," I said encouragingly

"Yeah." Chad's eyes widened again.

"Where's she from?" I knew that already, but didn't tell him.

"Winnetka, Illinois. Real rich town near Chicago."

No kidding. Even up here we knew about upscale suburbs.

"What does she do down there?" I asked

"Don't really know," Chad said, "but maybe charity work and stuff, whatever those rich ladies do." Probably, I thought, more stuff than charity work.

"She's divorced, isn't she? Who's her ex?"

"Big auto dealer named Bill Garrigan."

Even north woods cops knew about Garrigan Motors, a Chicago dealership empire that peddled Hummers, Acuras, Caddies, Land-Rovers, Mercedeses and BMWs to social underachievers who bought their status with expensive cars. Along M-64 I'd stopped quite a few costly SUVs with Illinois plates and GARRIGAN MOTORS affixed to their rear decks. Bill Garrigan had built up the empire from the single dealership he had inherited from his father, handed down in turn by *his* father, Nevil Garrigan, a pioneering Cadillac dealer. In the 1920s and 1930s Nevil had sold Caddys to Al Capone, Machine Gun Jack McGurn and other mobsters of his era. And Morrie Weinstein's father had been a Caddy dealer.

"Mm. Wonder what broke up that marriage."

"Ready for this, Steve? Morrie Weinstein."

I nearly knocked over my beer. "Morrie Weinstein?"

"Yeah. Mary Ellen said they had an affair ten years ago and Bill Garrigan threw her out." Chad's scruples against kiss-and-tell didn't extend outside the bedroom.

"She must have done okay in the divorce settlement."

"Sure did. Helluva house she's got on the beach."

I decided to plunge in as far as I could. "Tell me, how did you meet ?"

"In Frank's. Stopped in for a pasty and right by the produce stand she told me she liked my uniform. Got to talking and I guess we just hit it off. She invited me for dinner."

And dessert, I thought. "Even in the country the supermarket's a great place to meet chicks," I said unnecessarily. "Then you started seeing her regularly?"

"Couple, three times a week."

I shook my head admiringly, encouraging him. "Quite a looker she is."

"Yeah." He brightened even more. Pride of possession was written all over his face. He started in on his third beer. I hoped that would be his last. Big as he was, he could handle three brews without hitting the gong on the Breathalyzer, but not more than that.

"Hey, when we went fishing a couple of weeks ago, did Morrie invite you or did she?"

"She did."

"Cool. Surprising they still get along, considering their thing's all over."

"Oh, yeah. Said Morrie brought her up here and she just fell in love with the beach and Morrie helped her find a contractor to get that house built."

"Know much about her family? She ever talk about them?"

"Came over from Lithuania after World War II. Her dad was an auto mechanic and worked for Morrie's father. She was born here."

"The American dream," I said as I took another sip of Molson's. "What was her maiden name?"

"Pet-something, pet-rah—"

"Petrauskas?"

"That's it." He looked at me wonderingly.

"Very common Lithuanian name."

"I guess."

"Brothers? Sisters? Maybe she's got a knockout of a sister?"

"No, but she did mention a brother."

"He in the auto business too?"

Chad's brow furrowed. "Think she said he was in the Navy. No, he's out now."

Bingo.

"Hey, why you so interested in Mary Ellen?" Chad suddenly asked.

He was slow, but he wasn't dumb. I shrugged, then nudged him in the ribs and winked. "Two good reasons."

"Yeah, they're great," Chad said dreamily. Then he blushed.

Better change the subject. "Think the county will cough up for new cruisers?" The two older Fords had racked up more than 200,000 miles in just two years, and none of us thought they'd make it through a third.

"Beats me," Chad said, "but we gotta get 'em." The driver's seat of his cruiser was badly rump-sprung, thanks to the almost daily abuse of his two hundred eighty pounds, and the engine needed another ring job.

A little more everything and nothing, and we called it an evening. As we rolled out of Hobbs,' I was glad to see that Chad stopped after three brews. And he did not drive, but walked the two blocks home to the bachelor room he occupied on the third floor of Eli's house. This was a young man learning how to control himself. There's hope for him yet, I thought.

As I drove out the highway to my cabin, a knot of worry began to form at the back of my mind. There was more to Mary Ellen Garrigan, née Petrauskas, I was certain. Neither she nor Mike Anderson—Algis Petrauskas—had mentioned their kinship during our morning out on the *Lucky Six*. Wouldn't a brother and sister normally have done that? Nor had either she or Morrie Weinstein given a hint of their previous relationship, not that it was anybody's business. I decided to make it mine.

As soon as I arrived, I picked up the phone and called the Chicago Police Department. In a few moments I reached the sergeant on duty in Organized Crime, and told him what I was looking for. In a few minutes he returned to the phone.

"We do have a sheet on Morris Weinstein. No arrests, no convictions, but he runs with the mob. Often seen in company with Two Ton Tony Cella, he's a major capo, in restaurants and at racetracks, and out on his own fishing boat. Weinstein's father was a made man, provided Caddies to the gangsters before he sold his dealership to Francis Garrigan, also a hood."

"Francis' relationship to Bill Garrigan?"

"Father."

"Anything else?"

"Weinstein hasn't been seen in town for quite a while. Rumor is he moved up to your jurisdiction."

"He did."

"You have anything on him?" I could hear the sergeant clicking his keyboard.

"Not yet. Soon, probably."

"Keep us informed."

"I'll do that."

TWENTY-NINE

At my cabin late the next evening the doorbell rang through the steady thrum of driving rain on the roof. Momentous things had been happening at my cabin in the evenings quite a bit lately, and this occasion was no different.

Ginny stood in a voluminous yellow slicker on the deck clutching a large leather dispatch case, her expression set and unsmiling, as lightning crackled out over the lake and rain puddled around her. My mouth fell open. "Ah . . . ah . . . ," I said. Good thing the reservation orphanage hadn't named me Stevie Silvertongue. Finally I found my voice.

"Ginny, am I ever glad to see you! I've missed you so very much. I . . . I . . . There's a reason for what happened."

"I'm sure there is, Deputy," she said flatly, "but I'm not here about that."

"What?"

"Are you going to let me in or do I have to stand out here in the rain?"

Dumbly I stood aside and made little waving motions to usher her inside. "Ah . . . sit down. I'll make coffee."

With careful deliberation, avoiding my eyes, she removed her slicker, hung it on a kitchen hook, and strode to the dining table, placing the case upon it. "Never mind, thanks."

"Ginny, I . . ."

"We're not going to talk about it, I said. I'm here to see you as a law enforcement officer. I have some important information for you."

Her tone was stern, flat, and businesslike. She kept her eyes on the dispatch case. She pulled out a chair and sat down at the table, hands in her lap, spine straight, head bowed as if waiting for the host to say grace so that everyone could dig in. She reminded me of a balled-up porcupine, quills spread in self-protection.

Inwardly I sighed. So beautiful, so close, and yet so far. I pulled myself together. "What is it?" I said.

Like a Horace Wright county board report in the Herald, a Ginny Fitzgerald story does not unfold in big-city newspaper fashion, first giving the most important facts and then filling in the tale with subordinate details that grow less important the longer the story runs. She believes in beginning at the beginning in once-upon-a-time fashion, telling her story chronologically and letting the subtleties of narrative fill in the blanks. This is not a bad way to present an event, although impatient listeners, wanting to get to the meat of a tale quickly, might squirm and fuss and miss important nuances. With people like her I learned long ago to sit back and let their stories unroll. Maybe the patience is in the genes, generations of my ancestors having listened to Lakota storytellers spin yarns this way, refusing to hurry even when enemies lurked in the night outside the corral getting ready to steal the horses. But I really didn't know. I'm not much of a Lakota.

"It's about the Venture Mine." She opened the dispatch case and carefully removed a sheaf of yellowed old papers and envelopes, neatly stacked and tied with ribbon.

I skidded back a chair on the bare maple planks and sat down opposite Ginny. "Yes?"

"Last week I saw Horace's story about Andrew Carmichael in *The Herald*."

It had been a humdinger even for Horace, covering nearly a quarter of the bedsheet-sized front page with several photographs. Violence may be common but murder is rare in Porcupine County, and *Herald* readers snapped up stories about even century-old homicides. As I had thought he would, Horace had found a couple of Carmichael great-grandchildren living in Wisconsin and plumbed their thoughts about the discovery of the body of an ancestor neither had known and only one of them had ever heard of. They expressed only surprised banalities so commonplace that even Horace couldn't sweeten their quotes. But that still gave Horace the opportunity to make a few lugubrious editorial remarks about the fleeting nature of life and memory. He would have made a first-class true-crime author. The very end of the story gave details about a funeral and burial to be held in the home town of one of the survivors. I felt sure Horace had shamed them into paying for the services.

"And that reminded me about something I'd almost forgotten," Ginny said. "The day after I started the job at the Historical Society a few years ago, Edna Holderman came into my office staggering under a wooden box of papers almost as big as she."

"Edna Holderman?"

"You have the memory of a colander. Edna Holderman, the daughter of Gordon Holderman, late owner of the Venture Mine. Morrie Weinstein's mother."

I slapped the table. "Now I remember. Please go on." I had nearly forgotten my anguish over Ginny's unreachable presence.

"She said she was clearing out her house, getting ready to move into a retirement village in California, and she wanted her husband's papers to be preserved for future historians. 'They're just mining records and stuff like that,' she said. 'Nothing exciting, nothing we need now, but I want to give it to the society before it's thrown out in the trash.' I stuffed the box into a back room with a hundred other boxes at the society and simply forgot about it."

Ginny took a deep breath. "Then I saw Horace's story, and I suddenly remembered that box."

"What's in it?" I asked.

Having embarked on her careful narrative, Ginny would not be derailed from it. "It took me an hour to find the box," she said, "and then I had to vacuum maybe ninety years' worth of dust and grime out of the inside—the box was very old and had no top. It had been left open all the time the Holdermans had it. Much of the paper is brittle and I had to handle it carefully."

Ginny donned white cotton gloves and handed me a pair. Then she fished a portfolio out of the dispatch case, opened it and slowly and deliberately spread out the documents it contained, placing them gently on the table.

"Most of this stuff is just ore and assay reports, how many tons were brought up from the various drifts and sold for whatever price and so on, interesting only to an economic historian who specializes in mining." Her voice was brisk, that of the academic lecturer leading a seminar. She, too, had forgotten the awkwardness of our initial encounter and now had entered deep into her professional self. When she is like that I just sit back in admiration and take it all in. This time I had no choice.

"And here's a map of the mine in 1905. That was during its height, two years before prices collapsed and Gordon Holderman started managing the place as a tribute mine." Carefully she unfolded the yellowing paper, trying to keep it from cracking and disintegrating, and spread it on the table. The map took up nearly all the heavy maple table, four feet by six feet even without the two leaves I had never used.

The mine chart was almost identical to the smaller one I had seen on the wall of Morrie Weinstein's office. Like it, the old map showed seven drifts, each of them a good deal shorter than the ones on the modern chart.

"Um," I said, wondering where Ginny's presentation was going.

"Now here's a different map. It's dated 1920." She spread it over the older drawing. This one was smaller and cruder, its lines clearly hand-drawn in pencil, then traced over in ink. It was headed CONFIDENTIAL in large bold letters. Under that lay the legend EXTENSION BEGUN 1908 COMPLETED 1914. The map bore no Township and Range surveyor's coordinates to mark the mine's location on the surface of the earth. It had been drawn from memory, not to scale. It showed a modest mine of three horizontal drifts attached to a long vertical shaft. The lowest drift was marked 1,089 FEET. Unlike the others, this bottom drift was not closed at one end but open, leading off toward the west on the left side of the map, the two inked lines that outlined its dimensions fading into short broken lines. On the other side of the map, the eastern side, a small X at the end of the lowest drift bore the legend SILVER LODE.

I looked up at Ginny, my mouth open. "Silver?"

"Yes."

"Wow." Silver is often found in very small quantities with copper ore, mostly as tiny flecks in the rock, but late in the nineteenth century, rumors erupted that a large lode of mass silver had been found deep in what is now the Wolverine Mountains Wilderness State Park. Thousands of miners flooded in from all over the nation to seek their fortune, just as the Forty-Niners had during the California gold rush of 1849. The town of Silverton had grown up at the mouth of the Iron River to serve them, and had hung on to this day, even after the strike turned out to be a will-o'-the-wisp. Still, for more than a hundred years old-timers had related legends about a lost silver lode in Porcupine County.

"Where is this mine?" I asked. "Does anyone know?"

"I'm coming to that," Ginny said, pulling out a six-inch stack of pamphlets. I recognized them as old composition books made of cheap pulp paper, each page lined for handwriting. Most elementary and high schools used them well into the twentieth century for examinations, and some still did. As a small-town schoolboy myself I'd written countless quizzes and essays on them. Like the other documents in the dispatch case, their edges were yellow and cracked, but the wide blue fabric ribbon binding them was new. I said so.

"Yes," Ginny replied. "The old ribbon deteriorated as

soon as I undid the knot. Can't use rubber bands to hold these old chapbooks together—that would just crush the paper. There are a dozen stacks like these. I found them along with the maps inside a steel strongbox at the bottom of the wooden one. It was locked. I had to take the box to a garage to have the lock drilled out."

She took the top book off the first stack and slid it under my eyes, turning it so I could read the legend on the cover, in faded brown but still elegant Palmer Method handwriting:

JOURNAL
OF
GORDON HOLDERMAN
VOLUME ONE
1904-

I opened the first page. It was written in the same neat copperplate, in ink from a metal nib. "January the first in the Year of Our Lord 1904. Here begins the record of the life of Gordon Holderman, age 38, of Porcupine County, Michigan. On this day nine tons of ore were taken from the Venture Mine . . ." On I leafed, marveling as the everyday details of life of a foreman inside and outside a copper mine piled up on the pages. Holderman wrote a faintly fusty Victorian English, for the most part simple and serviceable but occasionally with a long, ornate sentence that was so gingerly balanced, like a round-bottomed boat with a high superstructure, that if it had been bumped at one end it would never have stopped rolling. He was extraordinarily painstaking with his grammar and spelling, frequently crossing out a misspelled word and sometimes substituting another. He must have been an excruciatingly slow writer.

No detail was too small to commit to paper. A cable was beginning to fray and by the end of the week the hoist would have to be shut down several hours for repairs. The men were grumbling about the rotted condition of the shoring in the Level Two drift and carpenters would have to be hired at great expense and sent down to fix the ceilings. Only two tons of ore was extracted January 10. A blizzard raged above ground, piling the snow too deep and sending the temperature too low — twelve degrees below zero Fahrenheit — for the horse teams to drag the crushed ore to the tram line two miles away where it would be hauled to the smelter at the Minesota Mine. Travel was so difficult that miners huddled in the bunkhouse rather than going home after work. Complaints about the cookhouse food were mounting. "Two men injured in a rock fall on Level Three. One will lose his leg, the surgeon says." There was no expression of regret or concern. Mining was a hard life, and miners were hard men.

"Does it go on like this?" I asked Ginny.

"More or less." She fished out another beribboned stack of composition books. New pink paper slips researchers used for placeholders instead of Post-Its, whose adhesive might harm delicate historical documents, peeked from some of its pages. "Take a look at this one."

Its cover was similar to the first, but the year was 1908. "You remember that Holderman became manager in 1907 and ran the Venture as a tribute mine?"

I did.

"Open to the first pink slip, please."

On "the twelfth of April in the year 1908," Holderman had written, "the air in the seventh level has begun to grow foul." Work would have to be stopped while a new air shaft was drilled. The surveyors had determined that the best place to start the vertical shaft lay half a mile northwest from the main shaft, where the rocky knob overlooking the Venture again met level ground. A half-mile-long horizontal shaft, six feet high by six feet wide, would have to be drilled from the farthest edge of the seventh level to meet the new vertical shaft. Fans atop the vertical shaft would pump air down and across into the mine proper.

"I think that might be the tunnel Morrie took me into when I visited the mine," I said. I shuddered when I recalled the panic that had welled into me when he turned off the lights. "But it's all fallen in now."

"Don't think so," Ginny said, leafing to another pink slip "Read this."

"The second of November 1908." At almost the point where vertical met horizontal shaft, Holderman had written, flecks of pure silver had appeared in the rubble. Tunneling a bit further revealed a vein of silver the thickness of a man's thigh. "I have sworn foreman Peterson and miner Carmichael to secrecy," Holderman wrote. "We have discovered this strike by our own honest sweat and justice demands we be those to profit from it. We shall not inform New York of our discovery."

And so began the conspiracy to cheat the owners of the Venture Mine.

In mounting excitement I leafed quickly through the rest of the chapbook, stopping now and then to read as carefully as I could the passages Ginny had set off with pink placeholders. Over the next year the three men and a dozen trusted and well-paid miners extracted the silver, at first carrying it through the horizontal air shaft and up and out of the mine with the copper ore, shipping the silver-bearing rocks aboard a lake steamer from Porcupine County to a smelter at the Soo where the foremen could be bribed to keep quiet. During this whole time the mine owners and stockholders stayed utterly unaware of the conspiracy. Within a few months the conspirators had cleared nearly seventy-five thousand dollars in profit, a huge sum for the time. So well were things going that the cabal decided to enlarge the vertical air shaft to six feet square, enough to admit a small skip capable of hoisting two tons.

In the next chapbook Ginny pointed to the Post-It marking the entry for the sixth of March, 1909. "Unfortunately

Andrew Carmichael has become untrustworthy," Holderman wrote in characteristically flat and neutral language, "and it was decided he had to be dealt with." This, I saw immediately, was the historical version of a smoking gun. If it had been discovered at the time it would have sent Holderman to the gallows.

He offered no further details about Carmichael's offense—who made the decision to dispatch him, or how it was carried out. In my mind's eye I filled in the missing facts. There was a brief meeting outside the shaft entrance. Harsh words, then pleading ones, a scuffle, and finally the sickening moist thunk of pickax against skull. The killers dragged Carmichael's body a quarter of a mile through tall white pines that had not yet met the logger's ax to a creek embankment where the still warm corpse was thrown, the contents of its clothing undisturbed, into a shallow grave. There it would lie for nearly a century before three cops chasing a couple of drunks through the woods in comic-opera fashion happened upon it.

And that galvanized steel building two of the officers had searched just the week before very likely concealed the entrance to that old shaft in the rock face behind. It did not take a genius to guess what was going on in the drifts far below. Expensive designer coca plants, poppy bushes, marijuana and God knows what else were being grown and harvested and maybe even refined in a lost section of the Venture Mine nobody knew about except Morris Weinstein and his gang. And I would have bet my snug little cabin on the lake, the home I loved and had sunk deep roots into, that Weinstein and his thugs had killed Frank Saarinen, Roy Schweikert and—yes, Danny Impellitteri, the hoodlum whose body had washed up on the beach. They had probably died because, one way or another, they knew too much.

"Exactly, Steve," Ginny said as I looked up at her. It was the first time all evening that she had addressed me familiarly. I took a deep breath.

"There's nothing to connect this drawing with the other, is there?" I asked, pointing at the maps of the Venture Mine and the extension.

"Nothing," Ginny said, "except that the extension map was lying on top of the main map in one envelope inside that strongbox. And, of course, the statements in Holderman's journal."

"Do you think Edna Holderman was aware of these maps and that journal?"

"Probably not. She wouldn't have given that box to the historical society if she had known."

"I recall you said Gordon died in 1956. Morrie is in his late forties, almost fifty maybe. If he was born before 1956, then Gordon could have willed the information in some form to his infant grandson, perhaps to be given to Morrie when he came of age."

Ginny nodded.

"However Morrie discovered his grandfather's—ah—adventure, it's pretty obvious he knows all about it. And he knows more than we do. That's what makes him dangerous."

"What are you going to do now?"

I thought a moment. "Consult with the allies. Bring in reinforcements. Alex and I can't do this alone, and in any case our bosses aren't going to let us. But now I think we may have almost enough evidence to plan a raid in force. I'll have to talk to the prosecutor."

Ginny looked into my eyes for the first time since she turned up on the doorstep. "Steve, please be careful," she said, concern coloring her voice.

"I will. Now can we talk about—"

"No!" She shook her head firmly, reached for her jacket, and was out the door before I could say anything more.

She left behind the journals and the maps. That was a message of a sort. I wanted to believe it was.

THIRTY

Two days later the better part of Porcupine County's law-enforcement establishment, plus a few outside troops, crowded into the county commissioners' chambers at the courthouse. Garner Armstrong, as prosecutor and the highest-ranking official present, chaired the meeting with his usual gentle but brisk authority at the head of a long, heavy oak table I suspected was left over from the cookhouse at a nineteenth century logging camp. The modern Porcupine County Courthouse is full of such stray heirlooms, most of them hand-me-down, government-issue items that nobody thought were valuable until a Chicago antiques dealer paying a speeding fine in the 1960s offered to quintuple it if he could have the county magistrate's massive maple roll-top desk. The magistrate, who knew something about turnip trucks, declined. Judge Rantala still uses it.

Eli and Gil sat as far apart from each other as they could, and gazed at each other and at me with barely concealed hostility. "They've both filed for sheriff," Joe Koski had whispered from behind his counter when I arrived that morning, "and they're both afraid of you."

Word had got out in the sheriff's department that Garner had approached me — I suspected from Garner himself. He is a canny politician who knows the value of a leak at stirring up action. But I was sorry that Gil had filed. He had done so, I thought, just to preserve his job with the county, not because he actually wanted to be sheriff. I suspected he worried that if I won the election I'd send him packing, for undersheriffs serve at the pleasure of the sheriff. I had no intention of canning Gil because I hadn't made a decision to run. But, I mused, if I did run — and win — I'd have to think hard about the undersheriff's job. Gil is superb in it, but could we get along? We are like night and day, alpha and omega, in our respective approaches to police work. And, needless to say, in our personalities.

Carelessly tilted in his chair against the far wall sat Chad Garrow, who had no idea what had been going on with the Venture Mine during the last few weeks but was about to find out. The night-shift deputies, portly Jim Haas and buxom Betty Allen, had been called in as well. Joe was manning the department's desk. We'd clue him in later. Lieutenant Jim Card, commander of the state police post at Wakefield, sat next to Alex. By rights Garner should have invited an investigator from the Drug Enforcement Administration, but like me, he can't stand the officious twits. Like federal agents everywhere, DEA guys always want to run the investigations, even in jurisdictions they know nothing about. Garner would inform the DEA only when he had to, and that would be at the very last minute before an operation began. We hoped it would end before the feds could bull their way in and piss everybody off.

"Alex, you're the ranking investigator in this case," Garner said. "Please bring us up to speed."

"I'll defer to Deputy Martinez, who knows more about this than I do."

Garner nodded to me. He, Alex and I had briefly rehearsed the opening of the proceedings before the meeting. Eli and Gil looked at me in surprise.

"Somebody dim the lights, please."

I turned on the digital projector — another of the many grant-writing trophies that made Gil such a valuable undersheriff — and the prosecutor's laptop computer, on which I had scanned all the facts and maps into the latest version of PowerPoint. Up here in the North Woods we enjoy not only hot and cold running water and flush toilets but also all the modern electronic conveniences of the big city. We in

Porcupine County government may not enjoy state-of-the-art technology in every department, but neither do we write with crayons.

First I projected on a blank white wall photographs of Morris Weinstein, Algis Petrauskas (alias Mike Anderson), and Mary Ellen Garrigan, explaining what I had learned about their relationships. When Mary Ellen's photo snapped on the wall, Chad gulped audibly and looked at me in consternation.

"Later," I mouthed to him, and put up the historical facts about the Venture Mine as well as the maps Ginny had given me. The whole presentation took fifteen minutes. I left nothing out, including my encounters with Mary Ellen at George's and on the beach, although I was careful to edit the more salacious details while leaving in Ginny's role in the events. At that everyone else in the room except Alex, in whom I had already confided, glanced at each other in sudden understanding.

When I turned off the projector and the lights came on, Eli swiftly bounded to his feet and said, "Very good, Steve, that was brilliant and really, really helpful. Now here's what we're going to do—"

Garner immediately thrust out long arm like a traffic policeman. "*I* am in charge here, Eli. Deputy Martinez has developed this case. He knows more about it than any of us except possibly Detective Sergeant Kolehmainen. I am going to give Martinez full field command, with the sergeant his backup, if that's all right with Lieutenant Card. And what's more, I will take strategic command myself."

I looked up in mock astonishment, as if surprised by Garner's words. Having a junior deputy run the whole show in the field was all but unheard of in law enforcement circles, even in Porcupine County. But Garner knew what he was doing. He was telling Eli Garrow that his day was done and new blood soon would be in charge of the department. Garner glanced at Lieutenant Card, who, having been informed of the prosecutor's intentions before the meeting along with Alex and me, nodded. Alex shot me a casual sidewise smile. Eli glowered. Gil smoldered. Chad gaped.

"Okay, Steve, it's all yours," Garner said. "Now what?"

"Alex?" I said.

The big detective leaned forward on the table. "This morning the forensics came back from Marquette on that Baggie of pot we found in the building at the clearing," he said. "Almost fifteen per cent tetrahydrocannabinol."

Everyone's eyebrows shot up.

"Exact same proportion as in the marijuana we found on the body of Danny Impellitteri, the Chicago hood whose body washed up on the beach in June. But we don't know that it's the same, and we don't know for sure that it came out of the mine. It probably did, but we have no proof. It could have been brought from elsewhere and dropped there accidentally, of course. Steve?"

"We know something's going on in that mine," I said "We don't know exactly what. We have pretty strong evidence to connect the two separate parts of the mine, and those also to the the suspicious actions Sergeant Kolehmainen and I witnessed at that clearing. But that pot doesn't constitute a smoking gun. Not just yet."

"Agreed," Garner said. "We're so close. But we can't move against Weinstein right now. The chances are that we're right, but what if we're wrong? We would not only damage the reputation of one of the county's most important employers but we would all look pretty stupid."

The prosecutor turned to me. "What next, Steve?"

"For the next week or so I'll find a reason to fly over that clearing every day. We don't know how often the trucks come. But if we spot them from the air or perhaps from the road, we can put an officer on stakeout at Matchwood and when the trucks come out, we can flag them down on the highway and check their loads. We'll get the General — excuse me, Judge Rantala — to sign an open warrant ahead of time."

Everyone knew the tactic. A cop could ask to see a

truck's load, and if the driver refused, detain him until backup arrived with a warrant. A prepared warrant saves time and bother.

Alex spoke for the first time. "Of course we'll have backup—at least three other units—when we stop the trucks. We'll be ready to go as soon as we get word of the stakeout."

"Yes," I said. "And we have to remember that we likely will have only about twenty-four hours, probably less, before Weinstein finds out that his load hasn't arrived wherever it's going. If the load turns out to be what we think it is, we'll have to mount the raid on the mine immediately."

"I'll have all my troopers equipped and ready to go," Lieutenant Card said. "Alex, see to it."

"Yes sirree," Alex said, eagerly cracking his knuckles. The old soldier loved action.

"Let's stress the importance of security," I said. "We don't want Weinstein and his gang to find out anything if we can possibly help it."

For the first time Gil spoke. "Yes. We can work out a code so any officers can report what they find when they find it without anybody else knowing." His oblique reference was to the forest telegraph. And cell phone coverage up here is still too spotty to be reliable. Only the landline is reasonably secure, but there are precious few call boxes out on the lonely highways.

In a few minutes we had drawn up an order of battle for our first wave of fourteen sworn officers—Eli, Gil, the department's five deputies, and eight troopers from Wakefield, including three who lived close by in Porcupine County. Within two hours we could bring in another couple of dozen reinforcements if we needed them—deputies from adjoining Gogebic, Iron, Baraga and Houghton counties, tribal policemen from the Lac Vieux Desert reservation, and several more troopers.

"Eli, we'll need you to stay at the department and help Joe with communications and liaison," Garner said.

"All right," Eli said grumpily. He clearly wanted to be part of the on-scene action, but he knew his enemies were at last trying to ease him out of the job he had held for almost twenty years. His shoulders slumped in defeat. I felt sorry for the man. But I knew he wouldn't go down without a struggle at the ballot box.

"Gil and I will lead three deputies and four troopers over the road to the mine entrance from Norwich Road," I said, carefully including the undersheriff in the chain of command. No use angering him by treating him as an underling. "Alex, will you take Chad and three troopers and wait by the clearing on the other side of the ridge for the rabbits to bolt from their hole? Chad, you know that area as well as anyone here, and I'd like you to help Alex."

"Whatever you say, Steve," Alex said. Chad, still looking astonished and upset at the events of the last half hour, nodded.

"And, Garner, wouldn't the start of the raid be the best time to notify the DEA? By the time they arrive things might be all over."

Garner beamed. "Just what I was thinking, Steve," he said.

The meeting broke up. On his way out Eli leaned toward me and hissed quietly, "Watch it, kid. You're in way over your head."

I didn't answer but looked at him sadly. It was just a defiant roar from an aging lion, and not the last one, either.

Gil didn't even glance my way, but stared stonily ahead as he stalked out of the room.

I caught Chad before he could leave and pulled him back by his massive elbow. When everyone else had left and we were finally alone, I said as gently as I could, "Chad, I'm sorry to lay all this stuff on you. And I'm sorry to have kept it from you all this time. But I had to."

"The bitch was using me, Steve," he said.

I took a deep breath. I would not have to worry about

Chad Garrow's loyalties. I decided to cement them firmly.

"She tried to use me, too," I told him.

Chad straightened and squared his jaw.

"Why?" he said. "Why would she do that?"

"I think she was acting at Morrie's request. I think he hoped to stay one boat-length ahead of us if we cottoned on to what he was doing in the mine. I think she was his spy."

"*Shit*," Chad said. He now understood completely. I could see him searching his mind, trying to remember if he'd revealed any sensitive details about the operation of the sheriff's department during his pillow talks with Mary Ellen.

"I'm going to ask you to do something difficult," I said.

"Anything."

"Until the raid starts, stay in touch with Mary Ellen. Do your usual thing, don't let her know anything might be up. We want to keep her in the dark as long as possible."

A small but wicked smile played on Chad's face. "I can do that."

I didn't ask the details.

THIRTY-ONE

Each afternoon for four consecutive days, I rolled out the Cessna and flew surveillance flights past the mine and the clearing beyond it, careful to stay 2,500 to 3,000 feet above the ground and on varying courses, never coming near my target more than once a day. I did not want anyone below suspecting that a lone aircraft was conducting a search. But the seven-by-fifty Bushnells closed the distance well enough. I couldn't make out anyone on the ground, but I certainly could spot eighteen-wheeler trucks. But each day I was skunked. The clearing remained empty.

Before I could take off on the fifth day, a radio call came in just before noon from a trooper at Matchwood, a semi-ghost town where Highway M-28 intersects Norwich Road on the way to the mine and the clearing. "Three boys heading for the barn," he said. For all anyone outside the law enforcement community knew, he was just talking about three troopers going off duty. But we in the task force knew the trooper had seen three big semis on their way north toward the clearing. As planned, he would follow the trucks in his unmarked cruiser, staying just out of sight, watching to make sure they turned off on the track to the clearing.

Ten minutes later I had my answer from the trooper. "The boys are home. Going off duty."

I called Alex on the landline. He had already heard.

"Steve, I'm putting on the stakeout at Matchwood now." Four troopers would rotate the twenty-four-hour job, carefully planned so nobody at the mine or clearing would be tipped off. Matchwood, an old logging town deserted long ago but for a few homes on its outskirts, is barely a bump in the road. Any cruiser, even an unmark, parked along the highway would stand out like a pink bullfrog on a lily pad. Luckily an old barn, half its roof collapsed, overlooks the intersection of M-28 and Norwich Road, and Alex had hidden a cruiser inside the barn with a clear view of the highway. We had figured the bad guys would want to load up and get away as soon as possible, probably within twenty-four hours, and so Alex's first man would take up the duty immediately.

I walked into Gil's office. "The trucks have arrived, sir," I said. "Shall we get things moving?"

He wasn't fooled by my deference—Garner had made it especially clear to him that I was in unquestioned tactical command of the operation—but this former Army drill instructor is a self-disciplined man. However he felt about an underling placed over him to run things, he was going to cooperate to the hilt. He nodded. "I'll send the word out now," he said evenly.

I felt better, much better, knowing that Gil O'Brien had my back.

Gil strode into the squadroom. "Joe," he said, "radio Chad and tell him to get ready. I'll phone Jim and Betty."

Joe keyed his mike. "Chad? Joe. Your package has arrived. Pick it up after your shift."

Everything was now set, each officer in the task force ready to go, with weapons and fresh ammunition, Kevlar vests—which most of us never bothered to wear on duty, despite the rules—at hand. I loosened my tie and flopped on a bunk in an open cell in the adjoining lockup. Gil did the same.

The hours ticked by. I lay awake, adrenaline coursing through my system. Finally, just before midnight, I fell asleep.

The call, from a tap in the landline along the highway from the hidden troopers at Matchwood, came just before four. "They're on the move," Alex said. "Three trucks heading east on M-28. I'm following with another unit behind me. Four officers total."

"We'll nail them on 45," I said. "Keep 'em in sight.

Radio silence as much as possible."

In an instant Gil and I rolled out to his cruiser. "Shall I drive, sir?" I asked. The junior deputy always does the driving, unless his superior chooses to.

"Suit yourself."

I took the wheel and we took off, headlights on but flashers dark and siren silent, and soon reached ninety miles an hour on U.S. 45 heading to Rockland ten miles south. At that hour the highway was deserted, and I slowed to sixty for the ninety-degree eastward curve just south of Rockland, the rear end of the cruiser skidding through the tight turn. One mile farther east the highway took a sharp right to the south, and after negotiating it I eased the cruiser up to ninety-five. In a few minutes we had bombed through darkened Bruce Crossing thirteen miles south, where M-28 intersects U.S. 45.

"Alex?" I called on the radio.

"With you. It's naptime. My undies are in a bunch."

That meant the convoy of trucks had reached Sleepy Hollow Road just north of Paulding, a hamlet seven miles south of Bruce Crossing. Four more miles and they'd be out of my jurisdiction, but Alex, as a state trooper, would make the official stop and arrest. And the trucks were running close together, like elephants in a parade, instead of spread out down the highway — which would make the stop easier.

"Natives?"

"Roger twice." That meant two Lac Vieux Desert Tribal Police cars from the reservation at Watersmeet three and a half miles south of the county line in Gogebic County were at the ready if needed to pinch off the trucks before they could escape. If not, they'd lend a hand in other ways.

"Ready?" I asked.

"On the move," Alex said.

When we were still two miles north of the trooper, I saw his flashers suddenly wink on, then the faint howl of his siren. I killed my headlights. In a few minutes Gil and I ghosted up behind a trooper's cruiser parked just behind the last truck, its blinding flashers camouflaging our arrival. Alex had stopped his unit in front of the first truck, blocking its escape. Six officers on the scene now.

I strode forward to the first eighteen-wheeler. Alex stood by the driver's door, seemingly relaxed as he examined the manifest. The two men inside sat quietly, with resigned expressions suggesting irritation at once again being harassed unjustly by law enforcement. I recognized neither of them. They were roughly dressed and unshaven, but they did not look like typical woods Yoopers. Their jackets did not bear the scrapes and stains genuine lumbermen's clothes would suffer from close encounters with branches, logs, and sticky pine pitch.

"Just a routine random check, Deputy," Alex said elaborately, milking the pecking-order scene for all it was worth. "They're carrying wood chips bound for Rhinelander. You know what those are, right?" I had to stifle a grin at Alex's studied theatricality.

I looked back down the line of trucks. Alex's fellow troopers stood by their drivers' doors, chatting unconcernedly with the trucks' occupants, no doubt commiserating with them about such routine harassment at such an early hour.

"Yes, sir," I said, ladling on the servility. "I do know. But perhaps it might be a good idea to take a look at the loads?"

"Well now," Alex said. "You've been going to school, haven't you?" He looked up at the men in the cab and rolled his eyes. They grinned. Alex is a magnificent ham.

"Do you mind if I take a look, sir?" he asked the driver, a dumpy, bearded fellow in greasy overalls. There was no edge of tension to Alex's courtesy. He *could* have done well in summer stock.

"No," the driver said, "but you'll have to climb up the side."

"Okay, but would you guys get out and stand by the cab while I check the load? Hate to ask you do that, but it's just routine." It is, but the crew's presence on the ground would keep them away from their CB radios and a panicky call to Morris Weinstein. We had not heard any CB activity as we pulled up behind the trucks.

Alex scrambled up the ladder and peered over the side. "Yep, wood chips, matches the manifest," he said, dropping from the last step lightly to the pavement, like a cat, making no sound.

"Wood chips," called the troopers from the other trucks. Like Alex, they had asked the two-man crews to step down and stand by the cabs while they checked the loads.

"Well now, guys, I think we're done here except for one thing. Hey, what's this?"

The two tribal police units from Watersmeet coasted to a stop on the opposite side of the highway, sirens silent but flashers full awake, dazzling the scene with the other cruisers like a rock disco at midnight. Cops keep flashers on at scenes not only to warn away oncoming traffic but also for psychological reasons, to intimidate and confuse, to keep their subjects off balance. It's hard to react belligerently when the night is lit up in blue, white and red fireworks.

"Hidy ho, Steve, Alex," said Sergeant Camilo Hernandez, the first of the four tribal officers to emerge from the cars. "What's up?" Camilo is not Ojibwe but a Tex-Mex *mestizo* from El Paso, "mostly Apache but with a little Spanish grandee thrown in," he likes to say. His Indian genes led the Lac Vieux Desert Ojibwe to hire him. He is a veteran cop and one of the odd ducks, like me, who washed up in the Upper Peninsula for reasons of his own. His partner was Benny Kramer, the "Finndian" who had once run for sheriff in Porcupine County.

"You missed all the fun, Camilo," said Alex. "We're just wrapping up here."

Camilo smiled and leaned against the truck's fender with one hand, the other casually at his waist. The other officers had wandered down to the second two trucks to chat with the troopers by the cabs.

"Uh, let me think," Alex said. "Oh, yes, now I remember."

He turned to the driver. "Mind if we open the trailer doors, sir?" he asked. "Just want to be sure."

Camilo and I slowly turned so that the truck's crew could not see our armed sides and unclipped our holsters. The officers at the other trucks, I knew, had done the same thing.

"You can't do that!" the driver said in astonishment. "The chips will just spill out!"

"Well, yeah," Alex said, "*if* they're chips."

"They *are*."

"You gonna open the door?" Alex's tone had shifted from crisp politeness to a soft menace.

"I can't."

"Then I will."

"It's not legal. You *can't*."

"Oh yes it is and oh yes I can. Here's my warrant. Give me the padlock key."

The driver turned and tried to bolt into the woods, but ran right into the muzzle of Camilo's Beretta, one inch from his nose. Swiftly I covered the other man with my .357.

"Hit the ground, all of you," Alex said. "Put your arms in front of you and spread your legs. You know the drill."

The six men all sullenly complied. They weren't dumb. They were outnumbered and outgunned. I quickly frisked the two in front of me, relieving both of them of Glock pistols and Buck knives concealed under their jackets and one of a snub-nosed .32 in an ankle holster. Then I cuffed them, hands behind their backs.

"The key?" Alex asked again.

The driver shook his head.

"Very well." Alex strode around to the rear of the trailer with a crowbar and hefted it, examining the padlock.

"Not going to pick it?" I asked.

"No need for finesse." Alex threaded the crowbar

through the hasp of the padlock and twisted sharply. With a cry of torn metal it sprang open. The six men leaning against their trucks jumped, but the clack of pistols being cocked squelched any intention they might have had of departing the vicinity.

"Showtime," Alex said. He threw open the doors and we played our Maglites on the interior.

"Wow," I said.

"Wow indeed."

Foot-high plants in flats sat stacked seven feet high along the sides of the van box. I recognized poppies and coca and marijuana but most of the rest eluded me. The pot plants bore huge iridescent blue-green leaves of a size that I'd seen only on mature eight-foot-tall bushes. A few cacti, six inches high, occupied one shelf. Peyote, most likely. But it was several large plastic bags of white powder at the front of the trailer that most interested us.

"Coke, probably," Alex said. "Heroin, too. Doubtless pure and uncut. This stuff would bring in a couple of million bucks wholesale, let alone on the street, and never mind the plants. Hands down this truck alone adds up to the largest dope haul ever made in Upper Michigan. And there are *two* more trucks behind us."

"And our adventure isn't over yet," I said.

"No, indeed."

Quickly the tribal police Mirandized the six suspects, then bundled them into their squads for the ride to the jail at Porcupine City, where they'd be kept on ice until the raid was finished. The tribal cops' own lockup at Watersmeet has only two holding cells and isn't state certified for holding prisoners for off-reservation arrests. Three tribal cops remained behind to drive the trucks to the police lot on the reservation, where they'd be guarded until the contents were moved to an evidence room at the Marquette state police post. It was the only one in the western Upper Peninsula big enough to store the haul in the three trailers.

Back at the cruiser Gil radioed Joe.

"Horses in the stable," he said. "Weigh the jockeys."
That meant we had made the stop and identified the suspect
cargo as illegal, and for all officers in the task force to meet at
the sheriff's department in Porcupine City.

We climbed in and dashed north at ninety-five miles an
hour, followed by the two state police cars. It was only five-
thirty in the morning, and sunup was still more than an hour
away.

THIRTY-TWO

At six-thirty we headed out of town and rolled in a three-vehicle convoy south on Norwich Road, flashers off, sirens silent and headlights out, proceeding slowly and as quietly as we could. I felt tense yet exhilarated, like a Lakota warrior embarking on a night raid against a Cheyenne village. A favorite tactic of the Lakotas was to hobble their horses outside an enemy encampment, creep on their bellies among the tepees and fall silently upon their sleeping antagonists, quietly slaughtering them before they awoke. The Lakotas would have understood the plan Gil and I had worked out at the sheriff's department, although they might have been puzzled by our intention to shed as little blood as possible. A dead enemy, they would have pointed out reasonably, is no longer a dangerous one. Times have changed.

Enough light from the fading moon and the false dawn outlined the faint asphalt ribbon through the trees so that we could navigate it safely at twenty-five miles an hour, but I worried that a deer or two would leap in front of the oncoming cruisers. Like most back-country Upper Peninsula tracks, even the paved ones, Norwich Road has no verge to speak of. The high and thick tree line crowds the shoulder, a dark curtain concealing large animals that seem almost eager to throw themselves before automobiles, like Southern Californians seeking an easy payday in fat insurance settlements. Norwich Road plays host to the largest number of deer-vehicle collisions in all of Porcupine County and, I suspect, all of Upper Michigan. The accidents are supposed to be reported to the local authorities, but drivers of old junkers don't bother. Only owners of newer cars who want the insurance payments go to the trouble of filing reports. Many drivers of both kinds keep their freezers stocked with choice cuts of fresh roadkill. Less paperwork for everybody. I don't mind, and even Gil doesn't.

But we were in luck. No bucks, does or fawns chose to commit suicide that morning, and at the Venture Mine turnoff, Gil and I and our squad of two other deputies and a pair of troopers rolled off onto the road leading to the mine. Alex and his crew headed farther south to the track that led to the clearing and the secret shaft hidden by the steel shack. A quarter of a mile short of the mine we stopped and parked our vehicles in the bushes beyond the verges, armed ourselves with riot guns and rifles, then hiked the rest of the way, whispering. In a few minutes, as the lights of the mine buildings came into view, we fell silent. At that hour only a skeleton night shift would be working the mine—the legitimate greenhouse mine, that is—maybe three or four caretakers. We had no idea how many Weinstein henchmen were about, nor whether they had gone to ground or where. But we were taking no chances.

Swiftly we separated into pairs and tiptoed around the edges of the mine property, concealing ourselves behind piles of lumber and darkened outbuildings. At the hoist house a lamp inside outlined the greasy ground-floor windows of the office. Silently pulling myself up to one window, I peeked inside and saw two middle-aged men. Both were known to me as longtime Porkies, hard workers and upright men, if a few cups short of a tea party. Ken Towers hid his long bearded face in a tattered old Motor Trend and Ralph Otwell slept at his desk, head thrown back, mouth open in that unconscious, fly-catching posture that always looks stupid and embarrassing when one is caught at it.

Neither man appeared to be a threat, but no cop ever takes that for granted—until after the subjects have been searched and salted away safely, to be sorted out later. I looked at Gil. He nodded and silently took up his prearranged station a few feet opposite the door. If it were locked, he would kick it in with a shower of splinters and I would roll into the room, riot gun at the ready.

But the door wasn't bolted. Gently I turned the knob, then slowly and silently swung open the door into the room. The sleeping man did not wake. The other kept his head in his magazine. When he saw my shadow on the floor, cast by the light behind me, Towers grunted, "Hiya, Denny."

"It's not Denny," I said, keeping my voice low, "it's the sheriff's department." I trained the riot gun on Towers while Gil covered Otwell.

Towers choked and Otwell nearly fell out of his chair.

"Sh!" I said sharply but as quietly as I could. "Keep your mouths shut! Get up and get against the wall!"

"But, Steve—what? What's going on?" Towers said as he quickly complied. Otwell followed. Both men looked stunned and scared. I knew they weren't the bad guys we wanted, but I didn't have time to explain.

"Something's going on," I said in a whisper as I searched Towers and Gil the other man, "but I can't tell you just yet. Please be patient with us. We just can't take a chance. We are not arresting you, but for your own safety we are going to put you in restraints until we find the people we're looking for. Then we'll release you and you can go home. Will you work with us?"

Poleaxed expressions still clouding their faces, the two men nodded. Swiftly Gil bound their wrists with plastic handcuffs and gently but firmly sat them in chairs along the wall.

"Please stay there till you're told to go," I said, glancing out the window. Three troopers squatted in the shadows just outside the entrance to the hoist house. "Who else is here?" I asked Otwell, the senior man.

"Denny Britton," he said. "He's down on Level Five watering the tobacco. Us three's the whole night crew."

"Call him up here—no, no, don't call him," I said.

213

"We'll go down and get him. Anyone else?"

"I don't think so. The boss came in last night about ten with a woman and went down into the mine, giving her the tour, I guess. But I didn't see them leave."

He turned around in his chair and peered out the window into the slowly lightening morning. "His car's still in the yard."

"The boss?"

"Mr. Weinstein."

"Did you know the woman?"

"Yeah. Mrs. Garrigan, that knockout blonde who's around here all the time with the boss."

I glanced at Gil. He raised an eyebrow.

"Is Weinstein often here at night?" I asked Otwell.

"No, not really. He's usually here for the eight-to-five shift. I see him coming in for the day when I knock off work."

"Anything seem unusual to you?"

"The boss was het up, worried about something. He didn't stop to chew the fat like he usually does when he goes down into the mine."

"Mrs. Garrigan?"

"She acted like she was scared about something. I don't know what."

Gil cut in. "They know we're here, Steve."

THIRTY-THREE

I thought we had achieved perfect surprise. Now we were going to have to hunt Weinstein and his men like terriers after rats, and that was a dangerous game, for they knew the tunnels and warrens of their burrow far better than we did. I stood back and took a deep breath.

Gil grasped my arm with a powerful hand. "You okay, Steve?" he asked, locking his eyes with mine. "Can you handle this?"

"Yes. Thanks." I took another deep breath. "We'll have to go to Plan B."

That scheme presumed an alerted Weinstein and his gang would try to make their escape through the old horizontal air shaft to the old silver mine and the secret entrance Gordon Holderman had had drilled through the earth from the other side of the ridge.

"I don't see any reason to think Weinstein knows we know about that part of the mine," I said. "Do you?"

"No," Gil said. "Those boys in the trucks never got off a transmission. Joe was monitoring the CB band on his scanner the whole time. And Weinstein doesn't know we saw those documents Ginny found at the Historical Society. Or does he?"

"No, I don't think so. I hope not. I don't know," I said.

"It doesn't matter," Gil said calmly. "He knows we're here. One way or another, he's going to try to bolt from his other hole if we chase him. And we've got a welcoming party just outside it, whether or not he knows it."

I felt a quick flash of gratitude for Gil's crisp levelheadedness. However he felt about me as a rival, this veteran cop wasn't going to let me down—or allow me to let myself down.

"Right. Let's get going."

Gil stepped out and with his hand-held radio raised Alex. "The moles know," he said. "Bar the door."

I doubted Weinstein and his gang could listen in from deep in the earth. If they did, it didn't matter, but I hoped Alex would achieve at least a measure of surprise.

"Copy," Alex replied.

"Let's leave the two deputies out here to watch the hoist house entrance and the road in," I said to Gil. "You, I and two smokeys will go down into the mine. The troopers will clear the first six levels and you and I will take the seventh and the air shaft. Then the troopers can follow us. Sound okay to you?" I wasn't just currying favor with Gil, but making grateful use of his long experience as a lawman. In police work as in anything else, two heads are often better than one.

"Roger. Sounds good. I'll be right behind you."

We left the room and crept into the cavernous hoist house, stuffing dark goggles into our pockets. Before we could reach the opening to the vertical shaft, the giant electric winch groaned and began to roll, its thick cables slowly hoisting the skip up from far below. LEVEL 5, the electric signboard proclaimed, then LEVEL 4 and LEVEL 3 . . . This was no speedster of an Otis skyscraper elevator but a copper-mine slowpoke, however modernized it may have been. The wait seemed interminable.

At last SURFACE flashed on the signboard, and the cage enclosing the skip rose into view. Gil and I trained our shotguns on Denny Britton as the hard-hatted nurseryman emerged from the cage, lunch pail in hand. He blanched as he saw our drawn weapons. "What the . . ." he spluttered.

In thirty seconds we had Britton politely cuffed, warned and seated in the office with Otwell and Towers, by now grumbling at their treatment but resigned to cooperation until the excitement had passed. If any of them ever had entertained suspicions that something they didn't know about was going on in the mine, such misgivings weren't visible in their resigned expressions. They were no threat to our backs.

"See anyone down there?" I asked Britton.

"No."

"Weinstein or anyone else?"

"No. I'm almost always alone all night except when Ralph or Ken's working in the other drifts."

"So the skip's been going up and down all night?"

"Pretty much. Like it always does."

"Thanks." I beckoned to Gil and the two troopers, and we returned to the hoist house.

"We'll all go down together," I told the troopers. "We'll drop you off at Level One. While you're checking it out, Gil and I will head on down to Level Seven. We'll send the skip back up to One, and you can sweep Levels Two through Six while Gil and I do our thing. Then you come down to Seven and back us up. If you hear gunfire or we call you on the PA system, you come right away. Okay?" They nodded, their faces grim. They had both been combat infantrymen in Iraq at the same time I was there. That gave me confidence that whatever happened, our backup would be there.

We donned miner's helmets, climbed aboard the skip and began our long descent into the bowels of the earth.

THIRTY-FOUR

In a few minutes we reached Level One and the troopers stepped out into the drift, Maglites at the ready and extra batteries in their pockets, although the long tunnels to the chambers were brightly lighted with bare bulbs hanging from cables stapled to the rough shoring that reinforced the rough rock ceiling. That was a good sign. If Morrie Weinstein and Mary Ellen were hiding in the old copper mine, they'd very likely have killed the lights in order to let searchers betray their presence with flashlight beams, the better to pick them off with gunfire. But I doubted that they had holed up in any of the seven drifts, all closed at their ends so far as I knew—except perhaps for the bottom one. The door at the end of it might be concealing the old air shaft that led to the secret part of the mine. Rats don't go to ground unless there's a way to get out. But we still had to search the drifts, just to be certain our quarry wasn't hiding somewhere, ready to make their escape upward once we had passed on to the levels below.

"Good luck, boys," I said, slapping the troopers on their broad backs. Then I pressed the LEVEL 7 button on the skip's control board and the cage slowly started downward again. As the rock wall unrolled upwards before my eyes, I fretted. What if an armed welcoming committee waited for us at the bottom? Gil and I would be bunched up inside the skip, unprotected by anything except our Kevlar vests, easy meat for bad guys armed with automatic weapons. I wished we had brought along slabs of armor plate to hide behind.

Past Level Two, as brightly lighted as Level One, then Three, Four, Five, Six . . . and with a soft mechanical clunk we ghosted to a stop at Seven. The drift was also illuminated. Dead quiet, not a soul in sight. Swiftly Gil and I donned the dark goggles we had brought down with us, exited the skip and dashed into the open drift, checking all the rooms, finding nothing except rows and rows of plants of every identifiable species on earth and then some. At the farthest room we fetched up against the heavy iron door marked DANGER. DO NOT ENTER. It was padlocked. I peered at it. "What the hell?" I said. "Another locked room mystery?"

If Weinstein and Mary Ellen had passed this way through the tunnel to the hidden silver mine, they could not have locked themselves in from the outside. A confederate would have had to do that, then make his escape up the skip shaft and out of the mine, but the caretakers would have been tipped off by the noise of the lift's machinery. But we had found no one on the seventh level. And on closer examination I noticed a thin and uniform layer of dust on the padlock. It had not been handled for many days, possibly weeks.

"Look at this," I said. Gil bent close and straightened up.

"They didn't go this way," he said. "Where then?"

I stared at the lock with pursed lips for several seconds. Then a light dawned in my brain as I remembered something I'd seen when Weinstein took me on the mine tour a few weeks before.

"I think there's an eighth level in this mine. Let's backtrack to the skip."

In a moment we reached the vertical shaft. The troopers above us had called the skip back up to descend to the second level, and the shaft lay open. We trained our MagLites down it. Water glimmered on the bottom about fifty feet below. The thick electrical cable I had seen on the tour snaked down for about thirty feet, then disappeared under a slight overhang. A rusty steel ladder firmly bolted to the rock wall descended just a short way past the cable. It was almost invisible from the seventh level. I wouldn't have noticed it unless I had been looking for it. Droplets of water sparkled on the rungs.

Nodding to Gil, I carefully climbed down the ladder and, thirty feet below the seventh level, a gentle breeze kissed my face. I switched on the Maglite and illuminated the opening to a long and darkened horizontal tunnel curving upward from the entry at a slight angle. I played the light on the damp rock floor. Two sets of fresh tracks, one large, one small, disappeared into the dark.

I called up to Gil in a harsh whisper. "Someone's been down here recently. I'll bet Weinstein and Garrigan came this way. This has got to be where Grant Holderman's old air shaft to the secret part of the mine starts. That steel door up on the seventh level probably just shuts off a collapsed part of the drift, like Weinstein said. This cable has to feed all the juice the secret part of the mine uses. Alex and I didn't see any outside electrical lines over the ridge into that clearing."

Gil nodded. "Ready when you are."

I climbed back up to the seventh level and rang the internal telephone attached to the cables running down the shaft. "First four drifts clear," the trooper said.

I told him what Gil and I had found. "Seven is clear. After you do Five and Six, come on down and follow us through the horizontal shaft I just found."

Gil clambered down right behind me as I descended the ladder for the second time. At the level of the air shaft, I swung out slightly to the left to step down onto the solid rock of the shaft floor. A few boards — pressure-treated pine of recent vintage — bridged the rocky footing of the tunnel. Its ceiling hung low, in places only five feet high, the breadth scarcely four feet. This was not a heavily traveled passageway for the transport of ore dug from a drift far ahead, but a true air shaft drilled to carry ventilation up through the mine. It was black as the inside of a bat.

"Mind your head," I told Gil. "If we see light ahead, we'll douse our flashlights."

Gil nodded silently. All the while we had been

underground, the undersheriff had followed my lead, once in a while stopping me with a tap on the shoulder if he thought he had heard or seen something odd. Maybe he resented the elevation of an underling to a position of command above his, but he did not show it. He was being the consummate professional, and I appreciated that mightily.

For long minutes we hiked, sometimes at a crouch under low ceilings, into the slowly increasing breeze. Twice my foot slipped on a wet rock but I caught myself, and once Gil's strong hand kept me from lurching into the jagged walls of the shaft. The long bore was not straight and true but took several slight jogs right and left as well as up and down, course corrections made by the miners drilling from the opposite end nearly a century ago as they drew closer to the original vertical shaft of the mine. Several times I thought I heard a faint scrabbling ahead, perhaps the scrape of a foot, and we stopped to listen carefully. That noise — if it was indeed a noise and not a figment of our imaginations — couldn't have been made by an animal, for the shaft was far too deep for even tunnel rats to find food.

After about half a mile of slow creeping I spotted a tiny glimmer of light ahead. Gil and I stopped, shut off our Maglites, and waited for our eyes to adjust to the darkness. Redoubling our efforts to stay quiet, we crept forward. After five or six minutes of silent progress, we fetched up against a sharp turn to the left, a bright light streaming onto the tunnel walls. I dropped to the ground, donned dark goggles and slowly peered into the light.

It was a large growing room, its rocky walls brightly whitewashed, fluorescent grow lights dangling from the ceiling like those I had seen back in the seventh level of the old mine. Rows and rows of two-foot-high marijuana plants, bushy and thick-leaved like the ones we had seen earlier that morning in the trucks we had stopped on U.S. 45, marched six abreast for twenty-five yards. Red poppy bushes lined the walls. No one was in sight.

"Cover me," I told Gil, and inched into the room, riot gun cocked and at the ready. Slowly and silently I crept forward, heading for the far end of the room, where an entrance tunnel no doubt led to either another open room or the vertical shaft. Remembering the map I had seen, I guessed we still stood at the far end of the drift and another open room or more lay ahead.

In a few seconds I reached the entrance to the tunnel. A ragged line of naked incandescent bulbs marched along the top of the tunnel—a short one, not more than ten yards long. Squatting, I motioned to Gil to come up behind me. "Stay here till I'm through the tunnel," I whispered. "No use us both getting caught like fish in a barrel." He nodded.

Again goggled, I peered into the room. It was just like the other one—empty, except for the lush greenery of narcotic plants. I waved Gil forward, covering him from threats ahead as he crept up behind me. As we stepped into the room together, Gil a step to the rear, a switch clicked somewhere ahead and pitch darkness enveloped the room, sucking the light out of our eyes like a black hole in space.

THIRTY-FIVE

Morris Weinstein chuckled savagely. "How does it feel, Steve?" he called from somewhere ahead. I opened my eyes as wide as I could, trying to draw in whatever stray electrons of light might have remained in the drift. "You're trapped like a rat, and millions of tons of rock's just waiting to drop on your head!"

I gripped Gil's arm behind me. Keep quiet, I fiercely willed him to understand. Stay quiet. Keep your Maglite off. Don't give Weinstein a target.

Gil patted my back reassuringly. He didn't need to be told those things. He was smart and experienced enough to know not to give a shooter even a muzzle flash to aim at in the dark. Wait for Weinstein to make the next move, then react.

"Getting nervous, huh, Steve?" Morrie called. "I bet you've already pissed your pants!" I did not, however, feel the slightest pang of claustrophobia. Maybe I would have done so under normal circumstances, but the tension of imminent combat kept me focused. Nothing engages the mind like the prospect of a gun battle.

Minutes passed. They felt like hours. Whenever fear edged into my heightened consciousness, I forced myself to think about the Big Water, its fish, the birds, the animals, the glory of life on the surface. The happy mental pictures I conjured thrust the terror of blackness out of my head. I breathed slowly and deeply. I can do this, I thought, and so can Gil.

More time passed.

Weinstein lost patience first. He fired a short burst from a MAC-10, the bullets ricocheting madly off the rocky walls, the frantic bedsheet-ripping roar of the heavy .45 caliber machine pistol reverberating throughout the grow room. Before decapitated branches and leaves could sigh and rustle to the floor, Gil and I each stood and fired a load of Double-0 at Weinstein's muzzle flash. We rolled to opposite sides of the room as he answered, the bullets gouging up sparks and shards of rock as they struck the spot where we had crouched. I nearly sprained my sphincter trying to present the tiniest possible target, for a .45 slug can take off an arm or a leg. My ears rang. I wished we'd had the foresight to bring along pistol-range earplugs. Gunfire in enclosed spaces can damage eardrums.

"Assholes!" Weinstein shouted. "Suckers! I can stay here for days and starve you out!" That meant he had plenty of food, water and ammunition. It also meant he was unaware of the welcoming party high above. Sooner or later Alex and his fellows would pick off Weinstein's henchmen and search the mine. Then we'd have him pinched between two parties of lawmen.

"Weinstein!" I called. "Do you have any idea what's going on on top? We've got officers surrounding the entry to the air shaft. We've got your trucks. Do yourself a favor and throw down that weapon, and I'll see what I can do for you."

"Fuck you!" Weinstein shouted as he ripped off another burst.

"Stay down!" hissed a trooper just behind us at almost the same time both answered with a double salvo from their riot guns. The heavy shot ricocheted wildly from wall to wall and ceiling to floor at the other end of the room, and my eardrums took another pummeling.

Now that the troopers had caught up to us, we had the advantage in manpower if not quite in firepower. But Double-0 buckshot isn't a bad close-quarters load, especially if you can't see your target.

"Aah!" Weinstein groaned in pain, then emptied his MAC-10 magazine in our direction. We heard the scritch and snick of another clip driven home, then silence fell in the drift. At that distance individual buckshot pellets wouldn't have done much damage, but they'd at least get him bleeding, maybe sap his energy.

A minute passed, then another. Down the drift echoed a faint sound of gunfire from up above.

"Last chance, Weinstein!" I called. "Drop it, or we'll catch you in a crossfire!"

"Ha!" Weinstein shouted defiantly. "So long, suckers!"

One more burst from his MAC-10, then we heard him scrabbling away down the tunnel. Before we could return fire, another fusillade of bullets hammered past us. They were from a different automatic weapon. To my ear it sounded like an MP-5, a short-barreled military machine pistol that's another favorite of drug runners.

"Come on, Algis!" Weinstein shouted. The scrabbling resumed.

Petrauskas. There were two of them, one to cover the other. We'd have to be careful. In the black we inched forward on our bellies, twice ducking behind rocky outcrops when Weinstein and Petrauskas took turns stopping to lay down bursts of suppressive fire. For the interminable span of perhaps five minutes, silence reigned in the tunnel, broken only by the soft clink of loose rock underfoot as our quarry made their way toward the skip that would take them up to daylight and into the sights of Alex Kolehmainen and his crew.

Once the noise of their footfalls had faded we rose and gave chase, Maglites pointing the way, stopping only to clear the view ahead of jogs in the tunnels. On we ran for a quarter of a mile. And then we fetched up at the old vertical air shaft, watching the skip recede upward and away from us, carrying Weinstein and Petrauskas.

I keyed the hand radio, hoping the vertical shaft would carry the transmission up to the troopers waiting above. "Alex? Steve. We're at the bottom of the shaft. Where are you?

What's happening?"

"Steve!" Alex almost crooned, relief palpable in his voice. "You okay? We're at the top of the shaft. Everything's secured up here. Three subjects down, four captured. One bad guy dead. One trooper wounded but he'll be okay."

"Alex, Weinstein and Petrauskas are coming up in the skip now. They've got automatic weapons. Be ready."

"Gotcha."

"Steve," Gil said, tapping me on the shoulder. He played his Maglite on the wooden planking underfoot, where a few droplets of fresh blood glittered. "Pinked him, but probably not badly."

We waited while the whining hoist hauled the skip to the surface. It stopped.

"Steve?" Alex's voice crackled on the radio. "They're not on the skip."

"Oh hell," I said. "They got off the skip at either the first or the second drift."

"Which one?" Gil said.

"Beats me."

"We'll have to flush him out."

Quickly I radioed Alex. In a few minutes two troopers, armored with loose steel plates they had found in the outbuilding, rode the skip to the first drift. They dismounted and sent the skip down to the third drift, where Gil, our two troopers, and I awaited. In a few minutes we emerged onto the second drift and searched. Nothing except rows and rows of Colombian and Huanaco coca plants and some other greenery we couldn't identify. Damp fog billowed out of misters hanging over the coca, mimicking the rainy season that spurred the plants to high-speed growth. My shirt began to stick to my back.

We radioed the first drift.

"Nothing, Steve," said one of the troopers. "But look what we found."

We rode the skip to the first drift and dismounted. The

huge room on the first level—bigger than the ones in the second and third drifts—contained a small-scale but complete drug laboratory for refining cocaine, with vessels and retorts, extractors and purifiers, cans of potassium permanganate, ether, acetone and hydrochloric acid, and copper piping. But first things first. Where the hell could Weinstein have gone?

"Look," Gil said.

A droplet of blood glistened in the dust on the floorboards.

"Is there a trail?"

"Here's another." The second droplet lay four feet from the first.

"And another."

The last speck of blood sat in front of a wooden skid, six feet by six feet, leaning against the rock wall next to the mouth of a large wall fan. Quickly we swept aside the skid, revealing a rough hole in the rock wall. A galvanized steel duct—obviously the vent for gases from the lab—occupied half the low straight tunnel, leaving just enough room for a man to scrabble through on hands and knees. Fifty feet on, daylight poured into the tunnel.

"He must of come this way," a trooper said unnecessarily.

With .357 in hand I crept through the tunnel and emerged into daylight, shouldering aside a bush, its leaves dried brown from the lab's exhaust gases, concealing the mouth of the bore. It lay in a low valley on the far side of the ridge, in view of the Venture hoist house just a few hundred yards away. Trampled grass showed Weinstein and Petrauskas' path directly to a Forest Service rut with fresh tire marks in the damp earth. Exhaust fumes still hung in the windless morning air.

"Damn," I said.

"Steve," Alex said, so close behind me I jumped. "He's after Ginny."

"*Ginny?*"

"Garrigan is singing. Just after we caught her coming out of the shaft, she started babbling. She said you destroyed Weinstein's dream, and now he's going to destroy yours."

"Jesus! Who's closest to Ginny's house?"

"Chad. I just sent him back to town for a couple of hazmat suits."

"Raise him, willya, and tell him to go straight to Ginny's. It may not be too late."

I broke into a dead run for the Venture yard and my Explorer, Alex and Gil close behind, radioing Chad on the run. We leaped into the vehicle and took off, scattering gravel.

"Talk to me," I told Alex as I wrestled the Explorer onto Norwich Road. Both he and I were panting from the sprint.

"Garrigan said Weinstein had a call yesterday from a mobbed-up mole in the Chicago police department who said the law in Porcupine City had been asking questions about him. Last night he decided to hole up in the old silver mine — he had no idea we knew about it — until he could make his getaway after the last load of trucks had been sent out. It wasn't until he spotted you and Gil coming through the vent tunnel that he finally cottoned on to the plan. By then, of course, we were in position in the clearing. One thug came out first, shooting with an AK, and we nailed him in a crossfire. Garrigan and the rest came out with their hands up. She's been talking to us ever since."

I barely heard him. "Ginny," I said. "Son of a bitch!" I pounded the steering wheel. We had reached the lakefront highway, but were still a mile from her house.

"Chad?" I called. No answer. "Chad?"

Just as I wrested the Explorer onto Ginny's driveway, Chad's voice crackled on the radio.

"It's over," he said.

THIRTY-SIX

"Ginny!" I shouted as I leaped, .357 in hand, from the Explorer, halted behind Chad's cruiser — I couldn't miss the neat row of .45 caliber holes stitched across its hood and through the starred windshield — and a muddy old Blazer. On a dead run Alex and I rounded the side of the house.

Ginny sat on a bench behind her kitchen, her .30-30 deer carbine held loosely in her hands. Chad stood beside her, riot gun in one meaty hand. Ten yards away, on the wooden steps to Ginny's deck, sprawled the body of Morris Weinstein, MAC-10 still in his right hand, the back of his head a grisly pudding. A neat round hole punctured the middle of his forehead.

Just above Ginny's head the door frame dangled, splintered by bullets.

"What happened?" I asked.

"Saw the whole thing," Chad said. "Weinstein got here just before I did, and as I got out of the cruiser he fired a burst at Ginny's door. I ducked behind the car and yelled, and he turned around and shot it up. But just as he turned to aim back at Ginny, she stepped out the door and fired. It all happened in two seconds."

I was surprised. But I should not have been. As a teenager Ginny had killed her first deer. She is as comfortable with rifles as I am, and she has a cool head in a crisis. It probably didn't matter that Chad had momentarily deflected Weinstein's attention. Ginny had the high ground on her deck and concealment behind the heavy logs of her house. She very likely would have used her advantage against Weinstein's superior firepower and won. He had no chance against this gutsy and very competent woman.

Ginny's shoulders slumped, a bleakness clouding her face, as she sat mired in the emotional shock that always accompanies such a terrible event. She had killed a man. Never mind self-defense, the taking of a human life, however justified, always forever alters the comfortable selfhood of a person. Any combat infantryman will tell you that. I had experienced it myself.

"It was a righteous shooting," I said, squatting next to her. "I'm sorry."

I did not touch her, but kept my physical distance, fervently willing an emotional closeness toward her. I was sorry not only for what she had just been through and what she still would have to go through, but also what had happened to us. But this wasn't the time or place to bring that up.

"Do you have somebody to stay with you until this is over?" I asked.

"I'll call Nancy Aho," she said. Calmly though a little shakily, Ginny stood and walked back into the house to phone Nancy. I wished very much that Ginny had asked me to be with her through the next hours and days. But the historical society docent was a strong, grandmotherly sort, the kind of person people naturally leaned on, and I knew Ginny would have a firm shoulder of support for the days to come. Police would interview and reinterview her, and print reporters and blow-dried cable television media creatures would yammer for sound-bite quotes. She would have to tell her story over and over again. It would be a long time before her life returned to normal — if it ever did. I hoped the press never discovered Ginny's secret life as Porcupine County's financial benefactor.

Meanwhile Alex had spread a tarp over Weinstein's ruined body. For the next half hour sheriff's cars, trooper's cruisers, DEA Hummers, and an ambulance rolled into Ginny's driveway while the authorities did their various things. Out of concern for Ginny, Alex asked all the officers to douse their vehicles' flashing lights — there was no need to intimidate or distract anyone — and when an arrogant DEA agent demurred, Gil quietly but vehemently threatened to stuff the fed's head up his nether region. The agent complied.

Alex and I were standing in the driveway when the thought struck us at the same time. *"Where's Petrauskas?"* we both shouted.

THIRTY-SEVEN

"Good God!" I cried. "What's the matter with us?"

"Simply forgot all about him," Alex said grimly. "Shit happens. We've just gotta clean it up now."

As we raced toward Porcupine City in the sheriff's Explorer, lights flashing, Alex raised the Porcupine River bridge tender on the radio. "Has the *Lucky Six* left harbor today?" he asked.

"She cleared the bridge forty-six minutes ago," replied the tender, who keeps careful score of all vessels' comings and goings. "It was going like a bat outta hell through the channel, too. Went straight out into the lake and headed due north."

Alex and I looked at each other. Weinstein must have dropped Petrauskas off at the marina on his way to Ginny's. Probably their plan had been for Petrauskas to pick up Weinstein in the shallow water off Ginny's cabin after he had killed her, and make their escape together aboard the *Lucky Six*. Somehow Petrauskas discovered things had gone wrong and was bolting off by himself. Maybe Weinstein was to have phoned him at the marina from Ginny's to coordinate the pickup, and when there was no call, Petrauskas had figured things out.

"We'll have to take to the air," Alex said as he turned to me. I looked at him. No sign of the fearful small-plane hater in his resolute expression.

"You bet. Let's go."

In ten minutes we took off in the sheriff's Cessna, heading north into the teeth of a stiff wind pouring down from Canada. To save time I had done the most cursory preflight examination of the airplane, checking only the oil and fuel and praying everything else was present and accounted for. We had plenty of fuel for a four-hour search if it came to that, for I had topped off the tanks after my last flight.

"Petrauskas won't be heading for the Soo or anyplace else on the American shore," I said. "He'll be aware that there's a BOL out for him." What other jurisdictions call APBs, or All Points Bulletins, we call BOLs, or Be on the Lookouts.

"Where's he going, ya think?" Alex asked.

"Canada. Straight north into the teeth of that oncoming gale. He'll hope to get lost in it and make landfall on a deserted shore somewhere during the storm and abandon the boat before the Ontario provincial police can get to him." Much of the Canadian shore of Lake Superior is unbroken wilderness even more isolated than Porcupine County, and it would be easy for a fugitive to conceal himself in the woods.

A long low front was rolling in from Canada, Flight Service had said on the radio, with heavy rain, low cloud, high winds, seven- to nine-foot waves and a good prospect of lightning. Already the plane was bouncing heavily in gusty turbulence as it shouldered through scattered low clouds, and we were still a good hour or so away from the oncoming front. I gazed down at the roiling whitecaps below, marching south under the wind in scattered but powerful ranks. A dangerous Lake Superior storm was building, and we were flying directly into it.

"He won't be making more than ten knots in that stuff," I said. "Any faster and he'd batter the boat to pieces against the waves. Let's see, it's been an hour now, and he'll be no farther than ten or so nautical miles out. We'll head due north and look for boats."

I throttled the Cessna's airspeed back to 110 miles per hour to reduce the impact of the bumps, and we droned out onto the lonely lake—so lonely that we saw only two boats, one a cruiser and one a sailboat, making their way toward Porcupine City Harbor as fast as they could, pushed along by the heavy chop. Alex busied himself arranging loaded 9mm magazines under his thighs, eight of them so far as I could see. He didn't want the clips to get loose and fall on the cockpit floor, perhaps jamming the rudder pedals. At the clearing he had relieved one of Weinstein's thugs of his Uzi and a knapsack of ammunition, carrying both down into the mine and then to Ginny's.

"I thank the sun, moon and stars that you had the foresight to bring that Uzi along," I told Alex.

"Weinstein had that MAC," Alex said, "and the Uzi just seemed like a useful equalizer. I thought we'd need it at Ginny's."

"Petrauskas probably has an automatic weapon of some kind, too. I know he's got a .30-'06 rifle in that boat."

"What for?"

I told him.

"Pirates," Alex repeated in soft amazement. "But now he's the one flying the Jolly Roger."

On the way I'd explained to Alex what we'd do. The passenger-window stop bracket was still detached from our night flight across Porcupine County, and again Alex could fold the window up where the airflow would hold it flat against the underside of the wing, allowing him to bring the muzzle of the Uzi to bear against a target abeam the plane. He'd have to loosen his seat belt, twist his body in the cramped space and fire left-handed, but it could be done. "You'll have a pretty good field of fire," I said, "but for godsake please don't hit the wing strut." With that shot away, the right wing would just fold up and we'd spin down to a watery grave.

"Won't," Alex promised. "Just give me a steady gunnery platform."

"I'll do my best," I said, "but there's a lot of turbulence."

A Cessna 172 does not make the world's best police aircraft, but the smokeys' helicopters all were hangared in

Lansing, 320 air miles to the southeast, and the nearest Coast
Guard chopper lay at Traverse City 230 miles distant. In the
Upper Peninsula, we make do with whatever we've got.

"How're we going to do this?" Alex asked. "I haven't
got a loud-hailer to tell Petrauskas to turn back and
surrender."

"That'd be futile." A thug fleeing a possible rap for
conspiracy to commit murder and possibly Murder One itself
isn't going to cooperate with the coppers, but desperately try
to escape.

Ten minutes went by, then fifteen. The wind against us
grew stronger and stronger, slowing the plane's forward
progress over the water to a mere eighty miles per hour. At
the point the GPS told me was ten nautical miles from shore, I
banked left. We'd fly for five minutes to the southwest parallel
to the Upper Michigan shore, searching all the way, and if we
saw nothing we'd just turn one hundred eighty degrees,
retrace our route and head ten minutes to the northwest. On
and on the plane droned.

Alex said, "This reminds me of the movie *Tora! Tora!
Tora!* Those lonely search planes way, way out over the wide,
wide sea, and noplace to land."

"Don't get all uptight on me now," I said.

"I'm okay. Never mind. Just making an observation."

At almost the fifth minute past our initial turn Alex
shouted "Sail ho!" as if we had been searching for a
windjammer. "Or whatever it is sailors say!"

I spotted the vessel ahead, throttled back and guided
the Cessna down through the growing turbulence to five
hundred feet above the waves, keeping its nose pointed at the
boat, itself bouncing madly as it shouldered its way through
the heavy chop. Alex peered at it through my Bushnells.

"Looks like a big cruiser," he said. "Tall flying bridge
near the stern."

"That's the *Lucky Six*, I'm sure. We'll have to do a flyby
to make certain, and order the skipper to return to port. Just

wave your arm out the window and point back to shore. Okay, battle stations."

Alex opened the window and folded it against the wing as the tempest of a slipstream raised a dust storm inside the plane. He loosened his seat belt and arranged his lanky body so that he could bring the Uzi to bear, but kept the weapon in his lap.

Down to three hundred feet we bounced, then two hundred, approaching the cruiser from astern. We could see a figure in the cockpit looking up at us. As we began to draw abreast, Alex leaned out the window and made a sweeping gesture, pointing back to land. The man turned, one hand on the wheel, and aimed a short-barreled weapon at us, trying to keep the barrel steady as the boat pounded and rolled in the surf.

"It's Petrauskas, all right. He's firing," said Alex. "I can see the muzzle flashes."

Whang! Whang! Two bullets struck the airplane's fuselage behind us and passed through.

"That's the *Lucky Six* for sure," I said, breaking off the approach before Alex could return fire. "I don't think we're badly damaged. The bullets didn't hit the control cables or anything else important." I tested the yoke and rudder pedals to be sure of of that. The plane responded as it should. I took a deep breath.

"That's it," I said. "An armed subject resisting arrest. That's the second time he's tried to kill us. We have good cause to use lethal force."

"Uh," said Alex. "Look." He pointed across me and out the pilot window. A stream of aviation gasoline gushed out of a hole in the bottom of the wing. Petrauskas had pinked us. Immediately I reached down and turned the fuel selector switch from BOTH to RIGHT, isolating the left wing tank. We'd lose no more fuel than the sixteen or so gallons remaining in that tank.

"Damn," I said. "Lucky hit. But now we have only

about two hours of flying left. That ought to be enough for what we need to do." I hoped very much that it was.

"How we gonna do this?" Alex said.

"We'll approach him from ahead," I said. "He's got to conn the boat, and that's a big, wide windshield in front of him. He won't be able to fire around it and drive the boat at the same time, especially in such heavy seas. He'll have to wait until we're going right past him, and that's a full-deflection shot, the hardest one to make. Likely the bullets will just pass behind us."

"Right," Alex said. "Let's do it."

I gunned the Cessna to draw well ahead of the boat, and at a range of half a mile wrestled the airplane around through the chop. Throttling back to a hundred ten miles an hour, I dropped the airplane to less than a hundred feet above the waves and headed directly for the *Lucky Six*, bouncing and rolling wildly in the mounting surf. We had the advantage. Turbulence or not, the plane held fairly steady between gusts while the boat pounded ahead, breakers crashing over its bow.

Then we were upon the *Lucky Six*. Alex fired burst after burst, pieces flying off the boat's superstructure as the bullets chewed it up, tall splashes bracketing hits as a ragged line of 9mm bullets walked through the hull. The Uzi's roar reverberated throughout the airplane, ejected shell casings ricocheting off the aluminum bulkheads. My ears rang even though, like Alex, I was wearing a noise-attenuating radio headset. Coupled with the painful noise of gunfire in a small enclosed space deep inside the mine, this was going to affect my hearing for days.

The figure at the wheel of the *Lucky Six* ducked, turned, and fired wildly as we swept past. His bullets, as I expected, passed harmlessly through our track way aft.

"Another approach," I said, "and then I'm going to circle the boat while you pour fire into it."

"Gotcha," said Alex, ramming a new magazine into the

Uzi.

The oncoming front had almost reached the site of the air-sea battle, low scattered clouds almost obscuring our view of the boat. A steady rain began to fall.

Again we flew through the ragged scud toward the approaching bow of the boat, and when the Cessna drew abreast of it I banked the airplane into a tight circle, fighting to keep the arc of the turn snug and true against the increasing wind. Holding the plane steady in the turbulence was like trying to break a recalcitrant horse, and Alex found it no easier to aim the Uzi. But although scores of bullets splattered the water wildly, he managed to pour clip after clip of nine-millimeter fire into the *Lucky Six*. Suddenly she slowed to a halt, rolling drunkenly against the building waves.

"Got him!" Alex shouted.

Petrauskas lay slumped and unmoving in the cockpit well of the cruiser as we circled. Alex looked at him through the Bushnells.

"Lot of blood," Alex said. I couldn't see that, but I could spot water pouring into the cockpit as the cruiser broached, its starboard side overwhelmed by the oncoming waves. The boat began to settle by the stern. Bullets, probably a score or more, had also holed the fiberglass hull. The *Lucky Six* clearly could not remain afloat for long before the Big Water claimed it forever.

The sky suddenly darkened as the full fury of the front rolled over upon us, nearby lightning flooding the cockpit.

"We're getting the hell out of here," I said, firewalling the throttle and pointing the airplane due south. The scattered clouds had formed into heavy unbroken scud, the ceiling barely 300 feet above the waves, driving rain cutting visibility to half a mile or less. I was now flying on instruments, keeping a careful eye on the altimeter and the wings level with the attitude indicator as I put the Cessna into a gentle climb through solid cloud, the airplane bouncing madly. Within seven minutes the clouds suddenly lightened and the airplane broke through into sunlight and smoother air. I set course for Porcupine City and in a short while, just as the fuel gauge needles were bouncing against the EMPTY mark, we landed.

Alex and I rolled the airplane into its hangar just as the the storm broke wildly over the shore, lightning shattering the tops of pine snags and the wind-driven rain drilling painfully into our faces.

"Think they'll ever find Petrauskas?" Alex asked as we climbed into the Explorer.

"His corpse might wash up on the beach somewhere east of here," I said, "and wreckage from the *Lucky Six* is bound to, but you know what they say."

"Lake Superior never gives up its dead," Alex said.

THIRTY-EIGHT

Later the same day, prisoners and bodies having been sorted out and salted away and both ends of the Venture Mine sealed as a crime scene, Prosecutor Garner Armstrong, DEA Agent William Underhill (the arrogant one), Undersheriff Gil O'Brien, State Police Sergeant Alex Kolehmainen and lowly Deputy Sheriff Steve Martinez (no longer tactical commander of the Venture Mine investigation), interviewed Mary Ellen Garrigan, resident of Winnetka, New Trier Township, Cook County, Illinois, in the county commissioners' chambers at the Porcupine County courthouse. The sheriff's tiny interrogation room being too small and too intimidating for the task, Gil had suggested the capacious chambers. "She's willing to talk," he said reasonably, "and let's make her comfortable." We drew the blinds against the yammering press and the bright television lights outside in the parking lot and got to work. It was an easy job, because Mary Ellen had waived her rights to a lawyer. She knew she faced hard time as a principal in a conspiracy involving illegal drug manufacture and sale as well as homicide, and wanted to make things as easy for herself as she could.

"I hope you Mirandized her before she started talking at the mine," I said before the interview began.

"Barely had the chance," Alex replied. "We had no more snapped the cuffs on her when she let loose with everything she knew. Chad actually had to clap a hand over her mouth before he could read from his card."

By common assent Gil, who is very good at interrogation, was in charge of the interview, Garner assisting. Chad set up the video camera and tape recorder and we began by noting date and time of day and the names of those present.

"Do you waive your right to remain silent?" Gil asked in a surprisingly gentle voice. He is a tough and efficient law-enforcement bureaucrat, and he has the personality of a dyspeptic crocodile, but he is not a bully. "Do you waive your right to a lawyer? Do you understand that everything you say in this room may be used against you at trial?"

"I do," Mary Ellen replied with quivering lips. Without jewels and makeup and clad in shapeless orange jailhouse coveralls, she had aged twenty years. No longer was she the glamorous and arrogant suburbanite, but a frightened felony suspect facing a prison term, a substantial one even if she cooperated to the hilt.

She signed and initialed the waiver forms and noted the date and time. At trial a defense lawyer wouldn't be able to claim she wasn't properly read her rights.

"What is your relationship with Morris Weinstein?" Gil began, still in a soft voice. I had seen him interrogate suspects many times, and knew that at any moment whenever he thought he was being lied to his gentle whisper could suddenly turn caustic enough to peel wallpaper off a ballroom. Fearsomeness was his natural disposition.

"I was his lover for six years. After my divorce we remained good friends."

"What is your connection with the Venture Mine drug operation?"

"He asked me to invest the cash settlement from the divorce in the Venture Mine—the legal operation, that is—so that he could show on the books that it was a going concern."

"He being Morris Weinstein?" Gil left nothing to chance.

"Yes."

"Was it a going concern, as you said?"

Not at first, she replied, although in the last few months the losses had dwindled to the point where the prospect of black ink seemed visible not far down the road. During the three years the nursery had been in operation, Weinstein had worked hard to build a brand name and goodwill among garden centers in the Milwaukee and Chicago areas, and, Mary Ellen said, he had taken great pride in the results. I wouldn't have argued with that.

"So the nursery was not just a front for the drug operation?" Garner asked.

"At first it was. All the time Morrie was building up the business, his main profits came from the bioengineered narcotic plants. But as time went on Morrie saw himself as a savior of Porcupine County. He loved the place and he liked the people. He was not completely a bad guy. I think that if the nursery became really successful he would have shut down the drug operation and gone completely legitimate."

Alex and I looked at each other. Under pressure from the feds, many Chicago mobsters had over the years invested their soiled money in clean enterprises. Mobsters being mobsters, however, their business methods tended to stay dirty. I doubted that even if part of his heart were pure, Morris Weinstein ever would have become much of an angel.

"What was Weinstein's connection to the Chicago crime syndicate?" Gil continued.

"He was a made man," Mary Ellen said. "As was his father."

"And your former husband, William Garrigan?"

"Him too. He was a big investor in Morrie's businesses. Including the Venture Mine."

The DEA guy looked up. "Let's take a short break," he said.

During the interval the agent called his superiors in Chicago to tip them off about Bill Garrigan's financial involvement. As he was making the call I quietly told him of the mole in the Chicago cops' organized crime unit, and suggested he and his bosses avoid any contact with it. When we returned, Gil asked Mary Ellen about the trucks we had stopped that morning, and their load.

The coca and poppy bushes, she said, were genetically engineered high-potency plants Weinstein intended to ship to growers in Peru and Colombia. The pot was on its way to northern California. All the greenery was trucked to a warehouse in a small Wisconsin town just over the Illinois state line called Wilmot, where it was divided and transshipped in vans to seaports, chiefly Corpus Christi and Los Angeles, to take ship for South America. Nobody in authority had yet cottoned on to this reverse flow of drugs out of the United States.

So much for biosecurity. Weinstein's benevolence extended only to legitimate crops.

"Those bags of white powder you saw in the trucks were just samples to demonstrate the potency of the plants to the buyers," Mary Ellen said. "That lab's not big enough to turn out much product. It's just a test kitchen."

"Tell us about the other men in the operation," Gil said. "Let's start with Algis Petrauskas, also known as Michael Anderson."

"My brother." Mary Ellen stifled a sob.

"I'm sorry for your loss. How'd he get involved?"

"It's a long story."

"That's okay, Mrs. Garrigan," Gil said almost languidly. "We have plenty of time."

Algis, four years Mary Ellen's junior, had followed her to New Trier High School in Winnetka. She had been one of the popular girls, a cheerleader and like nearly all her classmates college-bound for the University of Illinois, but Algis had been a square peg in a round hole. Tormented because of his ugliness, he lived up to his looks and became a vicious troublemaker and a thief, graduating from schoolyard bully to a thorough embarrassment to Mary Ellen's upper-middle-class family in the wealthy suburb. Their father, a prosperous banker, had washed his hands of his son after he was convicted of burglary as a juvenile at age sixteen and sent to St. Charles, the tough state reformatory for delinquents. When Algis turned eighteen he agreed to continue his so-called rehabilitation by joining the navy. After her brother's release from the naval prison, Mary Ellen persuaded Weinstein—still the wealthy and connected entrepreneur she had met while buying a Mercedes—to take Algis on as a gofer. At first Algis labored as an enforcer in Weinstein's loan-shark enterprise, softening up marks who couldn't come up with the vigorish, but Weinstein soon discovered Algis' small-boat expertise and made him the skipper of his yacht. Together they took fellow hoods as well as charter parties fishing.

"Did he take Danny Impellitteri for a cruise?" Garner asked. I perked up. This was the corpse that had washed up on the beach at the beginning of the case.

"Yes."

"What happened on that cruise?"

Impellitteri had been one of Weinstein's go-betweens with the South American drug lords, Mary Ellen said, and he had demanded a greater cut of the proceeds. Outraged, Weinstein ordered Petrauskas to dispose of Impellitteri in Lake Superior while the *Lucky Six* purportedly was in Lake Michigan. One foggy night Petrauskas suddenly caught Impellitteri unaware, pushing him overboard and immediately putting a bullet into the man's chest as he struggled in the water. No wonder, I thought, that Petrauskas had tried so desperately to escape. He was looking at life without parole.

"How do you know this?" Gil said.

"Morrie told me everything. He never kept anything from me. He loved to boast about what he did to people who crossed him."

"Tell us about Roy Schweikert and Frank Saarinen."

Schweikert, she said, had been a hit man before he discovered horticulture—even mobsters can have green thumbs—and killed Frank Saarinen. Frank had discovered the hidden mine, she didn't know quite how, and Weinstein tried to buy him off by enlisting him in the secret operation. But Frank's conscience interfered and Weinstein told Schweikert to get rid of him. Schweikert had followed Frank into the woods on the opening day of deer season and put a bullet into his head.

"What happened to Schweikert?"

"Bad attitude," Mary Ellen said. "He forgot who was boss and tried to run the dope growing operation the way he thought it should be. Morrie warned him several times to do it his way but Roy wouldn't listen."

One winter afternoon Weinstein and Schweikert went out on a "snowmobile monkey drunk" — that's when snowmobilers swing from trailside bar to trailside bar, in between snootfuls barreling across the wintry landscape at high speed. Weinstein induced Schweikert to get blind staggering drunk, put him on his snowmobile and pointed the machine at the thin ice of a nearby creek. As the alcohol-addled Schweikert struggled to gain his feet in the shallow water, Weinstein waded in and held him underwater until he drowned. The Gogebic County deputies wrote it up as still another snowmobile death. In that county that winter alone, seven snowmobilers had gone drinking, driving and dying.

"Mrs. Garrigan," I cut in, mindful of the fate of Andrew Carmichael almost a hundred years earlier, "were there any other homicides Morris Weinstein boasted about?"

"Yes," she said. "As I said, he loved to talk about killing his enemies. But they were all done years ago before he came up to Porcupine County."

The Chicago police, I was sure, would like to talk to Mary Ellen. Not that they could bring charges against a dead man, but they would be happy to clear a few cold cases.

"That's it for now," Gil said. Two hours had passed and Mary Ellen was visibly tiring. "We'll pick it up later."

"Just one more question?" I said.

"All right."

"Mrs. Garrigan, did you or Weinstein wonder how law

enforcement discovered the secret part of the mine?"

"Yes. How did you do that?"

"Never mind."

I did not want Ginny's role in uncovering the drug operation made public unless it was absolutely necessary to achieve convictions, and that did not seem likely. Mary Ellen was cooperating and Garner would present only enough evidence for the General to accept her guilty plea. With luck the Venture Mine Murders soon would be forgotten as the yammering reporters outside the courthouse fastened upon another crime du jour, the media circus pulling up stakes and moving to another town in search of circulation and ratings. Ginny's secret as the loving benefactress of Porcupine County would never be discovered.

The interrogation ended, Mary Ellen was returned to her cell, and the better part of law enforcement in the western reaches of Upper Michigan departed for their homes and families, if they had any. I headed for the door, too.

"Deputy," Gil said sharply. "I'll expect your report by tomorrow night."

I had to smile. He was back in command, and he was letting me know it.

"Afterwards, take a week off, will you?" he said in an only slightly softer voice. "That's an order. Besides, you've earned it."

"Yes sir, boss," I said.

THIRTY-NINE

Two evenings later I was relaxing in a canvas chair on the beach, squidging holes with my toes in the cool damp sand and belching softly as the westering sun descended redly through a clear sky into the lake. Alex and I had just put away porterhouses the size of hubcaps at George's while reliving the happenings of the last few weeks. He had not complimented me on my role in those events. Like Gil O'Brien, Alex does not think people should be praised for performing the jobs they were hired for—but he quietly worked on me to go to the courthouse and start the paperwork to run for sheriff. I said I'd think about it.

"Think long and deep," Alex had said in farewell. "But say yes. Say yes now so that before the local primary next August the whole county will have got used to the idea that it needs a new sheriff."

Sometimes the idea of the long-distance political campaign puts down roots even in the boondocks. The idea of running had been growing on me, but I didn't know whether I had the stomach for almost a year of campaigning. Still, as Alex said, all of Porcupine County now knew who had led the mission against the Venture Mine, and who had not. If I threw my hat into the ring, Alex said, with Garner's help Eli would be shunted farther and farther into the background over the next few months, keeping him—and the sheriff's department—out of trouble. With luck Eli would become the lamest of lame ducks while Gil, who actually ran the department anyway, kept on doing his job. But, I objected, with Eli out of the picture that would mean unbearable tension in the department between the undersheriff and me if I chose to run against him for sheriff.

A soft footfall sighed on the deck behind me. Every hair on the back of my neck alerted. These days momentous things tend to happen at my cabin, either with a knock on the door or a footstep on the floorboards, especially in the evenings. I turned and looked back.

It was Ginny with a soft smile on her face and an overnight bag in her hand.

She strode down the path and sat on the sand beside me before I could offer her the chair. I was dumbstruck.

"What brings you here, Mrs. Fitzgerald?" I said, trying to keep my voice even, but failing at the job. My voice cracked like a fourteen-year-old boy's.

"I'm here on another mission, *Steve*," she said, applying a slight spin to my name. It was only the second time she had used it since the day Mary Ellen Garrigan came between us.

I nodded dumbly.

Ginny gazed out over the Big Water, scanning the horizon and crinkling her eyes against the sun, the slight crow's feet I loved to kiss sending chills up my spine. Best to let her speak in her own good time. And, being Ginny, she took her own good time, starting at the beginning.

"I had a couple of visitors today," she finally said.

"Mm. Who?"

"The first one was Chad Garrow."

"Is he in trouble again?"

"Not with me." She looked down at the sand, a smile growing at the corners of her mouth.

"What did he want?"

"He said he didn't want me to think less of him because of his former relationship with Mary Ellen. He wanted to explain how he became involved with her and how ashamed he was of himself."

I knew the basics but didn't mind hearing the details. I nodded. "How did it happen?"

"You're the closest deputy to her house," Ginny said. "One morning a few weeks ago she waited until she heard on the radio that you were going to be out of the county, and then she called the sheriff's department to report that she thought someone had been trying to break into her house the night before. Naturally Chad was covering your beat and Joe Koski dispatched him.

"Chad said that when he arrived she was wearing a housecoat. She showed him a screwdriver mark on a window sill—Chad thinks she made it herself—and then told him she found him, in his words, 'absolutely fascinating.' He had such a stupid grin on his face when he told me that. But he had the grace to shake his head ruefully."

The silvery tinkle of Ginny's laughter broke the moment. "Now he didn't go into graphic details—he's both too shy and too much of a gentleman for that—but he did say that after a while she suddenly lost her housecoat. Of course she wasn't wearing anything underneath."

I had to smile, too, at the mental picture of Chad's testosterone-fueled consternation at Mary Ellen's display and the consequences, as logical as they were biological. Very, very few young men in good health could have had the fortitude to resist such an offer. Who could blame him?

But then Ginny frowned. "It grew from there. Chad visited her house almost every day after work. For quite a while, Chad admitted, Mary Ellen pumped him for information about the daily operations in the sheriff's department. And he told her. He said he didn't think anything he said was sensitive. He thought she just wanted to hear cop stories."

"He told me the same thing, too," I said. "But I don't think he spilled anything about the moves we made on Weinstein. He couldn't have, anyway. He didn't know about the investigation until the last minute, when we planned the raid. One thing, though. I asked him to keep on his visits to Mary Ellen even on the last day so she wouldn't suspect something was going on. He said he sure would. I wonder what he did. I don't think he'll tell me. Did he tell you?"

Ginny grinned wickedly. "Yes, he did. And I'm not going to betray a confidence."

"Hmph. All right."

"There was one other thing Chad told me that I *can* tell you."

I leaned forward on the chair, my expression intent.

"He told me what you had told him about that afternoon with Mary Ellen on the beach."

"I'm so sorry about that," I said. "I'm so *damned* sorry."

"So am I. I saw what I saw. I don't think you can blame me for reaching the conclusion I did."

"But it wasn't the right one."

"I realize that now."

"You do?"

"Yes, Steve."

"But how do you know I wasn't feeding Chad a line of bull?" I could have kicked myself for saying that. But I'm a cop. I think like a cop, which means I can't take anything at face value without checking it out—even anything I say myself—and it sometimes gets me in trouble.

"Because whatever else you are, Stevie Two Crow, you are not a liar." She calls me "Stevie Two Crow" only in highly sentimental moments. And her eyes were glistening. She placed her hand on mine.

Nothing more needed to be said. I took her in my arms, and she took me in hers, and we held each other tightly for an interminable time, so tightly that we both became breathless. We did not want the moment to end. We had been deprived of each other for so long. But I interrupted the proceedings.

"Why do you think Mary Ellen put the moves on me?" I asked. "Was she going to pump my brains for Weinstein the way she did Chad's, or did she just want to score her first Indian?"

"Sometimes a piece of ass is just a piece of ass," Ginny said.

"Your choice of words surprises me," I said primly.

"How else would you put it?"

I avoided the question. "Maybe she wanted all three—inside information, a boy in blue, and a lark with a Lakota."

"How uncharacteristically poetic of you!" Ginny chuckled.

I changed the subject. "You said you had two visitors today," I said. "Who was the second one?"

Ginny unwound herself from me, but not completely. "Gil O'Brien."

"Finishing up the proceedings?" I asked. Gil had conducted the formal interview with Ginny on her shooting of Weinstein. Nobody had had to tell me to stand aside because I was personally involved.

"Yes. He brought an amended statement for me to sign. The coroner had ruled self-defense, he said, and he wanted to tell me that the state and county will have no further reason to deal with me in the matter. I won't have to testify when Mary Ellen is tried. She's going to plead guilty to conspiracy and accept her sentence."

It had surprised me, I said, that Mary Ellen had rolled over and given up so quickly. "I wonder why."

"I went to school with lots of people like her," Ginny said. "They always play to the main chance. She married Bill Garrigan because he represented money and power, and she had an affair with Morris Weinstein because he represented not only money and power but also excitement. She knew from the beginning that if Weinstein was ever caught, her financial involvement in the mine would come out, and the best way for her to avoid a maximum sentence would be to cooperate with the police, to betray her friends. She uses people and she uses circumstances."

I sighed. "I wonder what's going to happen to the mine now."

After the drugs and narcotic plants had been removed the mine had been shuttered, its doors and gates padlocked, the legal crops abandoned deep below the ground to wither and rot. Morrie Weinstein had left neither survivors nor will. If any distant family member came come forward to claim ownership of the mine, the DEA would just seize the mine under drug crime forfeiture laws. I doubted that it would bother, preferring to let the county condemn the property for tax arrears and take it over. Workers would dismantle and carry away whatever could be sold, then the forest would be left slowly to creep back over the years and decades, concealing the mine and its history as it had so many other abandoned copper mines in Upper Michigan.

More than fifty people had lost their jobs, jobs that very likely never would be replaced. Some of them would leave the county for better opportunities elsewhere, as so many Porkies had done over the decades, shrinking the population even more. But many would remain, hanging on by the skin of their teeth, refusing to leave the land they loved, surviving any way they could.

Ginny broke my reverie. "There's more about Gil," she said.

"Hmm?"

"We talked about next year's election. Gil said Eli isn't going to give up without a fight, that he's going to run hard on his record. That's his right."

"Yes. He'll win if Gil runs against him. Eli has done too many things for too many people for them to turn against him easily. And if Gil should by some miracle win the Democratic primary, Eli will run as a Republican."

"But this is a Democratic county. You can't split tickets in the primary. I can't think many Democrats would cross over to the Republicans just to vote for Eli. Would he really be able to win as a Republican?"

"Maybe. Gil's no glad-handing pol. He's just not easy to like. He scares people."

Ginny nodded. "And if you run against Gil, you and he will just split the anti-Eli vote and Eli will win even bigger."

"How the hell did you know they'd asked me to run? I

thought that hadn't got out of the sheriff's department yet."

"Garner came to me about a week before Mary Ellen tried to put the moves on you at the beach and asked me what I thought," Ginny said sweetly.

I was outraged, but only momentarily. "All you guys were ganging up on me," I said, but without much conviction.

"How do you think Garner got to where he is as a politician?" Ginny said. "He knows that the whole family runs for office, not just one person."

"Family?" I was dumbfounded.

"Yes. And that's one reason why I told you I wanted to adopt a child. It's about time we became a family, whether or not you realize it."

"I have news for you, young lady. I *do* realize it." And then I told her what had been going through my mind that day on the beach, what I had been planning on telling her at dinner before Mary Ellen Garrigan spoiled the whole thing. I left out no detail.

Ginny moved toward me, and it was another while before we came up for air.

"Oh, there's one more thing," she said.

"What?"

"Gil asked me whether I thought you'd fire him if you happened to win the election."

The undersheriff serves at the pleasure of the sheriff. He can be let go any time and for any reason.

"Jeez, no," I said. "I couldn't possibly get along without him."

"Then why don't you tell him that?"

"How? I'd rather run naked through a patch of nettles than let my hair down with that guy."

Ginny sighed. "You idiots are so macho."

"I'll show you macho."

"All right, let's see what you got." She giggled.

And that was it for the rest of the evening, and far into the night.

FORTY

The next morning I drove to the sheriff's department in jeans and sweatshirt, for I was still on my week's leave. I walked in, sat at my desk and rummaged whistling through the drawers, pretending to look for something. All I could turn up was a withered apple core that must have been two deputies old and a ballpoint pen Joe Koski had given me for Christmas three years before. Its transparent barrel displayed a cartoon of a pretty girl in a bikini that slid off when you turned the pen upside down.

"I thought I told you to take a week off," Gil growled from his office across the squadroom.

I took a deep breath, stood and strode into his office, quietly closing the door behind me as the intensely curious eyes of Joe, Chad and two other deputies followed me in.

"What do you want?" The undersheriff did not raise his head but directed his gaze upward at me through hooded eyes, like a cantankerous eagle that had just missed a leaping trout in mid-snatch.

I scratched my head and shuffled my feet. "Um . . ." I said.

"I'm busy, goddam it. What is it?"

"Well, Undersheriff, I'd like to ask you a hypothetical question."

"Ask away."

"Suppose a guy decided to run for sheriff and another guy also decided to run for sheriff, too, because he didn't want to lose his job?"

Gil folded his arms, leaned back in his chair and drilled his laser glare directly into me.

"And the first guy told the second guy that no way would he lose his job if the first guy won because the first guy knew that he couldn't possibly get along without the second guy?"

"You're not making a lot of sense."

"Well, ah, what I'm trying to say is . . ."

"Deputy Martinez, you do what you have to do. I will do what I have to do." Gil slammed his desk drawer. He nodded curtly in dismissal.

"All right."

"But before you go, would you be ever so kind as to sign these reports you failed to sign before you decided to go goof off?" Abruptly he threw a folder on his desk. I opened it, stifled the urge to tell him that he had ordered me to take the furlough, and hurriedly scribbled my name on the sheets. It was as if we had never shared a couple of hours under fire, each of us depending on the other to cover his back. There is no stronger bonding experience among men than combat against a common enemy.

Just as I opened the front door, Gil called from his office. "Where are you going?" he demanded sharply.

"The courthouse," I said. "I'm going to pick up a petition for the election." The first step in running for a county office in Porcupine County is to submit to the county clerk a petition signed by a sufficient number of registered voters attesting that they support the petitioner's candidacy. In a place as sparsely populated as Porcupine County, only three to eight signatures are needed.

"Not so fast."

"Why?"

"I'll go with you." He slid back his chair and stood, still gazing at me, reached for his garrison cap, and buckled on his equipment belt as if he was going out on patrol. "I'm going to withdraw mine," he added almost casually. "For the good of the county."

He did not smile. But I thought I saw the beginning of a

crinkle at the corner of one eye. Or maybe Gil was just relaxing his gimlet gaze at me by a hair. It was hard to tell.

As Gil and I departed, not exactly shoulder to shoulder but with a full two feet of daylight separating us, I glanced back to see a beaming Joe Koski reaching for the mike with one hand and the phone with the other.

"It's happening," I heard him say before Gil and I walked out of earshot.

Jeez.

About the Author

Henry Kisor is the author of six Steve Martinez mysteries, *Season's Revenge, A Venture into Murder, Cache of Corpses, Hang Fire, Tracking the Beast* and *The Riddle of Billy Gibbs.*

He and his wife Debby spend half the year in Evanston, Illinois, and the other half in a log cabin on the shore of Lake Superior in Ontonagon County, Michigan, the prototype of Porcupine County.

He is also the author of three nonfiction books, *What's That Pig Outdoors: A Memoir of Deafness; Zephyr: Tracking a Dream Across America,* and *Flight of the Gin Fizz: Midlife at 4,500 Feet.*

He retired in 2006 after forty-one years as an editor and critic for the old *Chicago Daily News* and the *Chicago Sun-Times.* In 1981 he was a nominated finalist for the Pulitzer Prize in criticism.

CPSIA information can be obtained
at www.ICGtesting.com
Printed in the USA
LVOW10s2122170518
577556LV00012B/872/P